SEAGRASS
PIER

Center Point
Large Print

Also by Colleen Coble and available from
Center Point Large Print:

Hope Beach novels
  Tidewater Inn
  Rosemary Cottage

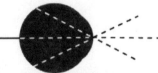

**This Large Print Book carries the
Seal of Approval of N.A.V.H.**

SEAGRASS PIER

A Hope Beach Novel

COLLEEN COBLE

CENTER POINT LARGE PRINT
THORNDIKE, MAINE

This Center Point Large Print edition is published
in the year 2014 by arrangement with Thomas Nelson.

Unless otherwise noted, Scripture quotations
are taken from the King James Version.

This novel is a work of fiction. Names, characters, places,
and incidents are either products of the author's imagination
or used fictitiously. All characters are fictional, and any
similarity to people living or dead is purely coincidental.

The text of this Large Print edition is unabridged.
In other aspects, this book may vary from the original edition.
Printed in the United States of America on permanent paper.
Set in 16-point Times New Roman type.

ISBN: 978-1-62899-220-5

Library of Congress Cataloging-in-Publication Data

Coble, Colleen.
Seagrass pier : a Hope Beach novel / Colleen Coble. —
    Center Point Large Print edition.
    pages ; cm
ISBN 978-1-62899-220-5 (library binding : alk. paper)
1. Large type books. I. Title.
PS3553.O2285S43 2014b
813'.54—dc23
                                                    2014019469

For my brother-in-law Harvey,
whose plot suggestions were
invaluable for this book.
Love you, brother!

❧ One ❧

The constriction around her neck tightened, and she tried to get her fingers under it to snatch a breath. She was losing consciousness. A large wave came over the bow of the boat, and the sea spray struck her in the face, reviving her struggle. She had to fight or he would kill her. She could smell his cologne, something spicy and strong. His ring flashed in the moonlight, and she dug the fingers of her right hand into his red sweater. The pressure on her neck was unrelenting. She was going to die.

Elin Summerall bolted upright in the bed. Her heart pounded, and she touched her throat and found it smooth and unharmed. It was just that dream again. She was safe, right here in her own house on the outskirts of Virginia Beach, Virginia. Her slick skin glistened in the moonlight streaming through the window.

The incision over her breastbone pulsed with pain, and she grabbed some pills from the bedside and swallowed them. *In and out.* Concentrating on breathing helped ease both her pain and her panic. She pulled in a breath, sweetly laden with the scent of roses blooming outside her window, then lay back against the pillow.

Her eyes drifted shut, then opened when she heard the tinkle of broken glass. Was it still the dream? Then the cool rush of air from the open window struck her face, and she heard a foot crunch on broken glass.

She leaped from the bed and threw open her door. Her heart pounded in her throat. Was an intruder in the house? In her bare feet, she sidled down the hall toward the sound she'd heard. She paused to peek in on her four-year-old daughter. One arm grasping a stuffed bear, Josie lay in a tangle of princess blankets.

Elin relaxed a bit. Maybe she hadn't heard glass break. It might still have been part of the nightmare. She peered around the hall corner toward the kitchen. A faint light glimmered as if the refrigerator stood open. A cool breeze wafted from the kitchen, and she detected the scent of dew. She was sure she'd shut and locked the window. The hair stood on the back of her neck, and she backed away.

Then a familiar voice called out. "Elin? I need you."

Relief left her limp. Elin rushed down the hall to the kitchen where her mother stood in front of the back door with broken glass all around her feet. The refrigerator stood open as well. Her mom's blue eyes were cloudy with confusion, and she wrung her hands as she looked at the drops of blood on the floor.

Elin grabbed a paper towel. "Don't move, Mom. You've cut yourself." She knelt and scooped the bits of glass away from her mother's bleeding feet. Her mother obediently sat in the chair Elin pulled toward her, and she inspected the small cuts. Nothing major, thank goodness. She put peroxide on her mother's cuts and ushered her back to bed, all the while praying that when morning came, her mother's bout with dementia would have passed. For now.

It was only when she went back to the hall that she smelled a man's cologne. She rushed to the kitchen and glanced around. The glass in the back door was shattered. *Inwardly.*

He's been in the house.

The neat plantation-style cottage looked much the same as the last time Marc Everton had been here. Seeing Elin Summerall again hadn't even been on his radar when he pulled on his shoes this morning, but his investigation had pulled up her name, and he needed to find out what she knew.

He put the SUV in Park and shut off the engine. Blue flowers of some kind grew along the brick path to the front door. A white swing swayed in the breeze on the porch.

He mounted the steps and pressed the doorbell. He heard rapid footsteps come his way. The door swung open, and he was face-to-face with Elin again after all this time. She was just as beautiful as he remembered. Her red hair curled in ringlets down her back, and those amazing aqua eyes widened when she saw him.

She leaned against the doorjamb. "Marc, what a surprise." Her husky voice squeaked out as if she didn't have enough air. Her gaze darted behind her, then back to him. "W-What are you doing here?"

"I needed to talk to you. Can I come in?"

She swallowed hard and looked behind her again. "I'll come out." She slipped out the door and went to the swing, where she curled up with one leg under her, a familiar pose.

He perched on the porch railing. "I-I was sorry to hear about Tim. A heart attack, I heard. Strange for someone so young."

She nodded. "His lack of mobility caused all kinds of health problems." She glanced toward the house again and bit her lip.

The last time he'd seen her she was pregnant. And Tim had thrown him off the premises. While Marc understood the jealousy, it had been a little extreme.

His jaw tightened. "I'll get right to the point. I'm investigating Laura Watson's murder. I saw a news story this morning about you receiving her heart."

She gulped and clutched her hands in her lap.

"That's right. What do you mean 'investigating'?"

"I'm with the FBI."

"I thought . . ." She bit her lip and looked away. "I mean, you used to be in the Air Force."

"I was ready for something new."

"Sara never told me you'd left the military."

He lifted a brow but said nothing. He doubted he'd often been the topic of conversation between his cousin and Elin. Eyeing her, he decided to lay his cards on the table. "My best friend was murdered while investigating this case. My supervisor thinks I can't be objective now and wouldn't assign me to the case, but he's wrong. I took some leave, and I'm going to find his killer."

She gulped. "Oh, Marc, I'm so sorry."

He brushed off her condolences. "The article said you received Laura's heart, that you've been having some kind of memories of the murder."

Her face paled, but her gaze stayed fixed on him. "Yes, it's been a little scary."

"Sorry to hear you've been sick. You all right now?"

When she nodded, a long curl fell forward, spiraling down her long neck to rest near her waist. He yanked his gaze back from that perfect, shining lock. Her hair was unlike any other woman's he'd ever met. Thick and lustrous with a color somewhere between red and auburn and lit from within by gold highlights.

Her hand went to the center of her chest. "I

had a virus that damaged my heart. I'm still recovering from surgery, but the doctors are pleased with my progress."

"That's good." He pushed away the stab of compassion. The only reason he was here was to find out what she knew about the murder. "So tell me about these visions or whatever they are."

Elin exhaled and forced her tense shoulder muscles to relax. She had to do this. But what if she told him everything and he didn't believe her? No one else had listened. Was it because she didn't know herself anymore and it came across to others?

His dark good looks, only enhanced by a nose that had been broken several times, had always drawn female attention. She'd vowed they would never turn her head, but she was wrong. So wrong. He'd haunted her dreams for nearly five years, and she thought she'd finally put the guilt to rest. But one look at his face had brought it surging back. The scent of his cologne, Polo Red, wafted to her, instantly taking her back to that one night of passion.

She'd been so young and stupid. They hadn't even liked each other, and to this day, she wondered what had gotten into her.

Marc opened the iPad in his hand and launched a program. "How did you find out she was your donor?"

"I have access to the records, and no one thought to lock me out." She twisted her hands together. "To explain this, I need to give you some background, so bear with me." She plunged in before he could object. "I've worked matching up donors with recipients for five years. I love my job."

"I know."

Those two words told her a lot. "Anyone who works with organ donation has heard the stories. They've even hit the news on occasion. Accounts of things the recipient knew about the donor. Things they should have had no way of knowing."

He nodded. "Cell memory."

At least he knew the term. "That's right. Within hours of receiving my new heart, I started having flashbacks of Laura's murder." She touched her throat. "I'm choking, fighting for my life. I remember things like the color of the murderer's hair. I keep smelling a man's cologne. I went to the department store to identify it. It's Encounter." She saw doubt gathering on his face and hurried on. "He was wearing a sweater the night he killed her. It was red."

He lifted a brow. "A sweater? On a Caribbean cruise?"

She bit her lip. "Maybe he put it on to prevent being scratched. I fought—I mean, Laura fought—very hard."

He didn't believe her. He hadn't taken a single

note on his iPad. She had to convince him or Josie would be orphaned. Mom would have to go to a nursing home. "He's stalking me."

His somber gaze didn't change. "What's happened?"

"Someone broke into my house the other night. I'd just had a nightmare about the murder, and I heard the glass break. At first I thought it was an intruder, then Mom called for me. I found her in the kitchen in the middle of broken glass. I cleaned her up and got her to bed before I looked around more." She shuddered and hugged herself. "The glass in the back door had been broken from outside. He'd been here."

"What makes you think it's the man who killed Laura?"

"Who else could it be? He knows I'm remembering things because it was in the newspaper. He has to silence me before I remember everything."

He closed the cover on his tablet. "Well, thank you for answering my questions, Elin. I'll look into your claims. I've heard about cell memory, but most doctors consider it part of the psychological trauma from organ transplants. Have you been to a doctor? Maybe the intruder the other night was a nightmare. You said you'd been dreaming. And he wasn't actually *in* the house, was he?"

She stayed put in the swing. "You have to

believe me. I know I sound like I'm crazy, but it's all too real."

His mouth twisted. "The police didn't believe you either, did they?"

She shook her head. "But they don't know me. You do."

His eyes went distant. "I'm not sure I do either. You seem—different somehow."

Her eyes burned. Everyone said that, but she didn't *feel* any different. Okay, maybe some of her likes and dislikes had changed, but it meant nothing. She was still Elin Summerall, Josie's mommy and Ruby's daughter.

The front door opened, and she saw her daughter's small hand on the doorknob. *No, no, Josie, don't come out.* Her daughter emerged with a bright smile. The red top and white pants she wore enhanced her dark coloring. Her distinctive hazel eyes were exactly like the man's in front of her. Maybe he wouldn't notice. A futile hope. Marc was a good detective, the best. Tenacious too.

"Hi, honey. Mommy is busy. Go back inside with Grandma."

Josie's eyes clouded. "She's sleeping. I want to go to the park."

Marc's gaze swept over Josie and lingered on her widow's peak. "This is Josie?"

There was no escaping this reckoning. "Yes. Josie, say hello to Mr. Everton."

"Hi, Mr. Everton. You want to come to my birthday party? I'll be five next month."

His smile was indulgent. "What's the date?"

"July 10."

His eyes widened, and Elin could almost hear the wheels spinning in his head, see him calculating the time. Tim hadn't come back for a month after that night.

He bolted upright, and his hands curled into fists. "I'd love to, Josie." His voice was controlled, but the look he shot Elin was full of fury and disbelief.

Elin forced a smile. "Go inside, honey. We'll go to the park in a little while. I need to talk to Mr. Everton for a few minutes."

Her daughter gave a final pout, then turned and went back inside. The door banged behind her as a final punctuation of her displeasure.

The silence stretched between Elin and Marc as their gazes locked. How on earth did she begin?

He paced to the door and back, then dug into his pocket and popped a mint from its package. He popped it into his mouth. "She's my daughter and you never told me." He spat out the tight words, and a muscle in his jaw jumped.

Marc struggled to control his anger. He'd instantly recognized Josie's resemblance to him instead of her red-haired mother. And Tim had

16

been blond. Josie's hazel eyes were flecked with green and gold, just like his. The dimple in her right cheek matched his. So did the shape of her face and her dark curls. And her widow's peak.

He paced the porch and looked at Elin. Her figure was enough to stop traffic, but their personalities had never really meshed. Except for that one night after her father died. Ravaged by grief, she'd shown up at his house looking for Sara, and he gave her a drink to calm her down. One drink led to another and another until they crossed a line of no return. A night they both regretted.

He saw hope and fear warring in her beautiful face. "Why?" His voice was hoarse, and he cleared his throat. "Why didn't you tell me?"

She bit her lip. "As far as I was concerned, Tim was her father. That was one of the conditions he made before we were married, that he wanted her to be *his* daughter."

"He's been gone for two years. You could have come to me as soon as he died." His gaze swung back to the door. Elin had deprived him of two years he could have had with his daughter. His fists clenched again, and his throat ached from clenching his jaw.

Her eyes shimmered with moisture. "The last thing he asked me before he died was to never tell you. H-He was jealous. I'm sure you realized that when you came here with Sara that day and he went into a rage."

He gave a curt nod. "So you never planned to tell me?"

Her chin came up. "No. I'd betrayed Tim once. I didn't want to do it again."

The fact he had a child still floored him. What did he do with this? "I'll talk to my attorney and draw up some support papers."

A flush ran up her pale skin. "I don't want your money, Marc! Josie is *my* daughter. Tim is her daddy, and we don't need another one. The only thing I need from you is for you to find that man and put him behind bars before he hurts me."

"I intend to." Surely she wouldn't keep his daughter away from him? He wasn't going to be one of those deadbeat dads, no way. "But I'm not so sure about that cell-memory stuff."

She wrung her hands. "I see your skepticism. Don't you think I know it's crazy? Everyone just says, 'There, there, Elin. You've been through so much. This will pass.' But it's getting worse! The dreams come nearly every night. You have to help me."

Against his will, he saw the conviction in her face. So what if it was some kind of hallucination from the heart transplant? Josie was still his daughter. He owed it to her to see if there was any truth to this. And his lack of control that night still haunted him. Her grief for her father had been a poor excuse for what they'd done.

He went back to his perch on the porch railing and picked up his pen. "Start over from the beginning."

ঝ TWO ঞ

Elin rolled over and looked at the clock. It was nearly two in the morning, and she hadn't fallen asleep yet. She massaged the pain between her breasts. The discomfort had lessened substantially this week, but the twinges reminded her every day of how fragile her life was.

What if Marc tried to take her daughter? Even trying to be part of Josie's life would be a complication Elin didn't have the emotional energy to handle. She flipped on her light since she wasn't sleeping anyway and reached for her MacBook.

She called up the real-estate listing again and stared at the house on Hope Island she'd purchased. Her father had been stationed on the quaint little island for three years during her teens, and she treasured the memories of time spent with her parents and sister. Maybe she could recapture that peace and learn something about Laura in the process. She felt well enough to handle the move now.

She heard a sound and raised her head. Was Mom up again? Or maybe Josie? She closed her computer and got up. After opening her door, she listened a moment but the sound didn't come again. Still, it wouldn't hurt to check. She moved on to her daughter's room, then relaxed when she saw Josie curled up with her stuffed bear. Elin went to the tiny room her mother occupied, barely bigger than a closet. She slept as well.

Though the sound must have been her imagination, she couldn't shake off the sense of unease. She stood in the hallway outside Josie's room and listened to the hall clock ticking. Nothing. Turning toward her bedroom door, she mentally shrugged at her nerves.

Something thudded as if someone had bumped into a wall. In an instant, she was in Josie's room and had her daughter in her arms. Josie barely stirred and only turned her face into Elin's chest. Elin clutched her and listened again. There was no phone in here.

A gleeful whistle echoed down the hall. Some-one was in the house, between her and the outside door. There was only one room in the house with a lock, and it also had a phone. To get there, she would have to go closer to the intruder, but she had no choice. She practically flew down the hall and into her office. As she slammed the door shut and locked it, she glimpsed a shadow rounding the corner.

A man laughed, a low chuckle from the other side of the door. Terror climbed in her throat. She backed up until her thighs struck her desk, then whirled and grabbed the phone. No dial tone, but her cell phone was charging on the other side of the desk. She shifted Josie to the other shoulder and snatched for her mobile and dialed 911. Thank goodness her little girl hadn't awakened.

"Someone's in the house." She whispered her address to the dispatcher. "Please hurry."

"There's a squad car two blocks from your location." The woman on the other end sounded calm. "Officers will be there in just a couple of minutes. Stay on the line until they arrive."

The doorknob rattled almost playfully, and the man's whistle came again. It vaguely sounded like a tune from *The Phantom of the Opera*. "The police will be here in a minute!" Elin shouted.

His fingernails raked against the door. "You shouldn't have told the police, Elin." His voice sounded distorted as if he'd deliberately masked it. "Everything I do is for you, you know. You should have kept quiet." A police siren wailed in the distance. His footsteps faded as he ran out the back door still whistling that same chilling tune.

He was the murderer, the man who choked her in her dreams. Cradling Josie, she sank onto the chair. No one believed her. She gazed down into her daughter's sweet face. He would kill her, and then what would become of Josie and her mom?

● ● ●

The salt-laden wind lifted Elin's long red hair off her neck as she dangled her legs above the ocean. Seagrass Pier seemed to go on forever and ever into the misty morning, and she wished she could walk out into those clouds and leave her problems behind.

She forced a smile as Marc's cousin, Sara Kavanagh, dropped to the weathered boards beside her. "You can't even see the horizon." Elin had fled to Sara's after the break-in a week ago, and the movers had brought her things two days ago.

Sara tucked a strand of honey-colored hair behind her ears. "It's like that a lot in the morning."

"I love it." One of her coworkers had told her this was where Laura spent the last year of her life, and Elin had fallen in love with it in a heartbeat. "It was built by a sea captain in 1905." She studied the grand old structure with its parapet walkway around the top. "His wife probably watched for him from the widow's walk."

Sara smiled. "Enough small talk. How are you doing, really? Was it hard telling Marc?"

Elin shuddered. "You should have seen his expression when I told him about the flashbacks. He really thought I was a crazy woman."

Sara hugged her, a firm embrace that brooked no nonsense. "You're not crazy." She waggled a brow. "At least not in the traditional sense. You'll be fine."

Sara was an EMT with the Coast Guard. She knew about medical things. Elin desperately wanted reassurance, but she feared there was none. Not for this. She still felt the dream's chill and power. "You believe me, don't you, Sara?"

"You know I do. That's why I was glad when you said you wanted to come here. To get to Hope Beach, the killer will have to come by ferry, and he'll be recognized as a stranger. This house is remote too. Not many know about it, and it's easiest to take a boat to get here. The dirt road takes forever." She turned her head and studied the lines of the house. "How did Kerri hear about this place?"

"We did some research on Laura after I started having the dreams. She worked here as a nursing aide all last year until the owner went to an assisted-living place. Then she went to work for the cruise line. When Kerri was searching for information, she ran across the listing. We'd just sold Mom's house before I got sick, and I really needed a bigger one if she was going to live with me long term. I thought we could move here and maybe learn more about Laura. I hope it doesn't take long for my cottage to sell."

"And you're close to me. Coffee dates, surfing, sunbathing. I love it!"

Elin studied Sara's dear face. They'd been

friends since high school. She knew everything about Elin except one important fact. She swallowed hard. "I had to admit something else to him, Sara. He guessed, and I couldn't lie. You're going to be upset with me for not telling you before now, but I'd made Tim a promise. I couldn't break it."

Sara's smile vanished. "I already know, Elin. Marc is Josie's father."

Elin's gut clenched. "How did you know?"

"I grew up with Marc. He's more like a brother than a cousin. I know what he looked like as a kid. Exactly like Josie. And you both acted totally weird at your father's funeral. Wouldn't look at one another. When Marc saw you coming, he went the other way."

That stung. Especially because it was true. "You never said anything."

"I knew you had a good reason for keeping the truth from me." Sara leaned over and hugged her. "I could give you a little space for love's sake."

Elin returned her hug. "You're the best friend ever." The truth should be told even if it was uncomfortable. "I went to his house looking for you the day Dad died. I was a wreck. He gave me a drink to calm me down." She rubbed her head. "We both drank too much. He'd just gotten word he was shipping off to Afghanistan, and I was nearly hysterical. The next thing I remembered was waking up in his bed. I was so mortified. It was wrong. We both knew it too. I mean, I never so much as looked at him that way."

"Don't I know it. He always called you the ice princess."

Elin shrugged. "Oil and water, that was always us. It was so out of character. He tried to talk to me that morning, but I grabbed my clothes and ran. To this day, it haunts me. I disappointed God and hurt Tim."

"Tim was injured shortly after that, right?"

Elin nodded. "As soon as he came home, I confessed. I couldn't marry him without telling him the truth."

"I bet he was mad."

Elin didn't like remembering the pain in his eyes. "He forgave me and said he understood. But I don't think he ever really got over it."

Sara leaned back on her palms. "What did Marc say when he realized he was Josie's father?"

"I think he could have murdered me." Elin examined the ends of her hair. She needed a trim. "I'm afraid he's going to want to tell Josie the truth. He didn't ask yet, but he will."

"Marc has always loved kids. What will you do?"

"I don't know yet."

Sara hugged her knees to her chest. "He deserves to have a relationship with Josie."

Elin shook her head. "I wish I could forget

what I did. God took me to the woodshed over my betrayal, and I still suffer a thousand deaths from guilt. But all that doesn't matter now. Laura deserves justice."

"I know. Marc will get him."

"I'm not sure he really believes me. I think he's just humoring me."

"What did the police say after the break-in? Didn't that make them pay more attention?"

"By that time they'd already categorized me as a crackpot. I believe they think I broke the window myself to convince them. And by the time they got there after he actually broke in, he was gone. I had no proof."

The sun had burned away the morning clouds, and she squinted in the glare to see two figures out front. "Mom and Josie are up. I'd better get them breakfast." She gulped the last of her cold coffee and got to her feet.

Sara rose too. "Since when did you start drinking coffee?"

Elin looked at the cup in her hand. "I guess about six weeks ago. It smelled so good one morning and I had some. I don't know why I hated it before."

They started for the house, and she realized she was happy for the first time in weeks. Something about this place spoke to her soul. The wind grabbed her fears and buried them in the sand dunes. She could breathe here, could see a future again. Marc and Sara would help her. She wasn't facing this alone any longer.

They reached the wide porch, and she stopped at the screen door. "What about you and Josh?"

Sara made a face. "There is no me and Josh. It's hopeless. He's determined not to let me past that guard he has up."

"Have you tried, I mean, *really* tried?"

Sara stared at her, then shook her head. "I guess not. I want him to realize he can trust me. I've tried to show him my character for the past two years, but I don't know if he will ever put down his resistance."

"What if you tell him how you feel? What's the worst that could happen?"

"You mean like how would I deal with the ridicule at the base when he runs the other way?" Sara grinned, but her eyes were sad. "I'm going to let God work on him. He'll do a much better job than I will."

"He always does." Elin opened the screen door and entered the house with Sara on her heels.

Josie ran to grab her leg. "Mommy, Grammy burned the bacon."

She smelled it then, the acrid smoke swirling from the kitchen. She rushed to the kitchen and found her mother scrubbing at a saucepan. "Are you all right, Mom?"

Her mother wore a white housedress over jeans. She teetered on red high heels, and three pink curlers peeked from underneath several spots in her blond hair, badly in need of a fresh dye treatment.

Her expression was vague as she glanced up. "There you are, Elin. I have breakfast ready."

The familiar sense of helplessness erased Elin's optimistic mood. Her mother's dementia had worsened recently, in spite of the medicine that was supposed to prevent the ministrokes that took her mother further and further away from her. How was she going to handle this too?

When Marc saw the name on his cell phone, he nearly didn't answer it. But his boss would just call back. "Hey, Harry. Sorry, I've got to run in five minutes. What's up?"

The man's gruff voice bellowed in his ear. "What the devil do you think you're doing? Did I or did I not specifically tell you to keep your nose out of this case? The next thing I know, you've taken leave and are poking around."

He set his jaw. "What I do on my own time is my business."

"If you compromise the integrity of this investigation, you'll be out. Do I make myself clear?"

"Perfectly." Marc couldn't keep the bite out of his voice.

Harry heaved a sigh. "Look, Marc, I know how you feel. But I don't even believe Will's death is related to this case. It was an organized crime hit. This wasn't the only case you two were investigating."

"I told you he called me and said he had a new lead he was sure would lead us to the killer. Will got cut off before he could tell me where to meet him. Two hours later he was dead. I find that a little too coincidental."

"It was a shot to the head. See, this is why I want you off the case. You have no objectivity right now. Take your time off, but use it to get your head back in the game. Work on restoring that car. Go play beach volleyball. Find a pretty girl and go surfing. You've been through the fire lately. You could use some distraction."

Marc gritted his teeth but said nothing. Harry would not dissuade him from doing what he knew was right.

"If I find out you're still poking around, I'm going to personally come down there and kick your butt. Got it?"

"Got it."

Marc was just going to have to be careful with his poking around.

❧ Three ❧

The scent of burned bacon still lingered in the air as Elin fitted several skeleton keys in the lock to the third floor. "One of these has to fit."

Her mother had fallen asleep on the sofa, and this seemed like a good time to explore. Sara held Josie, all arms and legs like a monkey, as they stood at the end of the second-floor hallway. They were both eager to see the rest of the house.

The lock finally clicked. Elin twisted the old black knob, and the door creaked open. Stale air rushed past her face, and she sneezed at the dust. "I don't think anyone has been up here in ages."

Sara wrinkled her nose. "I think we'll need that broom you brought."

Wielding the broom like a samurai sword, Elin ascended the wooden stairs, creaking underfoot like a leaky ship. "I love poking around old houses. You never know what you'll find. And the history of this place is fascinating. Dad always wanted a chance to explore here."

"I think I could do without finding anything that moves." Sara shuddered and climbed the steps behind her.

They emerged into a third-floor attic space. The rafters obstructed the headroom in a few places. Light streamed through the windows and illuminated dust motes thrown into the air by their movement across the wide plank boards. Boxes and crates crammed the space as well as old furniture, some of it shrouded by sheets and some if it gathering dust.

"Look at all this stuff." Sara set Josie down and lifted a corner of the closest sheet to reveal an old desk.

Josie giggled and crawled under it.

"Come back here, you little scamp." Sara pulled her out. "There might be spiders under there." She shivered and brushed a cobweb from Josie's curls.

Elin's adrenaline surged at all the great stuff to explore. The people who had put these things here were dead and buried, but what a wealth of stories she might find in all their belongings. "Constru-tion started in 1905 by Captain Joshua Hurley for his new bride, Georgina. He didn't live here long because he never came back from a sea voyage in 1907. The house stayed in his family until the owner put it up for sale, and I bought it. She was the last of the Hurleys and had no children. She was born here in 1930. Laura took care of her until she went into an assisted living place."

Sara hadn't moved from the center of the room. "So Joshua had a child?"

Elin nodded. "Twins, from what I've heard. A boy and a girl. At least that's what the previous owner told me. She said the family has always

31

looked for Georgina's diary collection, but it's never been found. There are all kinds of secret rooms in the place, I guess. I'd love to find her diaries. I'd give them to the family, of course. But I'd love to read them first."

"Did she remarry?"

"I don't know." She couldn't put her finger on why the history intrigued her so much. Maybe it was because Georgina had been a widow too. Elin still found the mantle of *widow* hard to wear. Every time she laughed or let herself forget about Tim for a few minutes, the guilt surged back as soon as she realized she was letting go of him.

"If generations of Hurleys haven't found it, then I doubt we will." Sara moved toward the biggest window and peered out. "Hey, what a great view! I wonder how we get to the widow's walk?"

Elin glanced around. There were probably some stairs up into the ceiling. She flipped on her flashlight and shone it around the space. A small closed-in area in the north corner caught her eye, and she walked over to check it out. A doorway opened on one side.

"Found it!" She put down her light and swept out the stairs with her broom. "There's a door at the top. I'm going up."

"Wait, Elin, it may not be safe!"

"The owner had a contractor fix everything on this place before she listed it. It's fine according to the home inspection." Elin mounted the stairs and struggled with the door of the cupola for several minutes until she found the right key to unlock it. It opened easily, and she peered into the sky. Over the wrought-iron railing, she saw the whitecaps rolling into the sand and smelled the fresh scent of the sea. Bird droppings marred the walk around the top of the roofline, and two gulls squawked when she put her right foot onto the balcony. She tested it before resting her full weight on it. It seemed solid, and she saw several areas of new wood the contractor had probably installed.

Sara was still muttering dire warnings below her, but Elin ignored her and put her other foot outside. The sea breeze lifted her hair, and she moved to the railing and looked out at the whitecaps. She could stay up here for hours. She shook the railing, and it didn't wobble. "The home inspector said it was sturdy. I could even put some deck chairs up here and come up to enjoy the view."

"Or just go down to the water, you silly girl," Sara called up.

Elin sighed and took one last look at the incredible panorama of sea, sand, and sky. A figure on the beach caught her eye. Who could be out here? No one walked this area. It was too far from the inhabited part of the island. She shaded her eyes but could only make out a general sense of size. Probably a man. He seemed to be walking slowly and looking for something. She watched him until he disappeared over a sand dune.

She retraced her footsteps and left the balcony to the gulls. "I love it up there. Go check it out." She scooped up her daughter. "Here, lock it when you're done." She handed Sara the ring of skeleton keys.

Muttering about the insanity, Sara went up the stairs. "Wow, you're right. It's pretty amazing. Almost like being in my helicopter."

"You see anyone? I saw some guy walking along the water."

Sara's footsteps came back to the door, and she stepped back onto the stairs. "I didn't see anyone. Maybe it was a fisherman."

"Maybe." But a sense of unease nagged Elin as they went back downstairs.

A bit of smoke still hung in the air in spite of all the open windows as Elin put away the last of the dinner dishes. Her mother sat on the back deck and pointed out birds to Josie. The clouds in Mom's eyes had rolled out and left her chattering like her usual self.

The doorbell rang, and Elin wiped her hands on a dish towel and went to open the door. Her brother-in-law stood smiling at her from the other side of the door, and she tensed. "Ben, what on earth are you doing here?"

His blond hair had been moussed and styled to stand up in a surfer style, and he wore khaki shorts and a blue shirt that intensified the color of his eyes. "I got stationed here a month ago and heard you had just come to the island. I thought I'd stop by and welcome you." He lifted a basket of fruit. "Josie loves pears."

"She does indeed." She took the basket from him. "Thanks so much. She'll be glad to see you. She and Mom are on the back deck."

He'd been married to her friend Kerri for a while, but they'd divorced about four years ago. He was Tim's half brother and had been to the house on occasion when Tim was in town. She could overcome her dislike for Josie's sake. The man had an ego the size of a whale.

She took him through the house and out the back door. "Look who's here."

"Uncle Ben!" Josie squealed and ran to him.

He swung her up into his arms. "You can't possibly be Josie. You're much too tall."

She giggled. "I *am* Josie. I'm going to go to school next year. Did you bring me a present?"

"Would I come to see you empty-handed?" He put her down and reached into his pocket. "What do you think it is?"

"A puppy?"

"In my pocket?" He rolled his eyes. "I don't hear any barking."

"It's candy!"

"Your mother would throw me off the pier." He slowly withdrew his hand, then handed her a small box.

She squealed and opened it. "It's a necklace! Look, Mommy, a dolphin necklace."

The blue and silver necklace sparkled in the sunlight. Elin smiled and fastened it around her daughter's small neck. "Very nice. Ben, you're spoiling her."

"I like to. I don't want her to forget Tim."

"Me neither." Not that Ben looked much like Tim, but it was still nice of him to think of Josie. Her frosty feelings began to thaw a little.

This move might be a good thing in more ways than one. Family was here. Sara was like her sister, and now Ben would be able to stop by on occasion.

꩜ Four ꩜

It was utterly ridiculous to live this far from civilization. Kalianne Adanete knocked at the front door of the only house on this point looking out on the Atlantic. The old house had good bones, but if she owned it, she'd tear this place down and build a fancy new house with an entire wall of windows that would take advantage of the spectacular view.

She smiled at the woman who answered the door. "Good morning. I'm here about the job helping the dementia patient."

She gave her name and looked her prospective

employer over. Gorgeous skin that made her aqua eyes stand out even more. In her late twenties with legs that probably got her a lot of attention from men. And that hair. Most men could only dream of having a woman with hair like that. That red wasn't from a bottle. And Kalianne knew fake color better than most since her first career had been as a hairdresser.

The woman smiled back. "Come in. I'm Elin Summerall. I appreciate you coming all this way. I know it's not an easy spot to get to. Did you drive or bring a boat?"

"I drove. Took me an hour though, so I think I'll bring a boat next time."

Kalianne followed her inside to a pleasant room. Painted pale blue, the gleaming wood floors and comfortable furnishings of overstuffed blue and white furniture made the large room feel cozier. Nautical touches adorned the lamps, tables, and walls. It was a room meant for relaxing with a glass of wine and an adoring lover. Not that she'd ever have that opportunity since this would never be her place. And the owner looked more like the kind of person into green smoothies and vegetable plates instead of parties.

Kalianne glanced around at the windows. They would be easy enough to leave unlocked. But she might not need to get back in when Elin was gone. There might be an opportunity to look around when she was watching the old lady.

"Nice room," she said.

"Thanks, I thought so too the first time I saw it. I can't claim to have done anything with it myself." Elin gestured to the sofa. "Have a seat. My mother and my daughter are having tea and cookies on the back deck. Let me go get them. I don't like leaving them alone."

Kalianne glanced around. The woman had spent a tidy sum on decoration. This sofa wasn't cheap. She dropped onto the sofa, then cleared her throat. This job would be hers, or she'd know the reason why. "About the job. How old is your mother?"

Elin stopped on her way to the door. "Fifty-five."

"Young for dementia." How awful to be senile so young. She pushed away the unwanted stab of sentiment.

Sorrow shadowed Elin's eyes and flattened her lips. "She started having ministrokes two years ago. We had her stable, then the strokes started up again a couple of months ago. She'd been insisting on living alone, but I made her move in with me just before we came here. She's starting to do dangerous things like leaving the stove on."

Kalianne noticed the dark circles under Elin's eyes. "And you need some respite care?"

Elin glanced toward the door. "I–I have some business I need to attend to, and I can't be here all the time. I'd like for you to come every day from nine to three. There might be times I need you to stay longer." She named a generous salary. "You brought references?"

Hiding her elation, Kalianne nodded. "Of course. Feel free to call them."

"I'll do that, and you'll hear from me in the next couple of days. But let me go check on Mom and Josie." She started toward the door.

An older woman, her hair awry, came through the door. She wore mismatched clothing and two different shoes. Her blue eyes seemed fixed on something only she could see. She looked younger than fifty-five with that fragility blondes could have. Kalianne suspected she might be a handful though.

"Where's Josie?" Elin's voice held more alarm than Kalianne would have thought. She started past her mother, but a little girl holding a cookie trailed after her grandmother into the living room. "There you are, Josie." The relief in her voice was palpable. "Mom, I'd like to introduce you to a–a new friend." She touched her mother's arm. "This is Kalianne. Kalianne, this is my mother, Ruby Whiteford."

Ruby held out her hand. "Hello."

Kalianne rose and took the older woman's limp hand. "Glad to meet you, Ruby. I hope to see you more often. We can do some interesting things. Do you like to garden?"

Ruby looked at Elin. "I–I think so."

Elin picked up her daughter. "She loves gardening. She'd like nothing better than to have a small plot out back with tomatoes."

"I love gardening too. And walks along the beach. Knitting too." As the woman brightened, Kalianne knew she'd hit the right notes with both mother and daughter. She'd get the job.

They chatted a few more minutes before she shook hands with Elin and headed back to the car she'd brought out from Kill Devil Hills. There was no cell service out here, so she'd have to wait until she got back to civilization before she called her brother to report on a successful day.

Marc drove his SUV off the ferry at the Hope Beach dock and headed down the narrow two-lane road to town. There was a good team assembled here, and he'd need their help if he was going to get to the bottom of what was happening to Elin. If it was even real. He still wasn't convinced her so-called visions weren't the by-product of the antirejection drugs she was on or the trauma of her surgery.

And she could have told him she was moving out here. Had she deliberately kept him in the dark to keep him away from Josie? He wouldn't put it past her.

A daughter. I have a daughter. The news kept surprising him. The anger at Elin had only intensified since he heard the news a week ago.

How did he assimilate this into his life? Josie deserved a father, a real father. Not someone on the sidelines, but someone who cheered on every accomplishment and celebrated every lost tooth. Elin had to agree to let him be part of his daughter's life. They could do that and be civil, couldn't they? If she didn't agree to his demands, he'd take matters into his own hands.

He parked in front of the Coast Guard station and walked in to ask for the team who had responded to the distress call out on the *Seawind*. He would have to handle this with delicacy, because if someone from the Coast Guard called Harry, the heat from his boss would only intensify.

He found the three men and Sara in a conference room down the nondescript tan hallway. Nodding, he shut the door and went to the head of the long table. "You all know why I'm here. I realize you wrote up a report on what you saw when you landed on the ship, but I want to go over it all with you personally in case there's some small detail you remember as we talk about it."

The guy in the Dodgers cap was the first to speak. "No problem. I'm Josh Holman, and this is Curtis Ireland. Sara you know, and the fellow across the table is Alec Bourne."

Marc gave Josh a hard look. He'd heard about the guy Sara was so crazy about. He shook their hands, then flipped open his iPad and navigated to his notes about the murder. "You found the

41

deceased, Laura Watson, on the aft deck level five under a pile of PFDs, correct?"

Sara answered first. "That's right. Only her hand showed from under the life jackets. Alec removed everything, and I checked her pulse. There was none. I noted the ligature marks on her neck and concluded she'd been strangled with a thin wire or cord of some kind."

"Most likely a guitar string, according to forensics." He turned to Josh. "You were aboard the ship as a passenger, correct?"

The other man nodded. "Just a vacation."

"Did you offer assistance when you heard about it?"

"I did. I placed the call for the team to come and help."

Marc watched Josh and noticed he seemed uncomfortable at the line of questioning. Was he hiding something? "So you filed a distress call indicating there had been a murder?"

"I did."

"The crew specifically told you it was a murder?"

Josh nodded. "The woman who summoned me said the deceased had been strangled."

Marc turned his attention to the other crew members. "Did you notice anyone with a particular interest in the crime? Anyone taking pictures or hanging around?"

The other three Coasties shook their heads. He

would have to talk to the ship employees. He thanked them, and the men filed out. Sara lingered until they were alone.

She walked to the coffee service and poured two cups. "You look like you could use something stronger." She handed him a cup. "You doing okay?"

"You knew about Josie."

She flinched at his accusation. "Elin told me this morning, though I wasn't surprised. I'd suspected it ever since Josie was about a year old."

That stung. "Why didn't you tell me?"

Her gray eyes were grave. "What good would it do, Marc? She was married to Tim at that point. Your interference would have caused them more problems."

He tamped down the rage roiling in his belly and took a sip of the coffee, then grimaced. It had been on the burner too long. "I want to see Josie."

"I'm sure you do." Sara bit her lip. "Would it do any good to tell you to take it easy on Elin? She's been through a lot, and these flashbacks, or whatever they are, have her really scared. I know you're angry—and you have every right to be— but think about what she's been going through."

"You think there's anything to that whole cell-memory thing? Sounds pretty sketchy."

She sipped her coffee before answering. "She's changed since the transplant. She drinks coffee for one thing, and she's always hated it. Even the smell."

He blinked. "Maybe her tastes changed."

"She started drinking it right after she got a new heart."

He grinned and set the coffee down. "Maybe she saw the light."

Sara's frown didn't ease. "It's more than that. She has always been a huge oldies fan."

He nodded. "Go on."

"She hasn't listened to her favorite *Forrest Gump* soundtrack in weeks. Now she listens to country music, especially Alan Jackson."

"That doesn't mean much." Though he shrugged it off, he frowned. "Anything else?"

"You're not taking this seriously."

"I'm helping her, aren't I? How much more seriously do you want me to take it?"

Sara pressed her lips together and shook her head. "She's always worn browns and tans. I've tried to get her to wear more color for years, and she always says her hair is enough of an accent color. But she had on a bright-green top yesterday. *Bright green.* She has always hated green."

He tried to recall if he'd ever seen her in a bright color but failed to remember a single time. She favored a caramel color.

"It's not just the colors though. She's totally changed her style. When was the last time you saw her in a dress or skirt with heels?"

"A few days ago." And her long legs had looked terrific in that skirt. But try as he might, he couldn't remember seeing her in a dress before that. Or heels. He hadn't gone to her wedding, but Sara had told him Elin wore tennis shoes under her dress, a fact that hadn't surprised him.

Maybe there was more to this than he thought. Or maybe nearly dying had messed with her head.

❧ Five ❧

"Woman, you are living in the outback!" Small suitcase in her left hand, Kerri Summerall stepped out of the boat and hugged Elin with her other arm. "But I have to say it's gorgeous out here. Look at that house!" She stared with awestruck eyes at the big house on the hill.

Elin had helped Kerri get the job with the organ procurement organization, or OPO for short, about three years ago after her divorce from Ben, and it had been fun working together. The two of them had even been mistaken for sisters, though Kerri's hair wasn't as vivid a red as Elin's, and she was three inches shorter than Elin.

Elin linked her arm with Kerri's and guided her up the path to the house. "I love it here, and Josie is thriving in all the sea air."

"And your mother?"

Elin's smile faded. "Slipping by the day."

"I'm so sorry." Kerri hugged her. "I'm here to cheer you up though. We're not going to work all day, are we? I brought my swimsuit."

"I've missed you. It's been hard to get used to working from home when I like office inter-action."

Kerri laughed. "You mean office drama? Is that a subtle way of asking if I've murdered Jean yet? And to answer that, no. She is still looking over my shoulder and questioning every organ I award. Without you there to act as a buffer, I've been keeping Walgreens in business buying antacids."

Elin laughed. "It's *so* good to see you! Why don't you tell her you're going to work from home too, and you can move right into my office."

Kerri groaned. "I don't have a good excuse like you did. Besides, you're the golden child who can do no wrong."

There was some truth to Kerri's statement. Elin had gone to work at the OPO when her father died. He'd been a cop and had been injured while apprehending drug dealers. He died before he could get the new liver he needed. Her uncle was the HR manager, and he'd encouraged Elin's interest in organ donation. He'd helped her get the job, and she knew she got a few perks no one else received. Right now she was so thankful for them. Without her uncle's intervention, she would be without a job instead of happily working from home.

They reached the house, and she opened the screen door for her friend. "I don't have it completely furnished yet, but it's looking pretty good."

Kerri gaped when she stepped inside. "Nice digs. On second thought, I'll see if Jean will put in for me to work from home. You've got a spare room?"

"Lots of them. Let me show you to your room. When you're done freshening up, the office is there." She pointed out the large room with big windows that looked out onto the ocean. "I'll be in here with iced tea."

"A siren song if I ever heard one. I don't really need to freshen up. Let's get our work over so we can play." She set her suitcase down by the door, then extracted her MacBook from the top zippered compartment. "We could have done this by phone, but I wanted to see you. I don't know what got into Dragon Lady, but she agreed."

Elin lifted the lid of her laptop and navigated to the OPO website. "You went to the hospital to check out the donor?"

"Just came from there. So sad. The family was happy to know his organs could be used though. He was fifteen and dove into a shallow pool. Broke his neck just above C4. They pulled him out and did CPR until the ambulance arrived, but brain death was declared a few hours later."

Elin winced. Nasty break. An injury above C4 would have required a ventilator for the victim to breathe. "We have such a large amount of organs to find homes for, this might take awhile. It depends on who we can reach."

Kerri's smile faded. "They are such a nice family too. Three kids. The dad is a pediatrician and the mom is a nurse. They are Christians too, which was a comfort. They immediately knew the scope of the injury when they saw the MRI. They'd like the organs to go to recipients as young as we can find. I think that's a reasonable request, but you know what Jean would say."

Elin nodded. "Follow the list. Maybe we'll get lucky and the first ones up will be children."

"Maybe." Kerri didn't sound convinced. She moved a chair around so they could share the desk and she could see Elin's computer screen. "What do we have?"

"Let me run a search for tissue matching." Elin executed a few keystrokes and let the computer do its thing. She noticed Kerri staring at her. "What?"

Kerri's smile was embarrassed. "I promised Isaac I'd say hello for him."

Elin's cheeks heated. "That's nice."

"I did my duty. The guy needs to learn to speak up for himself. Not that it would make any difference. You're not ready for a new relationship anyway."

Their coworker was nice enough. Early thirties with a kind manner and smile. He'd tried to get Kerri to set them up a few times. What would

Kerri think if she knew Josie's father was in the picture now? She should tell Kerri and get it over with.

"You have a strange expression, Elin. Is something wrong?"

Kerri had been a huge help to her when the dreams started. She'd assisted her in finding the donor's name and what had happened to her. She deserved to know the truth.

Elin shook her head. "Not really wrong, but things are a little different in my life right now. You'll probably hear about it sooner or later."

"You're dating someone?" Kerri looked a little crestfallen.

"No, no, nothing like that. Um, most people don't know this, but Tim was not Josie's biological father. I introduced Josie to her father a couple of days ago."

"What? B-But you've never said a thing." She studied Elin's face. "That explains why Ben used to make snide comments about you."

"About me?"

"He thought Josie didn't belong to Tim." She studied her fingernails. "I'm sorry, I shouldn't have brought it up."

"He's here on the island, by the way. He stopped by the other day."

Kerri rolled her eyes. "We have better things to talk about than my ex. So you told Josie's father about her? Who is he?"

"Marc Everton."

Her eyes widened. "Marc Everton?"

"You know him?"

Kerri shook her head. "Not personally, but I know the name. He's heading up that homicide investigation." Her expression cleared. "Thanks for telling me. I'll try to let Isaac down easy."

Elin didn't bother trying to explain her relationship with Marc wasn't like that.

Her cell phone rang, and she looked at the screen. *Unknown.* Maybe she shouldn't answer it.

"What's wrong?"

Elin stared at the screen a moment longer. "I don't know who's calling. It might be that guy. But it could be an important call that isn't picking up right." She slid her finger across the screen to answer the call. "Hello?"

No answer. Only the faint sound of "Music of the Night." Nausea roiled in her stomach, and she quickly disconnected the call. "It was him."

Kerri touched her arm. "Get your number changed. Now. At least he doesn't know where you live now. Once you get that changed, he can't contact you."

Elin nodded and called up her phone server. "I hope you're right."

The sea spray struck Marc in the face as his speedboat sliced through the rolling waves out to Seagrass Pier. It was a pretty spot on the north side of Hope Island. The widow's walk around the top was a lacy white that sparkled in the sun. The three-story structure looked like it had grown up out of the rocky knoll that looked out to sea.

A long fishing pier stretched out into the horizon. The pier looked like it could withstand about anything the sea threw at it. He motored past it into the small harbor where he anchored at a short dock. He tied up his boat, then strode up the pathway cut out of the rock. Maybe he should have called her first, but he didn't want her to throw a roadblock in his way. In the last ten days, all he'd thought about was his daughter. He didn't intend to go one more day without seeing Josie.

He reached the big front porch and saw the front door was open. Before he got to the steps, he heard giggling from the side of the house. He changed directions and headed that way. When he rounded the corner of the house, he saw Josie dressed in white shorts and a pink top.

She crouched beside an oleander bush and giggled behind her hand. "You can't find me, Mommy."

Marc's heart squeezed when he saw her dark curls and the shape of her face. *My daughter.* He wasn't sure he could ever forgive Elin for keeping Josie from him. For cheating him out of these years. Josie still hadn't seen him, and he let his gaze wander over her sturdy legs and feet encased in white sandals. Pink polish tipped her small toes, and a pink bracelet circled her left wrist. She was all girl. His parents would adore her, but he couldn't quite put his head around telling them yet. There was so much to figure out about the future.

He knew the moment she spotted him because her eyes went wide before she leaped to her feet and raced for the backyard. "Wait!" He went after her, but she'd already thrown herself at her mother's legs by the time he reached the patio.

Elin scooped up Josie and turned to face him. Her frosty gaze skewered him. "What are you doing here?"

"I came to see you. And Josie." He added the last in a firm tone. She looked beautiful this morning in a short khaki skirt that showed off her tanned legs. The bright-green top was an unexpected splash of color. Like Sara had said, he'd never seen Elin in bright colors.

"You should have called first."

"And you shouldn't have moved without telling me. Were you hoping I wouldn't find you?"

"Of course not."

He took a step closer, hating that his first meeting with his daughter was going so badly. Elin's tone hadn't helped. "Hello, Josie."

The little girl buried her face in her mother's neck and didn't look at him. Elin shifted her to the other arm. "She's a little shy. This is Mr. Everton, Josie. Remember him? Can you say hello?"

"No." Her refusal was muffled.

Elin's lips twitched. "I suppose you might as well come in since you're here. I was about to fix lunch. Would you like to join us?"

"Sure. Is your mom here?"

"She's inside knitting. I tried to coax her to the beach, but she didn't feel like coming outside." Elin put her daughter down and led her to the back door.

Marc followed her inside the back-porch area. A white washer and dryer were the only furnishings in the space, and the herbal scent of fabric softener wafted in the air. Through the whitewashed pine utility room was the kitchen. White cabinets lined one wall, and a vase of blue flowers atop the pine table added a welcoming touch in the dining area.

"Mom," Elin called.

Marc stood with his hands in his pockets. Elin's mother had always liked him, but would she still if she knew he was Josie's father?

Elin washed her hands, then poked her head through the door into the other room. "Mom, you want to help me fix lunch? We have a visitor."

When her mother didn't answer, Elin stepped through into the living room, and Marc followed her. The pleasant room was empty. A skein of yarn and knitting needles lay on the floor by the sofa. The front door was open to the porch.

A worried frown crouched between Elin's eyes. "The door was locked when I went outside."

"It was open when I got here."

"Did you see Mom?"

He shook his head. "I heard Josie giggling and went that direction."

"Wait here with Josie." Elin transferred her daughter's hand to his, then raced up the oak stairs to the second floor.

Josie's hand was so small in his. He liked the way her fingers curled around his before she snatched her hand back. "I'm not going to hurt you, honey. I'd like to be friends."

She stared up at him. "You're too big."

He crouched beside her. "Now I'm not so big. But it's good to have big friends. I can protect you."

"Mommy protects me." Her glare softened. "Mommy wants you to go away."

"What makes you say that? She was going to feed me lunch, remember?"

Her hazel eyes clouded. "Maybe you just scared her because you're so big. She yelled at you."

"She wasn't expecting me, but I'm Sara's cousin. You know Sara, Mommy's friend?"

Her expression brightened. "Sara takes me for ice cream."

"I'd like to do that too. And we can go for a boat ride. I can teach you to surf." There were so many things he wanted to say to his daughter, so many things he wanted to know about her too. It would take time to be part of her life, but in spite of his impatience, he had the sense the journey would be worth it. He handed her the pink gift bag in his hand. "I brought you something."

Her sudden smile made his heart surge. "What is it?"

"You'll have to open it and see."

She dug into the sparkly tissue and pulled out a box. "It's an iPad! My friend Mina has one. She plays games on it."

"A mini. I loaded some games for you too." He helped her open the box and pull out the tablet. "There are some princess games and a Mickey Mouse one."

She clutched it to her chest. "Can I play it now?"

"You sure can."

She clambered into a chair at the table and pushed an icon. She acted like she was an expert with it already. Kids took to technology so quickly.

Elin came back down the stairs at a gallop. "She's not in the house." Her panicked gaze went to the door. "She can't swim."

He rose and went toward the door. "She probably just went for a walk. I'll find her." Why was Elin so worried? Ruby was a grown woman. She was allowed to go for a walk by herself.

❧ Six ❧

"It has to be here somewhere." Ruby struggled through the waves lapping at her knees. Her husband had told her he'd hidden the ring in the water. If she could just find it, the discovery would erase the worry from the face of the young woman in the house. What was her name? It was on the tip of Ruby's tongue. All she knew for sure was she loved the pretty redhead and her little girl. But where was Owen? He'd been here just a few minutes ago.

She sat on a rock and rubbed her head. Why couldn't she think right? There were so many things she couldn't remember, and she didn't like it. It made her feel out of control and lost. But she wasn't lost. She was right here on the shore with Owen. He'd be back in a minute. They'd always been together, and he never left her for long.

Then she heard his voice calling her name. She turned around and saw him jogging toward her with the redhead and her little girl right behind him. She rose and waved. "Owen, I'm here."

He reached her, and she flung her arms around him. "Where have you been? I've been calling and calling for you." She pulled away and gazed up into his face. Had his hair always been so dark? And weren't his eyes more turquoise rather than hazel? He was taller than she remembered too. How could she forget what her own husband looked like?

She clutched his arm. "I can't find it. You said it was here, but I've looked and looked."

"What are you looking for?"

"The ring you hid for me. My engagement ring." The redhead's brow was furrowed. Didn't she know frowning aged a woman? She wanted to tell the pretty woman to always smile. Owen said he treasured her laugh lines. Her fingers found the tiny furrows at the edges of her eyes. Where was this place?

The redhead picked up her left hand. "Your ring is right here, Mom. It's safe and sound."

Ruby stared at the tiny diamond sparkling on her finger. It was worn, and the hand was wrinkled like that of an old woman. A twenty-year-old shouldn't have wrinkly hands. She pulled away from the woman's grip and put her hands in the pockets of her capris. The sun did funny things to her vision.

Owen put his arm around her and turned her toward the woman and girl. "It's time for lunch now, Ruby. Elin and Josie missed you. Elin can't remember how to make your chicken salad, and she needs your help."

"My daughter's name is Elin." Her thoughts began to clear a bit, and she looked past him to her daughter. It had been so long since she'd seen her, and she was all grown up. Someone had kept Elin from her. What enemy would do that? "There you are, Elin. I couldn't find you." Relief coursed through her, and she reached to gather her granddaughter up. "Josie, you've grown two inches since I saw you last."

"Grammy, you saw me at breakfast. I did eat a lot of cereal though."

Ruby started to shake her head, then bit her lip and said nothing. The little girl didn't need to be reminded of how little she understood the passage of time. She turned to stare at the woman again. "Wait, you're not Elin. Elin hates green. Who are you?"

The woman's eyes filled with tears. "Let's go fix lunch, and we can talk about it." She took Ruby's arm. "You can take a nap, and everything will be fine when you wake up."

"Oh, I hope so. I'm very tired. It will all be better after my nap." She clung to the young woman's hand and followed her to the big house on the hill.

Her mother and daughter were both down for a nap. Seated at the pine table, Elin sipped her coffee laced with lots of cream and looked at Marc over the rim of her cup. Her pulse still raced, but no amount of self-talk convinced her it was still a reaction from seeing her mother with the waves up to her knees. It was not knowing what Marc expected from her. And she really didn't want to share Josie.

"Your mom has Alzheimer's?" Marc's voice held sorrow.

She shook her head. "Her dementia is from ministrokes, but the end result is the same."

"I'm sorry. Can anything be done to help her?"

The words tried to stick in her throat, but she forced them out. "No. I've taken her to every type of doctor, and the damage is permanent."

He looked down at his coffee. "That has to be hard on you. The two of you have been so close since your father died."

"I'm losing her. She isn't the same person she used to be."

"The real Ruby is still there, Elin. Even if she wears her hair in an odd way or her clothes don't match. That fierce love she's always had for you is still there. I saw it in her face when she looked past me and saw you."

"She doesn't know who I am." The anguished admission burst past her restraints. "Losing her to death would be easier than this."

He nodded, his hazel eyes grave. "I can understand that. If there's anything I can do to help, let me know."

"She thought you were Dad today. You look nothing like him, not beyond brown hair. And yours is darker than his."

"I was who she needed me to be today. That

should show you she hasn't changed inside. She's just a little confused."

A little? How could he dismiss it so easily? She gritted her teeth. "What do you want, Marc?"

The softness in his eyes vanished, and he fixed her with a glare. "I would think the answer is obvious. I want to get to know my daughter."

She fell silent for a moment. How did she even answer that? She'd known the repercussions of telling him the truth would come, but she'd thought she would have a little more time. "It's too soon. And while we're talking about Josie, let's clear up the gift thing. I try not to spoil her too much. You should have asked before getting her that iPad. It was too much."

"Technology makes the world run, Elin. Every kid should know her way around an iPad."

She couldn't squelch the faint smile that lifted her lips. "Yours is never far away, I see."

"Never." He looked down and a muscle in his jaw twitched. "You should have told me about this a long time ago. The more I've thought about it, the madder I've gotten, Elin. You had no right to shut me out. Josie deserves better than that from you, and so do I." He put his coffee cup on the table and leaned forward. "I intend to be part of her life. If you try to prevent it, I'll take you to court."

His threat squeezed the air from her lungs. "You wouldn't do that."

His mouth flattened. "Just try me."

The intensity in his words made her stand and pace the wood floor. "It was the right thing to do. Tim deserved a chance at a happy family."

"You really think it was the right thing to live a lie all those years? To let him raise *my* child?" He shoved back from the table so hard that the chair fell back when he stood. "What kind of woman would be okay with that?"

Her fingers curled into her palms, and she wanted to hit him. "I told him about you, about the night Josie was conceived. He understood it was just a reaction to hearing about Dad's death. I–I had too much to drink—we both did. It never should have happened." She raked a hand through her red curls. "I've been tormented by guilt. Haven't you been?"

He pressed his lips together. "Yeah, I've had guilt, but that shouldn't stop you from doing what's right. And keeping it from me was *wrong*."

She looked down at her hands. "It was right for Josie, me, and Tim. He was happy with me and Josie by his side. He adored her." Her voice thickened, but she wouldn't cry. Not in front of him. Nothing she could do would ever really make up for her lapse that one night, her very great sin.

Marc stared at her as if he couldn't believe what he heard. "Play it any way you want, Elin, but make no mistake. I *will* be part of my

61

daughter's life. I want her every weekend. I'll pick her up on Saturday morning and bring her home after dinner on Sunday."

"It's too soon, Marc! She doesn't know you. Besides, I want her to go to church with me."

He raised a brow. "I want her to get to know my parents too, and we can do Sunday dinner together in Norfolk. You have to share her, Elin. You have no choice."

What right did he think he had to come in here and dictate how things would be? She rubbed her forehead where pain began to pulse. "This is more than I can deal with right now, Marc. How about Saturday afternoons for now? She needs time to get to know you."

His strong jaw flexed, and his eyes were like flint. "Fine. But eventually I will want her every other weekend. I'm entitled to that. Any court will award me that right."

He was right. She saw a dismal future stretched out ahead of her—a future of bickering and stress. She never should have told him the truth. What if she lost Josie to him?

☙ Seven ☚

Sunday dawned with overcast skies, but there was no rain in the forecast. Elin got the skiff out of the boathouse, then loaded up her mother and daughter for the trip around the west side of the island to town. After a week at Seagrass Pier, she craved human companionship. Would Marc be at church? She hoped he'd gone back to Norfolk. Surely he wouldn't stay at Hope Island until her stalker was caught. Not that he even seemed focused on her problem. He just wanted justice for his murdered partner.

She docked the boat, then walked down the street to the church. Josie whined and wanted to be carried, but Elin couldn't heft her far in these heels. Her ankles wouldn't take the stress.

"There's the church," she told her mother.

A steeple crowned the white clapboard structure, and the wooden double doors stood open in welcome. She entered and blinked in the room's dim light. Sara saw her and pointed to the pew where she sat. Several other people smiled her way, and her unease began to ebb.

"Honey, those heels are high enough to cause nosebleeds." Sara moved to the middle of the pew. "I hoped you'd make it. There's a church picnic following the service, and I brought extra food so you wouldn't feel funny about staying." Her honey-colored hair was in an updo, and her red dress made her gray eyes sparkle.

A smiling brunette with a toddler on her lap turned around and smiled her way. "I'm Amy Ireland. Sara has told me so much about you. Welcome to Hope Beach. We should get together for lunch this week. The kids could play together."

"I'd love that." *Ireland.* The unusual name struck a chord. "Is your husband Curtis?"

Amy nodded. "Do you know Curtis?"

It was too soon to explain why she was here. "I've heard his name from Sara. They're on the same team."

"You'll meet him soon enough. He's checking out some equipment today, but he'll be along in time for the picnic."

"You're a midwife, right? And know about herbal remedies?"

Amy brightened. "Oh yes. Sara told me about your heart transplant. If you're interested, I'd love to help you find the right remedies to keep your heart working at its best."

"I was about to ask that." Elin's biggest fear was her body would reject her new heart. She'd try anything to keep that from happening.

Sara introduced her to another friend, Libby Bourne, and the women chatted a few minutes. Elin began to relax. If Marc were coming, he'd be here by now. She could enjoy the day. The praise team took the stage, and Josie's hand crept into hers. Then Marc's broad shoulders blocked her vision as he moved into the pew and sat beside her. He wasn't smiling as he settled beside her and turned on his iPad.

She glanced at Sara. "Did you know he was coming?" she whispered.

Sara shrugged. "I invited him. He will be on

the island a few weeks while he's investigating."

He called up his Bible app, then turned to her mother. "Good morning, Mrs. Whiteford. You look very nice this morning."

And her mother *did* look attractive in her navy slacks and white blouse. It had been all Elin could do to get her mother not to wear the red capris and the orange tank top she'd put on first thing this morning.

Her mother simpered and took Marc's hand. "There you are, Owen. Elin wanted me to wear my red capris, but I told her you'd like these better."

Elin watched him smile and let her mother hold his hand. Should she intervene and explain to her mother that he wasn't her dead husband? She'd tried to tell Mom that Dad was in heaven, but it always upset her. The grief would strike all over again as if he'd just died. Church wasn't the place to cause a scene like the one that would blow up if she tried to explain.

She leaned over and whispered in his ear, "We're having a picnic on the beach after church today. You're welcome to come with us so Josie has a chance to get to know you better."

His lips flattened. "Fine."

She rose with the rest of the congregation to sing. Her mother let go of Marc's hand and reached for the songbook. Her clear soprano voice sang out with gusto, and Elin's eyes filled. Such a contradiction. Though she forgot her husband was dead, she never seemed to forget her love for Jesus. Did that mean her mother was still in there somewhere?

With his hand freed up, Marc moved closer to Josie. Elin's heart constricted at the longing in his face as he gazed down at their daughter. He stroked their little girl's soft curls, and she looked up at him. A wary smile made its way to Josie's face, and he scooped her up before she could protest. She leaned away from Marc a few inches, and her gaze examined his face. Then she relaxed in his arms and curled one arm around his neck. He grinned and chimed in with the song service.

He had a good voice, deep and resonant. Josie nestled against him in an even more trusting manner, and Elin resisted the urge to grab her daughter out of his arms. What if he grew bored with playing daddy and vanished back to Norfolk? Josie would be hurt. She wasn't one to quickly give her affection, but Marc's concentrated attention on her had quickly melted her reserve.

Elin's gaze fell on a slip of paper sticking out of her Bible, and she leaned down to retrieve it. It looked like it had been torn from a yellow legal pad. A single sentence slashed its way across the paper.

I found you.

• • •

"You're staring." Elin shook some pills into her palm and took them with a sip of water, then leaned back on the beach blanket.

She had grown more beautiful in the last few years. Maturity had brought new angles to the planes of her face. The shadows behind her eyes worried him though. "What's that? Headache?" He spared a glance toward his daughter who was building a sand castle with Ruby.

She shook her head. "Antirejection meds. And I'll need to take a nap here in the sun soon. I hate not being 100 percent."

"I thought you looked like something was wrong. You're just tired?"

She reached into her beach bag and brought out a yellow slip of torn paper. "It's more than that."

He took the paper and read it. "Where'd you get it?"

"It was stuck in my Bible this morning. I think he's found me." Her voice wobbled, and she bit her lip.

"I think you're reading too much into it. Look at the crude printing. Don't you think it looks like a kid wrote it? Maybe some children were playing hide-and-seek in the sanctuary. Or maybe it's been there awhile, and you just now found it."

"I read it every day. I would have seen it. And one of those kids today just happened to put it in my Bible? I don't think so." She regarded him steadily, her aqua eyes sad. "Why don't you believe me, Marc? You know I wouldn't lie about something like this. If I'm in danger, Josie is too. You need to take this seriously."

He fell silent at her question. No, she wouldn't lie about something like this, but her perception might be off from all she'd gone through. "I'm not saying the guy isn't after you, but I don't think this proves he's here on the island."

"You're not even going to check it out, are you?"

The disappointment in her voice stabbed him. "I didn't say I wouldn't check it out. I'll poke around and see if there are any new residents or visitors who have reserved a room for more than a week."

Her eyes lit with relief. "I have to live for Josie's sake. And for my mom."

The thought of someone harming her made his gut clench. He looked toward Ruby. "She seems okay today." The older woman patted sand into place without any sign of confusion.

She followed his gaze. "It comes and goes. Church seemed to ground her. She's been fine ever since the opening song."

"I'm really sorry. I wish I could help. You're hiring an aide?"

She nodded and reached over to pick up a handful of sand, then let it trickle through her fingers. "Every day I see her slipping away just like this sand. Memory after memory is just gone."

"I'm sorry." His gaze lingered on his daughter. The thought of fathering a little girl left him floundering. He knew nothing about being a father.

When he looked back at Elin, her expression betrayed no emotion. "If you hurt my daughter, I–I . . ."

He held up his hand. "Chill. She's not just your daughter."

The words hung between them, and color ran up her neck and splotched her cheeks. "You sound like you're still mad."

"I guess I am. Wouldn't you be mad if the tables were turned?"

She exhaled. "Fine. And I'm okay with you spending Saturday afternoons with her, but you need to give it some time. She doesn't warm up easily."

"Don't give me that, Elin. She warmed right up to me. I'm going to have my parents come to the island. It's time they met their grandchild."

"I–I have my mom to contend with. The new aide won't be working on the weekend. I think it's too soon for you to take her anywhere without me. She's not used to going with strangers. Invite them to come here. I have plenty of room."

He gritted his teeth. "I'm not a stranger. I'm her father. My mother was a nurse. She's used to dealing with dementia. You'll have to let me take her eventually."

Her eyes sparked. "Eventually, but not now."

"Fine. I'll have them come here."

Her slow nod finally came. "I hope you tell your parents before they arrive. It's going to be a shock."

Not nearly as shocking as the day he learned about his daughter.

❧ Eight ❧

The clock finally ticked over to three, and Elin swung her legs over the side of the bed. She hated the enforced rest time the doctor had prescribed. It make her feel weak and not in control.

She found Marc playing with Josie on the living room floor. He looked up when she entered. "Josie was telling me about a wonderful play area in the attic." He grinned. "She wants to show me some-thing up there."

So he'd quickly won Josie's affection. Elin wasn't sure how she felt about that. "I can show you. This way." She turned toward the stairs, and he lifted Josie into his arms and followed.

Elin led him to the attic door, where she fitted the key into the lock to the third floor.

Josie seemed attached to Marc's hip. She'd never seen Josie take to someone so quickly, especially a man. She flipped on the light and led the way up the stairs.

Standing in the center of the space, she frowned as she looked around. Something was different. She couldn't put her finger on it, not at first. Then she saw that someone had taken all the sheets off the furniture. On one side, she saw an old gold sofa that had to be nine feet long. And a fine, old high-backed chair. There was a pile of rolled-up rugs against one wall, and jumbled against the wall on the other side, she saw an open chest with old toys and dolls spilling from it.

"Someone's been up here." She moved to the trunk and put the toys and dolls back into the wooden box.

Marc set Josie on the floor, and she ran to look at the toys with her mother. "Where do you keep the key to this floor?"

"In the dresser beside my bed." She handed Josie a small china doll. "Be careful, honey. It's very old."

"She has a cute smile, Mommy. Do I smile like that?" Josie looked up at her and smiled, exposing only her front teeth.

Elin had to laugh at the cheesy smile. "Just like that." Her gaze locked with Marc's amused one.

She turned away quickly. What was she doing exchanging a moment of such intimacy with him? It was like he had really segued into being Josie's dad, and Elin wasn't ready for that. What about Tim? How did she even hope to keep his memory alive in Josie when Marc's strong personality would run roughshod over Tim's quiet ways?

"These are really old toys. I bet they're worth some money." He bent over and picked up a bear. "This looks like a Steiff. It's in really good shape."

She took the stuffed animal from him. When she turned back to the box, she discovered Josie had emptied it and was standing in it. "Josie, I was picking them up."

"I fit in here. It can be my house. Close the lid!" She sat down and hugged her knees to her chest. "I can pop up and surprise you like my jack-in-the-box."

"Okay, for just a second." Elin lowered the lid, holding it about an inch off the bottom from closing. "One, two, three!" She helped Josie push the lid up, and the little girl leaped to her feet giggling.

"Boo, Mommy!" She made a face, something between the doll's smile and a grimace.

Elin gasped and stepped back a step. "You scared me! My goodness. But let's pick all this up."

She smiled and lifted her daughter out of the box. The lace of Josie's shoe caught on something, and Elin paused to untangle it. The lace wound around a small curvature in the corner of the chest. She freed it, then lifted Josie out of the way and bent over to examine the bottom better.

Marc knelt beside her. "What's wrong?"

"There's a weird latch or something here." She tugged on it but nothing happened.

"Let me try."

His warm fingers brushed hers, and she pulled her hands back and moved away a few inches. He ran his hands over the bottom, then looked at the chest from the side. "I think there's a false bottom."

Her pulse leaped. "Maybe the diaries are in there. These toys are old. Look at that Tinkertoy set. They might have belonged to the Hurley twins." She told him about the missing diaries. "I mean, it's not a big deal, but I love history, and it would be fun to read about her life. I'd love to find them."

He nodded. "Let me see if I can figure out how to raise it without ruining the chest. It looks quite valuable."

He bent to his task and pulled on the latch. Nothing happened. "Got a screwdriver handy?"

"No, but try this." She handed him her key chain.

He took one of the skeleton keys and slipped it under the latch, then pried gently. There was a clicking sound, and one edge of the bottom popped up. He moved to the other side and did the same to the nearly invisible latch there. In moments, the bottom was loose.

He handed the keys back to her. "Let me lift it out of the way."

Josie clambered onto her lap and watched with interest. "It's a secret place?"

"It is indeed." Elin was afraid to hope there might be something important under there.

Marc slid his fingers under each end of the bottom and lifted. The material appeared fragile, and she prayed it didn't break. His hands caught on one side, and he paused to go more slowly, lifting first one end out of the way, then the other.

When he laid the false bottom on the floor, she leaned over the chest to peer inside. A gauzy material covered the contents, and it looked like it might tear at the slightest touch. She gently peeled back the layers to reveal three bound leather books.

"It's just books, Mommy. Dusty old books." Josie sounded disgusted. She scooted off Elin's lap and picked up the round box of Tinkertoys. "Can I play with these?"

"Sure." Elin couldn't take her eyes off the books. They had to be the diaries.

She picked up the first one and opened the cover. The fine leather was soft in her hands. The inside pages were yellow and a little brittle. She turned to the next page.

Georgina Hurley 1907

Elin closed the book. She would read it during her resting times. It might help her stay awake. She hated sleeping because of the nightmares.

• • •

She yanked on the bedroom door, but it wouldn't budge. He'd locked her in with that music blaring. He knew she hated the song "The Cold Hard Facts of Life." She shuddered as the Porter Wagoner lyrics about murder twanged their way down her spine.

She kicked the door, and pain shot up her leg. "Let me out of here!"

A knife blade slid under the door. "Sure you want me to open the door?" His voice sounded gleeful and way too happy about the fear in her voice.

She stepped back and looked around for a weapon. The heavy lamp would have to do. "You don't scare me." The thump of her heart told a different story. She grabbed her phone. "I'm calling the police!"

The knife disappeared. "You'd better not, Laura." His voice was cold. "I might just turn my attention to Sammie."

The blood froze in her veins. She stepped closer and pressed her forehead against the door. "You wouldn't."

But he would. She knew what he was capable of. The cell phone fell from her fingers and thumped onto the carpeted floor. "I won't call. Just go away and leave me alone."

The lock clicked, and she heard his footsteps clack rapidly away along the wood floor. The front door banged. She waited until she heard his truck engine rev up and pull out of the drive before she grabbed her cell phone and called her sister.

Sweat slicked Elin's skin, and she bolted upright in bed. Another nightmare. She rubbed her throat and swallowed. Just to be on the safe side, she padded down the hall and checked on her daughter and mother. Both slept, unaware of the storm rolling in off the ocean. She went back to her bed, unwilling to sleep again. Her gaze went to the diaries.

Flashes of lightning lit her bedroom as she snuggled under the sheet and opened the first diary. She'd been dying to read it, and she wasn't about to go back to sleep and fall into that nightmare again.

Written in my hand, February 3, 1907. Georgina Hurley

The February wind blew through Georgina's thin coat as she stepped off the ship onto Seagrass Pier and surveyed her new home for the first time. Her blood wasn't used to such dampness and cold, though Joshua had assured her it was nearly forty-five here today.

Joshua saw her shiver and wrapped his great-coat around her. "We'll soon be inside, love."

She thanked him with a smile. He towered

above her five-two height by at least a foot, and his dark good looks attracted every lady in his sphere. She'd been astonished when he began to call after dining at one of her father's soirees. When he'd asked her to marry him, she quickly accepted, and their marriage of six months had been quite harmonious. Most of the time.

But she didn't like the way her life was about to change. Joshua hadn't listened to her pleas either.

He dropped a kiss on her forehead. "It's a far cry from Cambodia, isn't it?"

"Very different." Her eyes took in the magnificent house towering over the sand dunes that seemed to go on forever. Three stories high, it was crowned with a lacy black railing and a cupola. The grand porch wrapped around one side, and the soft gray-green color seemed to blend into the hillside. The shutters could be closed to typhoon winds and storms. It had been built to withstand anything nature could throw its way.

She sent an appealing glance up at her handsome husband. "It's beautiful, Joshua, but I don't want to stay here. I want to go with you."

Impatience flickered in his eyes. "I know, I know." He offered her his arm and escorted her up the boardwalk to the house. "A ship is no place for a woman in a delicate condition. We both know that, Georgina."

He rarely used her name, preferring instead to call her *love* or *darling*. He must be displeased at her complaint. What would it take to get him to see she wasn't some shrinking violet of a woman but one used to making her own way in the world? She'd discovered new plants and had been places most women would be much too timid to venture. When was the last time she'd even been in the States? Ten years ago, perhaps?

She stepped into the house. A grand hall led to a large room on one side and a dining space on the other. A huge walnut staircase gleamed in the afternoon light. A fire coaxed her into the large parlor, and she shed her coat and approached the fireplace. "It's quite beautiful."

His expression was pleased as he surveyed the house. "The builder did a fine job. This is the first I've seen the completed structure myself."

She turned at a commotion in the entry. Four men lugged in her chests and luggage. "I should find our room so they can stow my belongings."

He put his hand on her shoulder. "The house-keeper will do that. You're a lady of leisure now, my dear. You must not infringe on the duties of our staff." He motioned to the unsmiling, middle-aged woman who appeared in the doorway. "Mrs. Winston, our belongings have arrived. Please get them unpacked. Oh, and we're ready for tea and some sandwiches."

Georgina pressed her lips together at his tone and moved so his hand fell away. She liked this less and less.

"Of course, Captain Hurley." She curtsied and turned to speak to someone in the room behind her, then scurried to lead the sailors up the large staircase.

A few minutes later a housemaid in a white apron and cap carried in a tray of tea and sandwiches. Georgina made sure to give her an extra-warm smile. "Thank you. What's your name?"

The maid, about seventeen with ruddy cheeks and bright-blue eyes, bobbed. "I'm Susan, Mrs. Hurley."

"I'm sure we will get along very well, Susan." Georgina removed her hat and placed it on the table by the sofa. "Is there sugar?" She'd developed quite a sweet tooth since her pregnancy.

"Yes, ma'am." Susan set the tray on the table in front of the sofa.

"I'll pour myself." Georgina moved to the table.

"Of course." Susan bobbed again, then practically ran for the kitchen.

She frowned at her husband. "Have you been terrorizing the servants? They seem quite timid."

"I made it clear when I hired them that I expect nothing but the best service. It's as it should be. I don't want you making friends of them either. They need to keep to their place, and you need to keep to yours. No fraternizing like you did aboard ship."

She curled her fingers into the palms of her hands and took a deep breath. "Joshua, you need to understand who I am. I'm not like your mother or your sister. I'm quite competent to do things for myself. I refuse to be some kind of matriarch who throws her weight around. I simply won't do it."

He blinked at her vehemence, and his mustache quivered, a sure sign of his displeasure. "You have a new role to fulfill, Georgina. You're my wife now. You'll soon be the mother of my child as well. I realize it will take some time for you to adjust to your new position, but there will be plenty of time here in the house to figure it out."

He wasn't listening to her. She fought the rising sense of frustration. His expectations were something she couldn't meet. She didn't *want* to be anyone other than herself. Her father had allowed her to travel with him all over the world, and she didn't take kindly to being relegated to such a constricted life.

But what were her options? She loved Joshua. Did that mean she needed to change herself, become some other person? Why couldn't he accept her for who she was?

∾ Nine ∿

The diary's cover was smooth and worn in Elin's fingers when she closed it. How many years had Georgina written in it? How many times had she picked it up and flipped through its pages? Elin glanced around the bedroom. It had been built with its own indoor bathroom right from the beginning, though bathrooms weren't that common back in 1907. This had likely been Georgina's room too. Had she sat by herself on her bed while the thunder rattled the windows and the wind threw whitecaps onto the sand? Had she ever been frightened living out here without her husband?

"What are you reading, honey?" Her mother stood in the doorway to Elin's bedroom. She wore pink curlers in her hair and a black nightgown. Her eyes were bright and alert. It was a good night.

"The storm woke you?" Elin patted the bed beside her. "This diary belonged to the original owner of the house. It's very interesting."

Her mother crawled onto the bed. "Who was she?"

Elin told her about Georgina and her adjustment to her new role. "I sympathize with what she was going through. I don't know who I am anymore either. I'm a widow, but I don't feel my life is over. I love my job, but lately I feel adrift from it, ever since my heart transplant." Her chest felt heavy.

Her mother's blue eyes softened. "I remember when I married your father. I'd had all these dreams of going to medical school and becoming a doctor. There were times after you and Abby were born when I wondered where that dreamy-eyed girl had gone. What had happened to all those plans?"

Elin had never heard her talk about that big of a dream. "Did you talk to Dad about it? You could have gone back to school."

Her mom nodded. "He didn't understand why I wasn't content with raising our two girls and being a mom. We grew up in the era of *Leave It to Beaver*. Your dad thought that should be enough, but I wanted more than washing dishes and taking cupcakes to school parties. I wanted to make a difference."

"You made a difference in my life and in Abby's." Elin took her mother's hand. "You volunteered a lot. And you got a job when I was ten or eleven."

"As a receptionist. Quite a comedown from my dream of being a doctor."

"I never knew you were unhappy."

"I never said I was unhappy." Her mother settled back against the pillow. "That's not what I meant. Contentment is found in your heart, Elin. It's not in a profession or in a relationship. Your roles don't define who you are. You define your roles. How you approach the different roles in your life is something you figure out for yourself. They don't make you someone different from who you are at your core. I realized when you were about eleven that no one else could be your mom but me. No one else could teach you values but me. I was glad I'd stuck it out."

Elin contemplated her mother's words. They

held a lot of wisdom, but they didn't answer the questions she had about how she'd changed since her heart transplant. Did Laura's memories change her? Did having different tastes mean she was more like Laura and less like herself? She didn't know anymore.

"Didn't you regret your decision?"

Her mother shook her head. "Not in the least. I could have gone to school when you went off to college, but by then I found my interests had changed. We evolve as women. Let yourself grow, honey. It's okay."

The phone on the bedside table rang, and she picked up the handset and looked at it. *Unknown.* That could mean a telemarketer, or it could mean her office was calling. She was tempted to let it go to voice mail, but it might be important. There might be a new donor she needed to find recipients for.

She clicked it on. "Hello." There was only silence on the other end. "Hello?" She pulled the handset away from her ear and looked at it. She appeared to still be connected. She put it back to her ear and said hello again. This time she heard the faint strain of music playing.

Her throat tightened. Was that a *Phantom of the Opera* tune? She couldn't tell for sure. Maybe it was her imagination. Before she could freak out, she clicked the phone off and practically threw it back onto its base.

"Who was that?"

Thunder rattled the windows, and Elin jumped. "No one was there."

"Then why are your eyes so big? And your mouth is trembling like you're scared."

"The storm has made me jumpy. That's all." That had to be all it was. It was likely her imagination that the music was the same. She'd heard it over and over in her head ever since he'd broken in. She was seeing danger around every corner, just like that silly note.

She was perfectly safe here.

The next morning Elin felt heavy and slow from lack of sleep. She sat on a beach towel under a dome of blue sky and watched Josie build a sand castle with her grandmother. Mom's eyes were as clear as the sky above, and she chattered with Josie as if she'd never called her by the wrong name. If Elin could only freeze this moment for all time. The scent of the sea, the squawk of the seagulls, and the warmth of the sun would be poignant reminders of a perfect day free from worry.

Mom squinted in the sun, then rose and dusted the sand from her hands. "We have a visitor."

Elin twisted to see Kalianne Adanete climb out of a dinghy at the dock in the tiny crescent of harbor. Elin got up and pulled on her cover-up as the nurse's aide approached with a smile. The woman had an air of competence in spite of her youth and attractiveness. Her denim skirt showed off shapely legs, and she wore her blond hair in a French knot.

Why did she feel such relief at the thought of help? This was her dear mother. Caring for her shouldn't feel like such a burden. The problem was, she was so afraid of failing her.

As the woman neared, Elin held out her hand. "Thanks for coming right away. I hope I didn't interrupt anything important."

"I was thrilled to get the call." Kalianne shook her hand, then turned to smile at Elin's mom. "Hello, Ruby. You look like you're having a good time."

"Josie and I are making a sand castle." The older woman's hand swept over the sand turrets and moat. "I remember you. You're one of Elin's friends from high school. Mary, isn't it?" She frowned disapprovingly. "You were always a bad influence on Elin. I'm sorry I had to forbid her from running around with you."

Elin's throat tightened. She should have known the clouds in her mother's eyes wouldn't stay gone for long. "You remember Kalianne, Mom. She's going to spend some time here and help us find fun things to do."

Her mother's nod was uncertain, and she turned her back to rejoin Josie at the sand castle.

Elin motioned for the aide to join her a few feet

away where they couldn't be overheard. "She was doing really well all day until now."

Kalianne patted her arm. "It's all right. May I call you Elin, or would you prefer Mrs. Summerall?"

She so liked this young woman. Her confidence strengthened Elin's courage. "Oh yes, please call me Elin. We're going to be seeing quite a lot of one another."

Kalianne glanced toward her new charge. "So where do you want me to start with your mom?"

Elin shaded her eyes as she looked into the afternoon sun to the west. She pointed toward the house. "She loves gardening. There's a plot in the backyard that just needs to be tilled. I found a tiller in the garden shed, but I'm not sure how to work it."

"There isn't a tiller made I don't know how to operate."

"I can get whatever plants or seeds you want too." Elin led her back to rejoin her mother and Josie. "Mom, would you like to have a garden?"

Her mother looked up. "A garden? Can I have tomatoes?"

"If we can keep the sea spray from wilting them," Kalianne said. "I think they'll be sheltered behind the house."

Josie jumped up and tugged on the new aide's hand. "Can I help too?"

Kalianne picked her up. "You sure can. I'll teach you how to weed and everything."

Josie pulled back and studied the woman's face. "I don't know. Will there be bugs? I hate bugs, especially centipedes." She shuddered. "They have too many legs."

"No centipedes allowed in my garden," Kalianne assured her.

"What about cats? Mommy hates cats." Josie looked to Elin for confirmation.

"That's right." She shivered. "You'll protect me from the kitties, won't you?"

"I'll shoo them away." Josie seemed in no hurry to get out of Kalianne's embrace.

Watching them, Elin smiled. They could be very happy here with some support from Kalianne.

Josie finally wiggled to be let down. "I'll find my sand shovel." When her feet hit the ground, she ran for the house and disappeared inside.

Elin picked up the beach towel and her *Superman* comic book to follow her daughter. "We'd better see what she's up to. Who knows where the shovel is. She'll have the entire contents of her closet in the middle of her bedroom."

Kalianne smiled and pointed to the comic book. "*Superman*? I have nearly all of them from the seventies. My dad collected them, and he gave them to me."

"You lucky girl. I pick them up whenever I run

into them. I don't have anything near a complete collection."

"Wouldn't it be nice to find a real man like that?"

It bothered Elin that her thoughts immediately went to Marc at the phrase *real man*. She had no interest in him that way. She glanced at her mom, who already looked more engaged and interested in life. It would be great to have Kalianne around.

❧ Ten ❧

The ice-cream shop wasn't busy on this Monday afternoon. Sara glanced around the room and didn't see Elin and Josie, but then, she was about ten minutes early. As she moved toward a corner table to wait, she heard her name.

"Sara." Ben's blue eyes warmed when he smiled up at her. Assigned here from Florida, he hadn't been in his new position long. He was the new head of IT. She hadn't had much contact with him yet and didn't even know his last name. In his late thirties, his blond hair had a casual cut. He was out of uniform and in khaki shorts and a light blue polo.

"Have a seat." He indicated the chair at his table.

"I'm waiting for a friend, but I'm a little early."

She glanced at the door before she sat down.

"Good work on that rescue last week. When I heard there were two kids aboard the sinking boat, I feared we'd have a fatality or two. The youngest was only two, right?"

She nodded. "It was pretty tense. Seas were running at twenty feet. The parents stayed calm though, and that helped."

His smile made her feel like she was in a spotlight. Was he *flirting* with her? Her cheeks warmed, and she couldn't force herself to look away. It had been awhile since such a handsome guy showed interest.

"Can I get you some ice cream? Or you can share my banana split."

"I'd better wait for my friend."

He leaned forward, his gaze intent on her face. "You're good at your job. I like that. I hope you don't think I'm being too forward, but I wondered if you'd want to go to dinner with me. Maybe take in a movie or something on Saturday. If you're free, that is."

Feeling tongue-tied, she glanced down at her hands. Josh wasn't making any moves in her direction. Wasn't it time she moved on from a hopeless relationship? Not that there had ever been a real relationship between them. She didn't owe him anything.

Ben's eager smile dimmed. "Earth to Sara."

"Sorry, you took me by surprise. I'd like that,

Ben. There's a new *Star Trek* movie hitting the theater in Kill Devil Hills."

His grin returned full force. "I'm a Trekkie myself. You're the local here, so you pick where we go. You have a favorite restaurant there?"

"Do you like Mexican? Bad Bean Baja Grill is good in spite of the unfortunate name."

He laughed, a nice sound that warmed her heart just a little. The bell above the door jingled, and she waved to Elin and Josie. "My friends are here. I'll see you Saturday."

He rose and stared toward Elin and Josie. "Elin, I didn't expect to run into you today."

Josie rushed to hug him, and Elin took her turn receiving a hug. "Ben, how great to see you again." She turned to Sara. "Ben is Tim's half brother. He introduced me to Tim actually. I didn't realize you two knew each other."

Ben sent an amused smile Sara's direction. "We just met since I moved to the island."

A warm feeling settled in Sara's chest. It felt good to know Elin approved of this new guy in her life.

Ben rested his hand on Sara's shoulder and gave it a little squeeze. "I wish I could stay and chat, but I need to get back to work."

The three of them stepped to the counter to order their ice cream. Elin studied Sara's face. "I sensed some chemistry between the two of you."

Sara's smile felt too big, and her pulse still

thumped against her ribs as if she'd just run two miles. "Maybe a little." She shut up until they had their order and were seated at a table in the far corner.

Elin scooped up pecan and caramel with her ice cream. "Okay, what's the deal? You are smiling like you just won the lottery."

Sara frowned at her. "Since when do you get something other than a hot fudge sundae?"

Elin looked down at her sundae. "Hot fudge didn't sound good today." Her brow furrowed, then cleared. "Don't try to change the subject. What's going on with Ben?"

A giggle tried to bubble up in Sara's chest, but she stuffed it back down. "He asked me out."

Elin reached over to wipe up a dribble of ice cream down Josie's front. "Did you say yes?"

"Um, I did." Sara took another bite so she didn't have to say more. She'd never been good at hiding anything, and Elin knew her too well.

Elin's eyes widened. "Seriously, you're going out with him? What about Josh?"

"That ship sailed a long time ago. If it was ever in the dock. Josh is never going to get over his fear of commitment, and my birthday is coming in two weeks. Do you know how hard it is to think about turning thirty without a prospect in sight?"

"You don't need a man to be complete. You're the most self-sufficient person I know."

Sara gave a heavy sigh. "Maybe that's the

problem. Josh doesn't think I need him. Is it too much to hope he might be jealous if he sees me with another guy?"

Elin took another bite of her sundae. "Josh strikes me as the type to use it as verification he was right and all women are fickle."

Sara slumped back in her chair. "You're probably right. Maybe I should cancel." She straightened. "No, I will *not*. I deserve a life, a family. I'm not waiting around on Josh any longer. It's amazing you know Ben. What can you tell me about him?"

Elin looked down at her ice cream. "Well, I dated him for a little while. Then he introduced me to Tim, and it was all over. I always felt a little guilty about that. You've heard me talk about Kerri?"

Sara nodded. "Your coworker friend."

"She was married to him for about a year, but it didn't work out. So be cautious, okay? Ben doesn't seem the type to settle down. At least he didn't with Kerri."

Sara's bubble of happiness deflated. "It's just a movie and dinner. Now let's talk about something else. How did Sunday go with Marc? He came over after church, right?"

"Yes." She glanced down at Josie, who was nearly finished with her ice cream. "Honey, you can play with the toys in the corner for a little while if you like."

"Yay!" Josie scrambled down from her chair and raced over to the small table and chairs that held crayons and toys.

"I didn't get a chance to tell you what I found in my Bible at church. Marc thinks kids were playing. I'm worried it's more sinister." She pulled a scrap of yellow paper out of her purse.

Sara stared at the words. " 'I found you.' That does sort of sound like kids playing hide-and-seek, but under the circumstances, it still feels off. Have you seen anyone out at Seagrass?"

Elin shook her head. "I'm having a security system installed though. I've been jittery ever since I got this." She glanced at her watch. "I'd better go. Mom should be done at the doctor's by now. That new aide is such a big blessing. She came early enough to fix breakfast."

"You can use the help." Sara watched Elin gather her belongings and her daughter, then head for the door. It was only when her friend was gone that she realized she still held the scrap of paper.

It wouldn't hurt to get it analyzed. She knew someone who could tell if a child wrote it.

Elin got her mother and daughter settled for the night. After the day in town, they were all tired, so she didn't even have to read Josie a story. Leaving the door cracked a bit, she headed to the living room where she took the herbal remedy she'd gotten from Amy. Maybe it was her imagination, but she was feeling better since she started it. She curled up with a suspense novel, maybe not the best choice of reading material with her current state of mind.

The evening held a bit of a chill, so she pulled a red chenille throw over her legs and opened her book. Something creaked and she looked up. Just the house settling or the wind. She turned the page of her book. Another sound came to her ears, a scratching sound as though someone was running his fingernail along the chalkboard in the kitchen.

A shiver ran down her spine, and she kicked off the throw. Even though she told herself it was nothing, the hair on her arms stood at attention. She got to her feet and grabbed a poker from the set at the fireplace. Wielding it like a baseball bat, she tiptoed toward the kitchen and winced when a floorboard squeaked under her feet.

The scratching in the kitchen stopped, and she heard the screen door slap against the doorjamb. At least that's what it sounded like. She froze, then retreated, reaching for the phone on the end table. There was no 911 on the island, and would the police even believe her? Without thinking, she dialed Marc's number.

He answered on the first ring. "Elin?"

"I think there's someone in the house," she whispered.

"Lock yourself in the bedroom with your mom and Josie. I'm on my way. Go now. I'll stay on the line." A door slammed and an engine started.

She took comfort from the fact he was coming. She tucked the poker under her arm, then rushed up the stairs to Josie's room. Holding the phone to her ear with her shoulder, she scooped Josie up. Her daughter didn't stir as she carried her down the hall to where her mother slept.

"I'm in my mother's room," she whispered. She shut the door and locked it, then slid to the wood floor and sat with her back to the door. She cradled Josie to her chest.

"I'm nearly to the harbor." His voice was urgent. "I'll lose you out over the water, but I'm coming. Do you have a weapon?"

"Just the fireplace poker."

"Better than nothing."

She heard his feet slapping something solid, and his breath was labored. A thud sounded. "Are you on the boat?"

"Yes. I won't be able to hear you in a minute, and I have to navigate out of the harbor. I'll be there in twenty minutes." His voice began to cut out.

Twenty minutes. That seemed so long. She didn't hear the rest of what he said because his voice was too garbled. She ended the call and pressed her ear against the door. Nothing.

She had difficulty regaining her feet with Josie in her arms, so she grabbed a blanket off the end of her mother's bed and laid her daughter on it.

She tiptoed to the window and gazed down into the yard. The tiny back-porch light pushed back the edges of darkness by only a few feet. Darkness shrouded the rest of the yard, and she saw no movement. Maybe the intruder had left.

She hadn't heard a boat approach her remote point, but maybe he'd cut the motor out in the bay, then rowed to shore. Or maybe he'd taken the longer dirt road. Was that the distant rumble of an engine? It was too soon for Marc to be here. A yellow glow of a boat light showed the craft moving away from shore.

He was gone.

She sagged against the wall, then went to take Josie back onto her lap. The little girl hadn't stirred, and Elin's mother still slept soundly. At least they wouldn't be awake the rest of the night the way she would. What had the man been doing in the kitchen, and why hadn't he come after her in the living room? Did he just intend to scare her to death?

Or maybe it was just a thief looking to steal something. It might have nothing to do with Laura's murder.

She wanted to explore the kitchen and see if he'd left anything behind, but she wasn't about to do so by herself. There was no reason to be stupid. The man could have left a booby trap behind. Or a bomb. Who knew?

It seemed an eternity before she heard the sound

of another boat engine. She laid Josie on the blanket again, then rushed to the window and looked out to see Marc tying up to the pier. He ran toward the house, and when he reached the back-porch light, she saw he had a gun in his hand. The tightness in her chest eased. She opened the bedroom door and rushed down the stairs, where she threw open the door and launched herself against his chest.

He stiffened, then his arms came around her and his hand smoothed the back of her hair. "Hey, it's all right. Did you see anyone?"

His male scent was like armor around her, and his embrace was a shield. She told him about the boat she'd seen. "I've been afraid to go into the kitchen."

"Good. I told you to stay out of there just before we got cut off." With his arm around her, he steered her toward the sofa. "You stay here while I check it out."

She shook her head. "I want to see. It sounded like he was scratching his nails on the chalkboard."

She clung to his arm as they advanced to the kitchen. He reached over and flipped on the light. Scrabble tiles lay on the kitchen table. They spelled out a chilling message.

Death.

✺ Eleven ✺

Marc couldn't tear his gaze from the ominous word on the table. He pulled out his phone and snapped a picture for proof. "I'm going to take this with me. You don't want your mother to see it. Josie can't read so she wouldn't know what it said, but it might upset your mom. I don't think you should stay out here alone."

When her chin jutted out, he knew he was in trouble. Her aqua eyes flashed and she shook her head, then moved to the cabinet where she took down a jar of Jif. She opened the lid and grabbed a spoon, then began to lick it off the spoon.

He took a step closer to her. "Look, I know it's upsetting to think about moving when you just got here, but I don't think it's safe."

"You believe me now. Or do you think I did this myself to get sympathy?"

He hadn't even considered the thought, but he allowed it to linger a moment before he rejected it. Elin wasn't the kind for histrionics. Her ice-princess persona liked control, and her first impulse had been to grab a fireplace poker and attack. Whoever had spelled out the word on the table was dangerous.

"You could stay at Tidewater Inn. That's a nice place, and we met Libby at church on Sunday."

The last of the peanut butter disappeared, and her spoon clattered into the sink. "I am so tired of running. If he can find me here, he can find me anywhere. I don't know what to do or where to go to get away from him."

He nodded. "It took me twenty minutes to get here. I could have found all of you murdered in your beds. At least in town or out at Tidewater Inn, you'll have other people around. People who could help if you screamed. I'm calling Libby."

"All right."

Libby answered right away, and he explained the problem.

"I wish I could help, but we're full for the next month. Could someone stay with her? Maybe some of the Coasties? Or a friend? There are five bedrooms in that house, and she's surely only using three. Tell her I'm praying for her."

"I will." He hung up the phone and turned to face Elin. "No room. You have a spare room?"

She nodded. "There is one upstairs and another one down the hall, both with their own bathrooms. I'd thought about taking the downstairs one for my master, but I wanted to be near Josie in case she cried in the night."

"I'm moving in."

She gasped. "You can't do that. I-It would cause talk."

"Rumors won't kill you. That man might. I don't want anything to happen to my daughter.

Besides, your mother is here. It will be perfectly respectable."

All the way out here on the boat, he'd been tormented by what he might find. What if the guy had murdered them all? He kept seeing visions of Elin's red hair splayed out on the floor and an even redder slash across her neck. Of finding his daughter dead. "I'll move my stuff in tomorrow, but in the meantime, you can show me the room." When she opened her mouth, he shot her a look. "I mean it, Elin. Nothing you say could make me leave here tonight."

"All right."

Her sudden capitulation shocked him, but he followed her when she turned and headed to the living room.

She went to the hall by the entry and flipped on the light. "This way."

His feet thudded on the gleaming wood floors as he went down the hall behind her. He peeked into the room. A king bed covered in a blue-and-white quilt dominated the large room. The pale blue walls made him think of a perfect day at sea. Seascapes hung on the walls, and a thick white rug anchored the bed. He nearly whistled at how beautiful it was. "Nice."

A soft smile lifted her lips. "I love this house."

"I hope your room is as nice as this. Pretty spectacular." When he turned back around, he nearly knocked Elin over. He grabbed her by the shoulders and steadied her. "Sorry." She didn't step back and neither did he.

She looked up at him. "Thanks for coming. I didn't know who else to call."

"I'm Josie's father. Of course you should call me." He cleared his throat, which had gone dry. Why was he suddenly seeing her from a different perspective? She'd always been too icy and controlled for him. The elder of the two girls, she had always been too focused on herself and what she wanted. When he settled down, he wanted someone with empathy and a carefree spirit.

He stared down at her. She seemed different now though. The air thickened between them. Her eyes were huge in her pale face, and it took all his restraint not to lower his lips to hers, just to see how she would react.

He dropped his hands from her shoulders and stepped around her. "This will be just fine. I'll see you in the morning." Stopping at the door, he waited until she exited, then closed it before he lost his last bit of self-control.

Elin wrapped her wet hair atop her head and secured it with a clip. Swathed in a white terry robe, she stared at herself in the mirror. Who was she? The heart that pumped under her ribs was changing her, forming her into someone she didn't know anymore. Fear suffocated her daily, and though she'd struggled to push it aside, it still

101

bubbled up every time she caught a glimpse of herself.

In her mind's eye, she had short dark hair, not long red hair. When she looked in the mirror, she expected to see dark brown eyes, not the aqua ones staring back at her. She swayed, suddenly dizzy, then sat on the toilet lid and closed her eyes. Her throat tightened, and she could feel something against her windpipe as he squeezed the life from her. His face was blurry, so blurry, but his hair was blond. And that cloyingly strong cologne he wore added to her lack of air.

"Look at me."

Had he really said that to Laura as she died, or was Elin jumbling it all up? She rubbed her throbbing head. She wasn't Laura, she was *Elin.* She loved oldies, not country music. Her favorite color was tan, not green. She liked chocolate, not caramel.

"Mommy?"

She opened her eyes and smiled at Josie, who stood in the doorway. "You're still in your nightgown. Get your bathing suit on, and we'll go swimming today."

"There's a man in the kitchen. Mr. Marc. He's cooking breakfast." Confusion filled Josie's hazel eyes.

"He's going to be staying here awhile."

And he's going to want to tell Josie he is her father.

She didn't know how long she could stall him. The thought of telling Josie made her shudder. She was too young to really understand, but she would still ask why she'd never seen him before they came here. She would ask questions.

Elin was beginning to question the wisdom of involving Marc in her life like this. She hadn't known whom to turn to, and he'd always seemed so strong. Strong in character, strong in faith, and strong in courage. She hadn't stopped to think of the complications involving him would bring. Had he been about to kiss her last night? She would have let him, and she didn't know where that urge came from. Maybe it was just the longing to feel a man's arms around her. Widowhood was lonely.

Josie tugged on her arm. "Come see, Mommy."

She let Josie pull her out of the room and down the stairs. The aroma of bacon made her tummy rumble, and she realized how hungry she was. When they reached the kitchen, Marc turned with a spatula in his hand. His gaze warmed when he saw her, and she realized she was still in her robe with her hair piled atop her head.

"You're quite domestic." She winced at the banality of her comment. "I mean, thanks for cooking breakfast. Josie was very excited about it. She usually gets a boiled egg and a bagel."

"Every growing girl needs bacon." He turned back to the stove. "Nice kitchen, by the way. All stainless, granite. Someone spent some money in here."

"I have found myself enjoying cooking here even though I always thought I wasn't much of a cook." She released Josie's hand, then opened the cupboard and took down blue-and-white plates. "Is coffee on?"

He nodded. "It's ready."

Josie helped her set the table, and Marc carried a bowl of scrambled eggs and a plate of bacon to the table. He pulled out a chair at the head of the table, the place where Elin usually sat.

She turned toward the doorway. "I'll get Mom."

"She went for a walk on the beach."

"What? You let her go by herself?" She sprang for the door.

He grabbed her arm. "You can't smother her, Elin. Where's she going to go? This point is pretty self-contained. She can't wander far. Besides, she was very bright this morning."

"Her mental state can change in an instant." She yanked her arm out of his grip. "She could drown, or she could wander in the woods and get lost. We haven't lived here very long, and she might not remember how to get back. And I'm *not* smothering her. I'm just concerned for her safety."

He frowned. "Suit yourself."

She started for the door again, but it opened and her mother stepped into the kitchen. Her cheeks were pink and her eyes bright with excitement.

"Mom, I was about to go looking for you." Elin bit her lip when her mother frowned. "I mean, it's time for breakfast."

Her mother's expression cleared, and she stepped to the sink to wash her hands. "I worked up quite an appetite. And I saw a whale blowing off the point. It was quite an exciting morning. I wished you were with me."

"I'd like to have seen that. I'm sure Josie would have been excited too."

Her mother came to the table and sat in the chair across from Marc's. "Maybe it will still be there after breakfast."

Elin pressed her lips together and sat down. Marc was already causing total upheaval in the household.

৵ Twelve ৶

Sara strained to hear over the roar of the helicopter as she leaned out the window at the boat in distress below them. "They're taking on water fast." Her medical-supply kit was fully stocked and ready.

In the cockpit, Josh nodded and maneuvered the craft lower until the powerful winds off the rotors kicked the waves even higher. On the boat deck below, Alec waved to let them know he'd arrived. He unclipped himself and motioned to the three men on the boat.

Sara frowned when one of them tossed two boxes overboard before rushing to where Alec was preparing to airlift them. Could this be a drug boat?

She spoke into the mic in her helmet. "Josh, did you see that guy throw something overboard? Looked like a couple of crates. Might be drugs."

"I noticed and sent a message to headquarters. A cutter is nearly here anyway, and they'll see if they can retrieve it."

He'd been impersonal and remote with her for two weeks. No flirting, no joking around. Even Curtis had noticed and tried to pry out any problems. One thing about Josh, he kept his real thoughts to himself. It was a good thing she'd given up. Nothing would ever get through that thick skull of his.

The Coast Guard cutter came into view below and zoomed toward the sinking boat. When the three men aboard saw the vessel, one of them dove overboard and started swimming for shore. Seagrass Pier was barely visible in the distance, but the swimmer struck out for it.

"One's escaping!" She pointed out the dark head, barely visible in the waves.

"They see him. No one is in danger, and my

engine is cutting out. I'm radioing Alec to ride back on the cutter. Something is wrong with this thing."

She nodded and sat back in her seat. Curtis exchanged a commiserating glance with her. It took only ten minutes to get back to the airfield. She yanked off her helmet and hopped out of the chopper. Let him be alone the rest of his life. She stalked toward the building to change out of her flight suit and head for home, but Josh called her name.

He jogged toward her. "Sara, wait up. Want to go get coffee?"

She put her hands on her hips as he neared. "What is with you, Josh?" When he blinked, she remembered Elin's advice and took a step closer, then jabbed her forefinger in his chest. "It's no secret how I feel about you. I've been in love with you for two years. One minute you flirt with me, and the next you act like we're strangers. I'm sick of the way you blow hot and cold. If you want to be with me, then say so. If not, I'm moving on. I'm not wasting my life waiting on you to make up your mind."

His blue eyes widened, and his smile faded. Nothing like drawing a line in the sand. Was she ready for him to totally walk away? She tipped her chin up and stared him down.

He took a step back. "Where is this hostility coming from? I thought we were friends."

"Friends. Is that what you call our relationship? Do you flirt with friends?"

His strong jaw flexed. "You know I care about you, Sara. We're good friends."

"Fine, if that's how you feel." She turned to go.

He caught her by the forearm. "Don't be like that."

"You mean don't expect anything to change? Don't expect you to finally tell me how you feel? Don't put any demands on you? What is broken in you, Josh? It's perfectly normal for a woman to want a man to show her how he feels. Most people want commitment and a love that will last."

"Love never lasts. I don't know anyone who has a perfect marriage."

"Marriage or any other kind of relationship takes hard work. Of course there are ups and downs. That doesn't mean it isn't worth it or that you're better off staying alone. Is that what you want? To die alone and unloved? Never to feel your child's arms around your neck or to wake up next to someone you love every morning? I don't want that kind of aimless existence."

He stared down at her with what looked like longing. "What makes you so sure that kind of thing is worth the risk? What if you roll over and hate the face next to you one morning? What about regrets?"

She wished he'd open up and tell her where all

these fears came from. His parents had a nasty, contentious divorce, but surely it was more than that. "The only thing I would regret is if I had a chance at happiness and threw it away. Some things are gone for good once the opportunity passes. You can't go back."

"What are you trying to say, Sara?" His voice was quiet.

At least he wasn't angry. She took a step closer. "I've always believed we could have something special, something that would last a lifetime. I think you believe it too, but you've been afraid. Now is the time to make a move."

Should she tell him she had a date? Would it push him the other way or make him realize he was about to lose her?

"What if things don't work out? What if our friendship is ruined by trying to bring romance into it? Don't those things worry you at all?"

"Life is always a gamble. The best things are worth fighting for. I think you're worth fighting for. I hope you feel the same about me. Do you love me, Josh?"

She held her breath after her question. Where was all this boldness coming from?

Something flickered in his eyes, a tamped-down passion she'd glimpsed a time or two over the past two years, and joy bubbled up.

She touched his face. "Say it."

His throat worked. "I–I care about you, Sara.

You know that." He backed away, and her hand fell to her side. "I'd better get back to work."

Her elation deflated, and she watched him retreat. It was over.

"So what have you found out so far in the diaries?" Marc adjusted a cushion and leaned back on the sofa.

He'd been here two days now, and he already seemed like a fixture in the house. Her mother catered to him, and Josie was never far from his leg. In shorts with his feet bare and his brown hair tousled from an ocean swim, he was entirely too male and too handsome for Elin's peace of mind. She didn't want this pull of attraction.

She averted her gaze and picked up the diary. "She was quite an adventurer. Have you ever heard of Isabella Bird?"

"Sure. A Victorian lady who traveled to the outer reaches of the world—Japan, Hawaii, Tibet. She was a naturalist, I think."

Elin tucked her feet under her and opened the leather-bound book. "Georgina was like that. She traveled with her father who went out looking for exotic species of orchids and other plants for Victorian gardens. His specialties came from Cambodia, a place she loved. So she didn't take to the conventions of married life. She wasn't used to being told what to do by a man."

"Sounds like a spitfire."

"I like her. I've just gotten to the part where one of her friends from Cambodia has come to see her."

APRIL 24, 1907

Chann hung back until Georgina rushed to hug him. He looked so different without his conical hat and his krama, a scarf the Khmer people used for everything from carrying babies to protection from the sun. About thirty, Chann was tall for a Cambodian with shiny dark hair and a ready smile that warmed her from the inside out. His gray suit fit him perfectly.

She flung her arms around him. "I wasn't expecting you until next week." He held himself stiffly, and she realized she'd embarrassed him. Stepping back hastily, she gestured for him to follow her to the parlor.

"Please be seated. I'll ring for tea. Joshua should be home soon." She quaked a bit at the thought of his reaction. He'd been quite upset when she told him Chann would be stopping by for a visit. It was only by threatening to leave herself that she got his agreement to let her friend stay.

Her husband's jealousy was growing old.

Chann didn't smile. "I can only stay a moment. I've been followed."

She studied his face after his surprising announcement. That explained his somber appearance. "By whom?"

Instead of answering, he rummaged in his valise and withdrew a folder. The handsome leather tooling depicted a Cambodian couple in traditional dress. "Can you keep this for me?" His fingers stroked the leather as if it contained something very dear to him.

"Of course." She didn't ask what it was. It was none of her business.

"Tell no one you have it, Miss Georgina. Not even your husband. Hide it somewhere safe. I'll be back for it when I can." His voice was a whisper, and he glanced through the open window behind her before thrusting the leather folder into her hands.

"Are you in danger, Chann? What can I do to help?"

He held her gaze. "Nothing and no one can help me. I must help myself."

She looked down at the pouch. "What's in it?"

"It is best if you do not know, Miss Georgina. Keep it well hidden. As far as you know, I came for a short visit, nothing more."

Before she could ask any more questions, she heard Joshua's heavy tread on the porch. Without stopping to think, she flew to the door and down the hall to the kitchen, then up the back stairway. Luckily no one was in the kitchen. She had the leather pouch tucked into her skirts in case she ran into one of the servants.

The stairs to the third floor stood open, so she

rushed up them and looked around wildly for a place to stash the leather folder. There. She tucked it away, then returned downstairs. The coast was still clear, so she ducked into her room and smoothed her hair while she waited for her high color to subside. When she heard Joshua's unmistakable footsteps in the hall, she sat on the edge of the bed and pasted on a smile.

He rapped at the door, then opened it. "Georgina, are you all right? You have a guest in the parlor." His grim tone told of his displeasure.

"I'm being a terrible hostess, but I needed a moment." She fanned herself, and his frown eased. "I knew you would be along soon to make him welcome."

"Of course, of course. And quite right that you should wait for me. We don't want any wagging tongues." He held out his hand. "I told your friend I'd fetch you."

She put her hand on his arm and rose. "Thank you."

He stared down at her as if trying to see into her thoughts. "Did you know he was coming today?"

"I did not. The last word I had was he would arrive next week. I was surprised to hear he had arrived."

"I quite dislike how free you are with other men, Georgina. You must behave more decorously. Men can get the wrong idea."

How quickly he had discontinued the use of his

pet names for her. They'd been here nearly three months, yet his high standards had become more exacting and his disapproval harder to bear. What had he ever seen in her? She hadn't changed, but his view of her had soured.

"Chann is my friend, Joshua. He's like a brother to me, but nothing more. If I had wanted to marry him, I would have. Father would not have prevented me."

His lips twisted. "Your father gave you too much license."

She wanted to fly to her father's defense, but she pressed her lips together and turned toward the door. Nothing she could say would change her husband's mind.

Elin closed the book. "Can't you just picture her life here? And what an exotic existence she lived before coming here. I would like to travel like that, see strange and wonderful places."

"Sounds like her husband was a jerk."

She couldn't think with his gaze on her. "It was a different time back then. I think she would have fit in this era much better."

"And you would have fit there."

She frowned, unsure how to take his comment. "Are you saying I'm timid and easily manipulated?"

"You like to keep the peace whatever the cost." His gaze sharpened. "Though maybe not so much anymore. The old Elin wouldn't be searching for the murderer so tenaciously. She would have tried to block out the problem by suggesting the killer just get along before she went back to following all the rules and being the perfect daughter."

She should have been offended, but a bubble of laughter in her throat surprised her. And Marc too from his expression. "Was I really that bad?"

He grinned. "Only worse. You seem different now. I think losing your dad made you grow up some."

"It did." That was a better answer than saying getting a new heart had changed her.

Marc found himself watching Elin over the next couple of days as he looked online for clues and made calls in his covert investigation. The gentle care she showed her mother and Josie touched him and made him watch her even more. She laughed more, in spite of the circumstances, and didn't obsess about the small things.

On Wednesday morning, he met her and Josie at the bottom of the stairs. "Things have been stressful lately. I recommend a little R & R for all of us."

She wore a cute tan sundress splashed with orange flowers. Her curly hair was caught up on top of her head, and she looked about twenty. Her eyes brightened. "What did you have in mind?"

"It's a surprise." He put his hand atop Josie's

head and looked at Elin. The real surprise was she didn't shoot him down. "I guarantee you'll all like it."

She tipped her head to one side. "Do I dare trust you?"

Josie danced around her. "Yes, Mommy, yes! I love surprises."

"Your mommy does too. She just doesn't know it yet."

A hint of color stained her cheeks. "Give me a hint."

"It involves wind and sand."

Josie antics grew more energetic. "Yay! A day at the beach!"

"Not exactly. Grab your flip-flops and let's go."

For the first time, a hint of worry swam in Elin's eyes. "What about Mom?"

"She'll love it too. She's already down by the boat."

"You left her alone? Marc, you have to learn you can't do that." Elin brushed past him and hurried to the window where she peered out. "I can't see her."

"That's only because you can't see the harbor well. She's standing guard over the sunscreen and sunglasses." He opened the front door. "Come on, we're wasting daylight."

The smile started to return to her face. "Okay." Taking Josie by the hand, she exited and hurried down the walk toward the harbor.

Marc locked the door behind them, then jogged

to catch up with her. "There's Ruby, right where I left her."

"Gramma!" Josie tore her hand from Elin's and raced to join the older woman standing beside the boat.

Ruby's eyes were bright when she turned to face them, and Marc saw the way Elin relaxed. What must it be like to always be conscious of danger lurking around the corner? Not just for her but for her mother and Josie.

He picked Ruby up in his arms. "Let's get you onboard."

She giggled like a girl as he splashed through the water with her, then set her on the middle seat before going back to shore for Josie. His daughter practically climbed his leg like a tree when he reached for her. He set her atop his shoulders and gave her a ride to the boat. Reaching under the seat, he extracted her flotation vest and cinched it around her.

"Don't forget Mommy." She settled into the seat beside her grandmother.

"Oh, I won't." Smiling, he waded back through the knee-high waves to Elin, who was staring at her sequined sandals with dismay.

"I'm going to ruin my new shoes."

"We can't have that." Before she could protest, he scooped her up too.

Her arms came around his neck, and he caught the scent of her perfume, a light and sweet smell that made him want to hold her closer. Her hands touching his skin felt soft and tentative as if she couldn't believe she was in this situation. Her eyes widened as she stared up at him. The moment seemed to stretch out forever as he stared back. Something changed inside him as he studied the faint blush on her cheeks. Awareness flickered to life in the depths of her clear aqua eyes. Something indefinable shifted between them, and he had to force himself to set her in the boat when he reached her seat.

Her long lashes swept down and obscured her expression when he set her down. "Thank you." Her voice went husky.

"No problem." He vaulted into the motorboat and settled at the helm, then fished his key out of his pocket and started the engine.

He reached for his water and took a gulp to quench his suddenly dry mouth. Turning back around, he gazed at his three passengers and pointed. "We'll be there in five minutes."

He couldn't turn back around fast enough after finding Elin's gaze on him. The engine responded to the throttle and zoomed quickly toward the stretch of beach in the distance. At the time when he'd come up with this idea, a beach all to themselves seemed a fun idea.

"Kite flying?" Elin wound her fingers around the ball of string and couldn't hold back the incredulous laugh that burst nervously from her throat. "I haven't flown a kite in years."

"I thought so." Marc looked entirely too smug and handsome as he helped Josie get her kite up in the air. "I'm going to teach you to be spontaneous."

Her cheeks heated. His statement indicated he planned to be around for a while, that they were going to have some kind of relationship. And what had happened between them when he carried her to the boat? The frisson of awareness she'd felt had shown in his eyes too, and his arms had tightened around her.

The wind yanked at her kite, and she ran out some string to let the breeze carry it up toward the puffy clouds scuttling by. Her kite was a Wonder Woman one in red, white, and blue. He'd brought Josie a princess one, and her mother ran along the lapping waves like a kid with her dolphin kite. Elin's worries slipped away like the tide.

Josie's kite was in the air, and Marc let her handle it by herself after showing her how to keep it floating. He jogged to the top of a sand dune with Elin. "Looks like you need help."

His warm hands closed over hers, and her knees went weak. She lost her balance on the soft sand and sat on her rump. The wind yanked the kite up, and she lost her grip on the string. She and Marc grabbed for it at the same time, and he fell onto her.

The air rushed out of her lungs, but it wasn't as much from his weight as from the feel of his skin against hers. She hadn't been this close to a man since Tim died, and the sensation felt . . . nice. Too nice, in fact. She snatched her escaping breath back and jumped to her feet.

He got up too, brushing the sand from his bare legs. Her gaze followed his big hands to the muscular curve of his thighs and calves. She turned away quickly. What on earth was wrong with her? This was *Marc*. Not some new suitor who would welcome her unruly thoughts.

❧ Thirteen ❧

"So he just turned and walked off?" Elin couldn't believe Josh was so pigheaded. "What did you do?" The sand was warm on her bare feet. A gull fixed its black eyes on her and stared, probably waiting to see if she would drop a crumb for it.

Sara stooped and picked up a perfect shell, then dropped it in her bag. "Came here for sympathy." Her laugh was forced.

The scent of rain hung in the air from the dark, low clouds overhead. The women walked along the cove just north of the pier where driftwood and shells collected. Elin had been glad to leave Marc's suffocating presence at the cottage. Ever since their kite outing yesterday, she'd found herself uncomfortable around him. What if he noticed the way she looked at him? She'd die of embarrassment.

"I have a feeling this was the final straw." Elin couldn't blame her. Sara had been more than patient.

Sara's eyes glistened, and she nodded without saying anything. She probably couldn't discuss it without letting the tears fall. Elin wished she could talk some sense into Josh. "I'm sorry, Sara."

"I'm okay." She sighed and reached for her purse. "Oh, and that note you got at church? I had it analyzed. It was likely written by a male in his thirties or forties."

Elin swallowed. "So it wasn't a kid."

"I'd hoped it was. Try not to worry."

"Let's talk about something else." Elin forced a smile. "You have your big date on Saturday. Have you run into Ben any more?"

Sara shook her head. "I saw him from a distance yesterday, but he didn't see me. I'm trying to look forward to it, but right now I wish I could cancel it and stay home. I'm not sure I'm ready. I don't want to get into any kind of rebound relationship. Talking to Josh today, I realize it may be a long while before I'm over him."

"I think you should go. Maybe he'll see you or hear about it, and it will make him jealous."

"You said you were worried it would prove to him that women are fickle."

"It doesn't sound like you have anything to lose though."

Sara picked up another shell. "That wouldn't be fair to Ben. Besides, I don't think Josh cares enough to be jealous. He was able to walk away today after I told him I loved him. That tells me everything I need to know." Her throat was choked.

"I guess so." A crate scraped against the rocks just offshore. "Hey, look at that. What do you suppose it is?" She waded into the water toward it before the current carried it back out to sea.

Sara waded out with her. "We had a rescue earlier this week, and I saw one of the men aboard throw a couple of boxes over. It was right out there." Sara pointed offshore. "This might be one of them." The two women steered the crate to shore, then dragged it onto the sand. "We'll need a crowbar to get it open."

Elin turned toward the house. "I'll go ask Marc to bring one."

Sara frowned. "Wait, he's here? You didn't say anything about it when I called for you to meet me. I wouldn't have pulled you away."

"There was a break-in Monday night." Elin told her friend about the scare. "So he insisted on moving in."

"He's *staying* with you?" Sara's expression turned worried. "He thinks the threat is that serious?"

"I was going to go to Tidewater Inn, but

Libby had no open rooms. Full-on tourist season."

Sara stopped tugging on the top of the crate. "So you think it was the same guy who killed your donor?"

"Yes. It's creepy the way he's playing with me."

"Could it be someone else? Someone who gets his kicks out of scaring women? That's all he's done so far."

That gave Elin pause, and she shrugged. "It could be anyone. An article ran in the newspaper about my cell memories, remember? Someone could have read it and decided to start scaring me. I would love to believe it wasn't the murderer, and this guy is just some sick jokester." She remembered the Scrabble letters and shuddered. "It doesn't feel that way though. I'm sure it's him."

"That was in the article too. He could be playing to everything he knows about your memories."

"It feels like the same man though. What if he decides silencing me isn't enough and goes after Josie or Mom? I have to help find him and put him behind bars where he can't hurt anyone else."

"Have you tried pulling up even more memories?"

Elin shivered at the thought. "I don't know how to do that. I try to remember more, but it's all blank."

"What if you got some of that cologne and maybe a man's red sweater? You could go out on a boat with them and see if they trigger anything else. I'll help you. It's worth a try."

Elin found it hard to breathe. "It's terrifying when the memories come. I hate them. But I don't want to just wait around for him to try again either. I guess I'm game to try it. I'll have to go to Virginia Beach or a bigger city to find the cologne. It's uncommon. I ought to check on my house too. A college student is house-sitting, and I haven't heard from her for a few days. I have visions of the place being trashed during a party. She's supposed to be keeping it clean for real-estate showings."

"I'm ready to get away for a day. I'm off tomorrow. We could run over to Virginia Beach, check on your house, then shop a bit."

"Okay. I'll see if Kalianne can keep Mom. She's not a good traveler. And my sister, Abby, wants Josie for a couple of days."

"Let's leave about nine. I'll meet you at the dock with my car." Sara squinted toward the house. "Your knight in shining armor is outside."

"I stopped believing in fairy tales a long time ago. Life never seems to turn out the way we expect." She started for the house. "I'll see if we can find a crowbar."

Marc waved at her, and she wished she could stop her pulse from galloping every time she was around him. Why was that happening when she'd never looked at him that way before?

• • •

The two women stood close together as though they were talking about something personal. Sara's smile seemed forced as he stopped in front of them.

Marc held up the crowbar. "Took me a minute to dig it out of the garage. This the box?"

He eyed the crate at their feet. It bore no distinguishing marks and seemed a typical storage unit. At first the top resisted his attempts to open it, but the crowbar finally slid under the lid and popped it loose. He pried it off the rest of the way with his hands. The inside seemed to be filled with only shredded rubber, but he flung the wet packing material out of the way to reveal plastic-covered, white, oblong packages.

"Heroin," Sara said. "I thought they were drug smugglers. I should see if they caught the one who jumped overboard. I can identify him." She pulled out her cell phone. "Oh wait, this doesn't work here."

"Go closer to the house so it logs on to the Wi-Fi. Then you can use it."

Sara nodded at Elin and walked toward the house to deal with her call.

Marc shoved his hands into his pockets. "I checked into your break-in. The police located the skiff used to come out here—at least they think they did. It was the same type as one stolen from the dock in Hope Beach, and it showed up onshore down the sand from Tidewater Inn."

"Did Libby or Alec see anything?"

He shook his head. "Alec is the one who found the boat, and he called it in."

"Why do they think it's the same one?"

He didn't want to have to tell her, but someone would spill it to her anyway. "They found your name carved in the side of the boat with a skull and crossbones beside it. Your full name."

She shuddered and took a step back. "Sara had an idea about trying to jog my memory. She wants us to go out on a boat with the killer's cologne and a red sweater." She hugged herself. "It scares me though. What if she takes over more and more?"

He didn't like the way the color drained from her face. " 'She'? Who do you mean, Elin?"

"Laura. I'm becoming Laura." She rubbed her forehead. "I see things she saw, like things she liked. Sara thinks I haven't noticed how much I've changed, but it terrifies me. What if I lose who I really am?" She swallowed hard and turned to look out to sea.

He followed her gaze out over the whitecaps. There was a boat, just barely visible at the horizon. He put his hand on her shoulder. "Traits can change like the sea, Elin. You might like coffee now or hate oldies, but you're still you down inside. Your daughter is the most important thing to you. You would do anything to help your mom. You love your job of matching organ donors with recipients because you feel such purpose in helping others. Quit worrying about extraneous things, honey."

Something flickered in her eyes at the endearment that slipped out, but she turned toward Sara before he could identify if it was irritation or warmth.

"Did they catch the smuggler?" she asked Sara.

Sara shook her head. "And they think he might be dangerous. The drug boat is registered to Devi Long, a known drug smuggler on the run from the authorities in Florida. He is believed to have killed at least three men so far, but he's eluded the authorities at every turn. Here's his picture."

She turned her phone around to show them a good-looking Asian man in his forties.

"He leaped overboard just offshore here and swam this way," Sara said. "You both need to be careful. He could still be lurking about."

"It's possible, but I'd guess it's far more likely he had someone pick him up. Did the Coasties find any sign of him when they searched here?" He'd seen them picking through the seagrass and brush for a couple of hours before getting back on their cutter and cruising off.

Sara shook her head. "No sign at all."

The wind lifted Elin's long red hair and blew it across her face. She swiped it out of her eyes. "Could this Long have been the man who broke in the other night?"

"No. He swam ashore yesterday. The break-in was on Monday night." He understood where Elin was coming from. Any other intruder wouldn't be nearly as terrifying as Laura's murderer finding her.

"Oh, right."

She looked so small and scared standing there on the beach in her bare feet. The sundress she wore showed off tanned arms that looked eminently touchable. He averted his gaze.

"We'll find the guy, Elin. I won't let him hurt you or Josie." He glanced at his cousin. "Elin says you have an idea about helping her remember more details about the killer. Smart. I could wear the red sweater and cologne."

Sara tucked a honey-colored lock behind her ear. "That's a little too threatening, I think. Let's just try having her smell the cologne and touch the sweater. We don't want to scare her to death. We could go out tomorrow night after we get the cologne. It was nighttime, right?"

Marc had studied the file over and over. "About midnight. Moonless night, too, so really dark." He glanced overhead. "Should be a good night for it. It's supposed to be like this for the next three days."

Elin's face showed she was anything but excited about it. "Just stay close to me, okay? If I start having an intense flashback, I'll need you two to bring me out of it." She swallowed hard. "Sometimes they're pretty scary."

He wished they didn't have to put her through it, but they had to find this guy. Sooner or later he was bound to find a soft spot in their defense.

❧ Fourteen ❧

Finally the house was empty. Kalianne would be undisturbed for the entire day since Elin had gone to Virginia Beach. Once Kalianne was sure Ruby was sleeping soundly in her chair, she headed to the hall bedroom with a flashlight. Where on earth should she look first? The house was old. Were there even any guarantees it was still here?

She wanted to check Marc's room first, mostly because he intrigued her. Though she'd put on her most seductive smile and tried her best, he hadn't noticed her as more than a fixture. He had eyes only for Elin, which peeved Kalianne a bit since the woman was at least eight years older than her.

His room was set up like a master. About fifteen feet square, it held only a sleigh bed and matching dresser with nickel pulls. He'd put out no pictures or decorations, not that she expected it of him. Most guys didn't think about the niceties like that. She opened his closet and found only four pairs of jeans, a pair of khakis, and six shirts. The dresser held underwear and socks, nothing personal. Disappointed, she shut the top drawer and checked out each one in turn, only to find them empty.

She went to the attached bathroom next, pausing to sniff his cologne and sigh. His toothbrush and deodorant were in the cabinet with his comb. She plucked a dark hair from the comb and rolled it around in her fingers before dusting it off in the wastebasket.

So impersonal. She didn't know him any better than she did this morning.

Next she checked out the office. Nothing. Then she headed upstairs to the old lady's room. It was one of those rooms that appeared not to have been used much over the years. It still had the original plaster walls, unlike the other bedrooms that were covered in newer drywall. She tested the wide floorboards for movement, but they all appeared solid. After opening the closet door, she removed the shoe boxes and other storage boxes from the shelves and pressed around on the back of the closet walls. When she found nothing, she flipped on the flashlight and shone it around the ceiling area and floor.

Was that the outline of a hidden panel? Kalianne grabbed the chair from the corner and dragged it into the closet, then mounted it and moved her hands around the panel. It didn't move, but there had to be a way to open it. She began to press each corner. When she touched the third corner, she felt it shift. With renewed interest, she pressed harder, and the opposite corner popped loose, allowing her to pry the panel off.

She shone her light into the space. The illumination revealed only dusty rafters at first. She stood on her tiptoes and poked her head cautiously into the space. There. What was that brown thing? Her fingers barely reached to the far rafter, and she snagged the leather tie around it. Once it was safely in her hands, she stepped down from the chair and turned, eager to take a look at the hidden stash.

"What are you doing in my room?" Ruby's voice sounded bewildered.

Kalianne spun around. "Um, I was looking for your new shoes. I thought you might like to wear them."

Ruby swayed a bit on her feet, and her hair stuck up in places from the way she'd been sleeping. "I have new shoes?"

"Red ones," Kalianne improvised. "You said something about them before you fell asleep."

"I love red." Ruby came toward her. "That's mine."

Before Kalianne could react, the old woman grabbed the leather pouch from her hands. Kalianne tried to grab it back, but Ruby turned and rushed away. Kalianne followed, but Ruby was up the stairs to the third floor before she could blink. As she yanked on the door, she heard a click.

She rattled the knob. "Ruby, unlock this door!"

Ruby giggled from the other side like a child playing hide-and-seek, then her footsteps went up the stairs. Gritting her teeth, Kalianne rushed down the hall to the stairway to the first floor. There were keys around here somewhere, but she wasn't sure where Elin kept them. Rummaging through the drawers in the kitchen, she found nothing. Next she checked the drawers in the side tables in the living room, but the keys weren't there either. Maybe they were in Elin's bedroom.

She raced back upstairs and down the hall to the master bedroom. She hit the jackpot when she yanked out the top drawer on the bedside table. Her fingers closed around the ring of keys, and she turned to hurry to the third-floor stairwell. It took another few minutes to figure out the right key, and she fumed the entire time.

She unlocked the door and threw it open, then stomped up the narrow staircase in an angry staccato. Her brother owed her big-time for this.

With great effort, she pitched her voice low and soft. "Ruby, where are you?"

A giggle to her left answered her, and she turned but didn't see the old woman. "Come out, come out, wherever you are. Olly, olly, oxen free."

Ruby burst out from behind an old piano with a delighted grin on her face. "I fooled you!" She did an awkward dance under the eaves.

"You sure did. Now where is the leather pouch you took from me?"

Ruby's grin faded. "Pouch? I don't have a pouch."

Kalianne gritted her teeth. "I had it in your room. You took it and ran."

Ruby took a step back at Kalianne's sharp tone. "I don't have a pouch."

"A leather folder. It had a leather tie wrapped around it. This big." Kalianne measured it out with her hands.

Ruby shook her head. "I don't have it. I'm hungry. I think I'll make some soup."

She turned and hurried down the stairs. Kalianne stomped after her. She would get that pouch no matter what it took.

Josie kicked her feet against the back of the seat. "I want to see Aunt Abby. Now."

"We're almost there, honey." Elin could see the red metal roof of her cottage from here as she turned the corner into the cul-de-sac. "Quit kicking the seat." Josie had been impatient when they stopped at the mall to buy the cologne, and Abby had texted her several times as well. "There's Aunt Abby's car." She pulled in beside her sister's blue Camry and shut off the car.

Sara hopped out on her side. "I'll get Josie out."

Elin climbed out and hugged her sister. "You look great, Abby. I've missed you."

Abby returned her hug. She smoothed the pink sweater over her curves. "I've lost five pounds."

Her sister was on a perpetual diet, even though her generous curves looked good on her. In her late thirties, she wore her blond hair in a perky style with the ends flipped up. Her husband was a dermatologist and didn't want her to work, so she spent her time perusing fashion magazines and volunteering at a local senior center. They had no children, though not for lack of trying, and Abby liked to take Josie for the weekend every chance she got since they lived only twenty minutes apart.

"Aunt Abby!" Josie pelted toward her aunt. "You haven't been to see my new room."

"Not yet, bug, but I'll see it when I bring you home." She turned and looked at Elin. "I should be there by dinner tomorrow. We can go out for seafood. Charles is out of town at a seminar so I can stay the weekend."

"Perfect." Elin opened the back door and grabbed Josie's small case, then stowed it in her sister's backseat. "Have fun."

"We will." Abby buckled Josie into the car seat she always had in the car for her niece, then went around to the driver's side. "I knocked on the door, but Lacy didn't answer. Her car is in the garage though. Maybe she's sleeping in."

"I've got my key. See you tomorrow." Elin waved as they pulled away, then turned toward the house. "I don't like it that she isn't answering the door. I have a feeling the house is going to be trashed."

The house looked normal. Still the same neat and clean cottage she'd taken such pride in. The grass hadn't been mowed in a few days, but it would be two or three more before it needed a trim. The flower bed had no weeds.

Sara followed her to the front door. "Have you talked to her since you left?"

Elin shook her head. "I've tried to call her a few times this week but just left messages. She hasn't called me back. She has finals though. I suppose she could be neck-deep in studying with no time for reassuring me that she's taking care of my house."

She mounted the big front porch and stepped to the red door. There was no sound from inside. She pressed her finger firmly on the doorbell. A dog barked and she frowned. "She's not sup-posed to have pets. She assured me she would have someone else take care of Max."

Sara glanced at her. "You love dogs. I've never known you to complain about a dog's presence in your house."

Elin's irritation faded, and she remembered nuzzling her golden retriever when she was growing up. "I don't know why I said that." She pressed the doorbell again, and the barking grew more frantic. "I'm going to use my key."

She inserted her key in the lock and opened the door. "Lacy? It's Elin." The dog, a tiny Yorkie, leaped against her leg. "Hey, Max." She leaned down and picked up the dog. "What's that smell? It's like rotten meat."

The women ventured farther into the house. The living room seemed fine at first until Sara pointed out an upended table. Pieces of a broken blue vase lay scattered around it. Something didn't feel right. The house was too still, almost waiting. And that smell . . .

Still carrying Max, she moved to the kitchen. Two saucers were in the sink along with a coffee cup and a red glass. Max's food dish held only two pieces of food, and his water dish looked murky as though it hadn't been freshened for several days. The strong odor came from the over-flowing trash can.

"I'm not sure she's here, but I'm surprised she'd leave Max all alone." There had been a doggy door in the kitchen when she moved in. She nudged it with her foot and it opened, so Max had been able to use it.

Sara turned back toward the door to the living room. "Let's check the bedrooms."

They went back through the living room to the entry and headed up the open stairway to the second floor. "Lacy? Are you all right?" Elin had no sense that anyone else was in the house. The silly girl had likely gone off with friends without a care for little Max. Some people didn't deserve to have a pet.

Lacy's room was the first one on the right, and it was empty. The bed was made, and the room appeared as though it wasn't being used. Lacy's things weren't on the dresser. Sara opened the closet. Empty.

"It looks like she left."

"And didn't take Max?" Elin shook her head. "Let's check the other rooms."

Elin's bedroom door hung partway open, and she saw a pale hand on the carpet. She gasped and flung the door fully open. "Lacy!"

Lacy, dressed in Elin's blue negligee, lay on the beige carpet. She wore a long red wig, and it lay spread out around her head.

Sara leaped to her side and placed her hand on her carotid artery. "It's barely pulsing."

"She's dead, isn't she?" Elin asked.

"She's been strangled with a wire, but her heart is still beating."

Sara pulled out her phone. "I'm calling for an ambulance and then the police."

Looking at her young friend, Elin knew the ambulance would be too late.

❧ Fifteen ❧

Police cars lined the street around Elin's house. Marc showed his ID, then pushed his way through the throng of neighbors and officers to get to Elin. This had to have been a huge shock to her. She'd been nearly incoherent when she called him.

He found her seated in the pale-blue living room with Josh beside her. Marc surveyed her shocked white face, then moved to sit beside her. "You okay?"

Her lips trembled and she nodded. "I can't believe it."

He glanced at Josh. "How'd you hear about this?"

"Scanner." Josh pressed a glass of water into her hand.

Marc should have been glad someone was caring for Elin, but he didn't like that Josh had gotten here so fast. What was he doing in Virginia Beach anyway? Marc popped a mint into his mouth.

He took Elin's hand. "What happened?" He listened to her describe what they'd found.

"She died shortly after she got to the hospital, but at least they saved her organs."

The fact the dead woman had been dressed like Elin disturbed him. Had she been the intended target, or had the killer forced her to dress up like Elin as a warning? Either way, the killer was escalating.

She turned her head to whisper to him. "The responding officer is the one who came after he broke in the first time. I think he believes me now. If he'd only listened the first time. None of the detectives believed I knew anything about this guy." She rubbed her head. "I wish I could remember more. He has to be stopped. He's killed two women now."

"That we know of."

She sucked in her breath. "Could it be a serial killer?"

"Maybe. The method of killing is the same."

Sara came through the kitchen door with a coffee cup in her hand. "It's fresh with cream."

"Thanks." Elin wrapped her fingers around the cup and took a sip. "My stomach is in knots. I just want to get out of here. Do you think we could go?"

"I'll check with the officers. They already interrogated you both, I assume?"

Sara nodded. "At great length."

It had taken Marc three hours to get here by the time he caught the ferry and drove through the traffic. He didn't doubt the police had hammered them with questions. He found the detective in charge who told him they could leave, but that someone would be out to ask more questions tomorrow.

"Let's go," he told the women.

Elin rose. "Let me rinse out my cup first."

He followed her into the kitchen, away from the hubbub going on in the rest of the house. "Do you know how he got in?"

She shook her head. "The police are checking all that out. They asked for permission to get my phone records to see when I last spoke to her. I think it was a week ago." She shuddered and hugged herself. "I should call Lacy's parents. They don't know yet."

His gaze roved over her pale face and trembling mouth, her shadowed eyes. She was much too fragile to be the one to deliver such horrific news. "The police will do that. You can stop by once the shock has worn off and offer your condolences. Where do they live?"

"In Charlotte. She was their only child." Tears welled in her eyes. "I feel like it's my fault. He wanted to punish me, didn't he? I think he forced her to dress that way. She saw my negligee once and laughed at it, saying she wouldn't be caught dead in something so matronly on her wedding night. She wouldn't have tried it on for fun. And where did she get that wig? She was a college student. There was no money in the budget for something that expensive. The police said it was human hair."

Seeing her cry tore him up. He started to embrace her, then realized he didn't have that right. She wouldn't welcome such familiarity from him. "You need to take some medicine or anything?"

She shook her head. "I'm fine."

He popped another mint, then stuffed his hands in the pockets of his jeans. "The police will get a lot of clues from here. They can track down where he bought that wig, and I'm sure they'll find some forensic evidence. They'll be combing the place for hair and fiber."

She brushed the tears away. "I'm going to stop him. Lacy was my friend, and I loved her. Seeing her like that made me realize just what a monster he is. I'm going to do what Sara said and go out on the boat tonight to see what I can pull up from Laura's memories."

At least she was saying *Laura* and not *me*. "I'd like to come along."

She rinsed out her cup and turned it upside down in the dish rack. "All right."

"Did you call your sister and tell her about this?"

She shook her head. "Not yet. I don't want to worry her. Josie will pick up on it."

He pulled out his phone. "She should be warned. What if this guy decides to go after her too?"

Elin's eyes grew enormous in her white face. "Why would he do that?"

"He's sending you some kind of message. We have to figure out what that is. And keep everyone you love safe while we do it. Give me her number."

She rattled off the number, and he punched it into his phone. "Abby? It's Marc Everton."

"Why, Marc, I haven't spoken to you in years. Elin's all right, isn't she?" Her voice sharpened from curiosity to worry.

"She's all right, but the house sitter isn't." He briefly explained the situation and heard her gasp softly on the other end of the phone. "Is there anyone there with you besides Josie?"

"No, Charles is out of town. Why?"

"This guy seems to have a vendetta against Elin, and he's taking it out on people she cares about. Engage your security system. I'll tell the police to have an officer sit outside tonight."

"You're scaring me. Are you sure that's necessary?"

"No, but I don't want to take any chances. Not with you and not with Josie." His little girl had already wound him around her little finger. He'd kill anyone who threatened her. "On second thought, let's all stay together tonight. We'll come get you both. Then I'll be able to watch all of you."

When he ended the call, he found Elin staring at him. "Thank you for watching out for us." She shivered and hugged herself.

He wasn't sure how long he'd be able to protect

them. Killers were good at finding a weak link in their targets' defenses.

Elin rubbed her burning eyes and turned on a desk lamp. Dusk was falling, and she was tired after the events of the day. She'd go to bed early, but Lacy deserved worthy recipients of her organs. She took a dose of her herbals and opened her laptop. From the living room, she heard Josie's excited squeal and Abby's measured tones. At least they were all here together.

She picked up the phone and rang Kerri.

"I was just about to call you," Kerri said. "You working on Lacy's donation? I'm so sorry, Elin. Are you okay?"

"As good as I can be, knowing he was after me." She told her friend about Lacy's attire.

"I'm at the hospital and I noticed her dress. That's just freaky. Do the police have any leads?"

"They had a bunch of forensics people there, so I hope so." Elin opened her list of recipients and sorted them by blood type B, then by tissue type. "Ready to get to work?"

"Ready." A volley of key clicks came from Kerri's end. "You want to take heart and lungs? I'll call the rest."

"Okay." This was her favorite part of the job—calling the recipient's doctors and letting them know they had an organ. "I'll call you when I'm done on my end. Good luck." She ended the call with Kerri, then placed the first call to the doctor of the recipient who needed the heart.

She was smiling when she got off the phone from the final call. A sixteen-year-old boy was about to get a new heart. Elin's smile faded when she thought of the pain Lacy's family was going through right now.

A soft knock sounded behind her, and she turned to see Marc in the doorway. Her heart always seemed to hiccup when she spied him. His sleeveless T-shirt showed off muscular arms and a flat stomach. His dark hair curled a little at the nape of his neck, and when he turned those hazel eyes her way, any thoughts in her head dried up and blew away.

He leaned against the doorjamb. "About ready for the boat trip?"

Dread curled in her belly. She didn't want to immerse herself in the night Laura died.

She forced a smile. "I'm ready. Let me close out of here."

"Did you find recipients?"

"Yes."

He frowned. "You don't sound all that excited."

"I-It's the thing we're doing on the boat." She clasped herself. "You have no idea what it's like to have memories that aren't mine. It's like I'm dreaming with everything distorted and frightening."

His gaze softened. "I'm sorry. We don't have to

do this if you don't want to. The day has been stressful enough."

Shaking her head, she shut the lid of her MacBook and rose. "I can't sit back and do nothing. He was in my house, Marc! He's not going to hurt those I love. I don't trust what he might do next. We have to figure out who he is and get him behind bars."

"You don't have to convince me." He took her arm. "I've got two guards walking the perimeter, and we won't be gone long."

The heat from his fingers warmed her skin. If she leaned in closer, she'd be able to smell his cologne.

"Elin?"

She blinked. "Sorry, I was woolgathering. I'm ready."

His grip on her tightened. "You're sure? Maybe this isn't the best evening to do this. I don't think he'll try anything with me here. Having a man in the house is likely to scare him off."

A man in the house. What an appealing thought. She liked walking into the kitchen in the morning and seeing him there, coffee already brewing. She'd never dreamed how quickly she would acclimate to having him around. Or how quickly their hostility would turn to . . . something else. She couldn't quite name it yet. Attraction for sure. But maybe more than that.

Smiling to reassure him, she led the way out of

the office and nearly mowed down Kalianne, who was hovering outside. "Is everything all right, Kalianne? Where's Mom?"

"Oh fine, fine. But she won't eat. I fixed her some supper, and she thinks she ate already. She hasn't eaten enough today to keep a bird alive."

How sweet of Kalianne to be so concerned. "What did you fix her? She's gotten to be a picky eater, though she used to be willing to try just about anything."

"I fixed beef and noodles with mashed potatoes. And I brought brownies I made last night. She looked at them, then turned away. I thought she loved chocolate."

"She does. Let me check on her. She's in the kitchen?" When Kalianne nodded, Elin went down the hall to the kitchen.

Her mother had already put on her pajamas and fuzzy slippers. She wore a terry robe too even though it was eighty degrees outside and not that cool inside even with the air-conditioning. She sat at the large white table staring blankly at her plate of food. Her fork had fallen to the floor beside her napkin.

Elin stooped and picked them up. "That looks good, Mom. Enough for us too? I'm a little hungry, and I'm sure Marc is starved."

He followed her to the table. "I'm famished. Noodles. There's never been a better food invented. Did you make these, Ruby? I've lusted after your noodles for years. No one makes them like you."

Mom brightened a little and smiled up at Elin. "I made them, I think. Didn't I, Elin?"

She went around to the other side of the table. "He's right—you make the best noodles in the world, Mom. You roll them out by hand and cut them nice and thin." She pulled the bowl to her and ladled some onto her plate. "Yum, it smells wonderful. Do you have enough salt?"

Her mother hesitated, then picked up the clean fork Elin had placed beside the plate. She scooped up a forkful and placed it in her mouth. Chewing reflectively, she finally smiled and nodded. "They are pretty good, if I do say so myself. What do you think, Owen?" She looked expectantly at Marc.

He glanced at Elin but moved to an empty chair and got some noodles. "They're great, Ruby. Thanks for making them for me."

Tears glistened in her eyes, and she put down her fork. "I'm confused. You're not Owen." She rubbed her hand. "What's happening to me? I am losing myself." She pushed back from the table and ran from the room.

Kalianne hurried after her, calling her name.

Elin knew the feeling her mother was experiencing. There were times she wanted to run crying from the room too. In another few months, would either of them be the women they were a year ago?

✺ Sixteen ✺

The motorboat rocked in the waves offshore. Pinpricks of light from the house's windows looked like fireflies on the hillside. The wind tangled Elin's curls, and she wished she'd thought to tie back her hair before coming out here tonight. Was this really a good idea? Nervousness rippled over her spine and heightened every sense: the smell of the sea, the roar of the engine, the taste of the salt on her lips.

Abby hadn't wanted her to do this, and she was likely watching out the window at the boat's lights offshore. She would be praying for Elin too, a thought that comforted her.

Marc's figure loomed in front of her, and he sat beside her. "You look like you're about to jump overboard. We don't have to go through with it."

"I can do this." The words bolstered her flagging courage. "I have to figure out who he is. He might have done this before, and he might do it again."

"It's a brave thing to try. Sara and I will be right here with you. If it gets too scary, we won't press you." He reached over and took her hand.

She clung to his strong fingers, then forced herself to release them. "I don't want to have to do this more than once, so let's find out all we can."

She looked around the boat. It was a forty-five-foot vessel with a large deck area. Not at all like the cruise ship where Laura died. Would this even work? Maybe they should have tried to get aboard the same kind of boat.

The engine cut off, then Sara stepped toward them. "Ready? Let's go around to the other side of the boat. Laura was found on the aft deck. I've got the cologne."

"And I have the red sweater." Marc rose and held out his hand.

Her fingers curled around his, and his strength gave her courage to stand. If she could hold his hand the entire time, she might make it through this. She dreaded the memories, the dreams. This was the first time she'd ever consciously tried to re-create what happened that night. What if she wasn't Elin Summerall when this was over? What if Laura's memories crushed out her own?

She forced herself to walk with Marc to the other side of the craft. At the first sight of the life jackets, she stumbled. Those bright-orange flotation devices brought a hazy memory floating to her. And the smell of the canvas, moldy and pungent, made her feel as though she had no air.

Marc steadied her. "You okay?"

She managed to smile and nod. "Fine." His skeptical gaze remained on her face, and she lifted her head. "I'll be okay. Let's get this over with."

"Okay, I've tried to re-create as much of that

day as I can remember." Sara pointed to the life preservers. "She was under a pile of PFDs. Her feet were here." She moved to the end of a bench just to the left of the orange pile.

Elin edged closer, though the stronger scent of mold made her want to retch. "What was I—she—wearing?"

"White shorts and a red tank top. Her hair was up in a ponytail, and her feet were bare."

Elin's hand went to her throat. She could almost see a woman's outline under the pile of life jackets. Her breathing came hard and labored in her chest. She couldn't breathe, and she took a step back.

Marc's warm hand touched her back. "Ready to try this?"

She nodded, unable to speak, wishing she could change her mind. But Josie was counting on her. She had to protect her daughter.

Marc pulled out a length of piano wire. "He used something like this to choke her." He opened the bag in his hand. "Here's the sweater. I doused it with the cologne."

Elin's fingertips had no feeling in them as she closed her hand around the sweater Sara thrust at her. She stepped to the railing and looked out over the dark water . . .

She'd seen Theo kissing another woman, and all she wanted to do right now was cry. Laura staggered to the railing and rubbed her damp eyes. When a footfall sounded behind her, she thought it might be him following her to apologize. Well, let him try. If he thought she would forget it, he was very wrong. Then she caught a whiff of the cologne. It wasn't Theo. She stiffened and turned to go, but strong fingers gripped her arm.

A voice as smooth as a calm sea whispered against her neck, "Don't go. I was looking for you. Just for you." His hand touched her upper arm, then moved to the back of her neck. "I could kill her for you. Theo would never kiss her again. You don't deserve that kind of treatment. Or do you?" His fingers brushed her neck before the tweak of a hard pinch made her flinch.

Her limbs turned to ice. She pulled away and started for the inside deck. He snatched her back before she'd gone two feet. His breath hissed through his teeth, and he slammed her back against his chest. She struggled to get away, but the alcohol she'd had left her dizzy and unsteady.

His breath smelled of wintergreen, and he pressed his lips against the side of her neck. She caught a glimpse of a red sweater. His strong cologne made her gag, and she felt light-headed. He must have practically bathed in the stuff. He kept her pinned, and she couldn't move her head more than a few inches. His hand was clamped around her arm, and a signet ring with the letter *R* glittered in the bit of deck lighting.

He released her, and she fell to her knees. She caught a glimpse of something shiny as he whipped it over her head. Then something choked off her air. She brought both hands to her neck, but she couldn't get even a finger under the thin wire around her skin. Her eyes fluttered, and she sagged to the deck.

She was drowning, drowning. Her lungs burned, and she struggled harder, then crashed into a pile of orange life vests. The musty scent was the last thing she remembered.

Through a fog, Elin heard Marc say her name, felt Sara touch her arm, but it was as if she were numb and couldn't move. She tried to speak, but she couldn't form her lips into words. Who was she? Where was she? Where was Theo? Was she dead?

Her vision faded to a pinprick, and the musty scent of the life preservers grew stronger as she sank into their embrace.

The boat rocked in the waves as Marc leaped forward to catch Elin before she could hit the deck. He hadn't liked the look on her face before she went limp. If this re-creation had harmed her, he didn't know how he could live with himself. He shouldn't have let her do it.

He eased down with her in his arms and pulled her onto his lap. He brushed her long red hair out of her face. "Elin, it's all right. It's over." Her long lashes didn't move. Her face had lost all color. He looked up at Sara. "Any ideas on bringing her around?"

She knelt beside them. "Let me get some water from the galley." She rose and hurried to the port side, flipping on the deck lights as she went.

His anxiety heightened a notch as he studied Elin's face in the brighter light. Sara returned with a glass of water. He glanced up at her. "What just happened in her memories?"

Sara's mouth trembled. "Even her movements weren't her own. She never tosses her hair the way she did while remembering Laura's murder. She walked differently too."

"You think it really is possible she could become someone else?"

"I think so, Marc. There's something going on we don't understand."

He didn't want to believe it, but Elin clearly knew something she would have no way of knowing without picking up some of Laura's memories.

Her lids fluttered, and she began to stir. A bit of color came back to her cheeks. "Don't touch me, Theo."

Theo? Marc raised her head a bit. "Elin, can you open your eyes?"

She grimaced, then flung up her hand. She blinked and opened her lids. "Marc? What happened?" Her expression changed, and her hand went to her throat.

Relief flooded him. Elin's voice, Elin's expressive face. "You're fine. We're on the boat, remember? You were trying to remember what happened the night Laura died."

Her eyes widened. "I remember. I *was* Laura. I smelled the cologne, and I saw everything just like it happened."

She seemed to realize she was on his lap and struggled to sit up. He eased her into a seated position but didn't let go of her in case she fainted again. She seemed in no hurry to stand.

Sara knelt beside them on the deck. "Here, drink this. How do you feel?" She uncapped the water and handed it to Elin.

Elin gulped down half the water. "I feel a little shaky. But I remember so much more. There was an *R* on his ring." She began to recount what she'd seen when she smelled the cologne.

"Who is Theo?" Marc asked.

Her face fell. "I don't remember. Laura was mad at him, though, when she caught him kissing another woman. He was drunk. Maybe he was a shipboard romantic interest." She inhaled and shook her head. "The man offered to kill the woman Theo was kissing. I think he likes killing."

She shuddered, and he knew she was remembering finding Lacy. She made no effort yet to pull out of his arms, and Marc was content to keep her right where she was. Her softness was just as he remembered it. That night had been etched into his memory for all time.

"Anything else you remember?" he asked.

"His breath smelled of wintergreen, like the pink candy. Or wintergreen gum." She touched her throat again.

"Do you remember what Theo looks like? Any memory of him?" Sara asked.

She shook her head. "Nothing, sorry."

He realized he was enjoying the feel of her in his arms, a dangerous position. He shifted her a bit. "I think I'd better find this Theo and talk to him. I can look at the passenger manifest. Full name might be Theodore. That's not a common name, so we might hit pay dirt."

She finally made a move to get up, and he released her. Sara helped her to her feet, then held out her hand to him. He took it and got up.

Sara hugged Elin. "I'm sorry we put you through this. It's over. You want more water?"

Elin shook her head. "It's okay. At least some good has come of it. If we find this Theo, maybe we'll get some answers." She looked to Marc as if searching for confirmation.

He nodded. "I have a copy of the manifest on my computer. Let's see what we can find out." He walked back to the helm where he'd stashed his laptop. Sara flipped on the light in the small room, then she and Elin settled on the bench seat behind him while he opened the file.

He swiveled in the pilot's chair to face them. "There are two Theodores. Theodore Jensen and Theodore Farmer. Either one ring a bell?"

The tiny lines between her brows furrowed, then Elin shook her head. "I just remember Theo, no last name."

He jotted down the phone numbers and addresses of the two men. "There's a guy with a last name of Theobold. That might be him too. One of them lives in California and one lives in Florida. This other guy lives in Virginia Beach. Let's call him first." He pulled out his phone and punched in the Virginia number first.

The call rang three times before a male voice answered. "If you're selling something, I'm hanging up."

Marc put on a stern tone. The guy's attitude really bugged him. "This is Marc Everton with the FBI. I'm investigating the murder aboard the *Seawind*. Is this Theo?"

"Yeah." His voice was more respectful. "I didn't see anything. And besides, someone already interrogated me."

So he *did* go by Theo. "Right, but I'm trying to discover if you knew the deceased, Laura Watson, at all."

"I don't think so." His voice held a wary note.

"What does that mean? You either knew her or you didn't." Something about this guy put his hackles up.

"Look, you know how it is aboard ship. Love 'em and leave 'em. I played around with a few women. It was a long cruise—two weeks. Plenty of time to play the field. I didn't get all their last names, but yeah, there was one Laura. It could have been her."

"Did anyone ever show you a picture of the deceased?"

"Nope."

He is lying. Maybe shock would loosen his tongue. "Did she cause a scene when she caught you kissing another woman?"

"Who told you that?" Theo snapped.

"Is it true?"

"Look, it was totally uncalled for. We'd spent one night together, and all of a sudden she thinks she owns me. There was no reason for her to go off like that." His voice rose. "She slapped me and stalked off."

"What happened next? Did you go after Laura? Maybe you wanted to teach her a lesson." Could this be the killer? Every instinct told him the guy was hiding something.

"Get real, man. Why would I do that when a pretty woman was all ready to offer condolences, if you know what I mean."

Marc could almost hear the man's smirk in his

voice. He gritted his teeth and tried to get past his dislike. "So you didn't see her after she slapped you?"

"Not for even a second."

"Can anyone corroborate your whereabouts after the incident?"

"If I knew the chick's name and number, I'd give it to you. Her first name was Bambi. Can't be too many of them on the list."

Marc ran his gaze over the manifest. "Try again. There was no Bambi aboard."

"Maybe it was a fake name. Look, I have to go. If you have anything else to say, you can talk to my attorney."

Marc heaved a sigh. How did he go about finding this Bambi? He'd bet a hundred bucks this guy wasn't as innocent as he claimed.

❧ Seventeen ☙

The seat cushion was hard under her thighs, a comforting sensation that proved she was Elin, not Laura. She was here aboard the boat with Sara and Marc. The vision or whatever it was when she'd smelled the cologne and had a surge of Laura's memories wasn't real. This was real. Sitting here under the stars with the boat rocking in the waves.

Marc ended his phone call. "The guy is hiding something."

"Like what?" Sara asked.

Marc's gaze went to Elin, and she felt the intensity of it. He must have disliked that Theo because his hazel eyes were blazing. "The name Bambi mean anything to you?"

She started to shake her head, then stopped. An image of a woman floated in her memory. "I–I don't know. Maybe. Theo was kissing a woman with big blond hair. Obviously dyed and the ends were tipped with hot pink. I think that might be her name."

Sara lifted a brow. "Fake name?"

He shrugged. "Got to be."

"I think her real name was Barbara. She was older than Theo. Maybe forty." Where were all these details coming from? Elin couldn't consciously recall them. What if they were made up by her desire to get answers? But no, she could swear she'd actually seen the woman.

Marc leaned over his computer and perused the list again. "Seven Barbaras. I'll get some records pulled so we can check the birth dates. Maybe we can find the right one. She might have seen Theo go off to confront Laura."

Had there been a confrontation? Elin couldn't remember, but it didn't feel right. She couldn't remember ever speaking with this Bambi either. Maybe it was all a dead end.

Sara put her arm around her. "I think we'd better get her home. She still looks like she might keel over any minute."

"Yeah." Marc swiveled back around and started the engine. The boat putted slowly toward the boathouse in the harbor.

"I need some air." Elin rose and went toward the door to the deck. When Sara started to follow her, Elin shook her head. "I'll be fine. I want a minute by myself. Maybe something else will come to me."

Sara sank back onto the cushions, but the worry didn't leave her eyes. Marc glanced at Elin with a lifted brow but then nodded. She escaped into the damp night air. The waves lapped against the bow of the boat, and the stars twinkled down as if it were any other night. And maybe it was. Most people would look up into the sky and revel in the gorgeous sight. But this night was just like the one when Laura gasped her last, and Elin felt the young woman's presence keenly in this moment.

Was she here, inside her? Or just her memories? Elin didn't even know if Laura had been a Christian, though she hoped so. It might be comforting to know for sure of her final destination. One thing she knew for sure—what she felt wasn't a spirit. Wherever Laura had gone, the journey was a permanent one, just like the Bible said.

The chugging of the engine lulled her thoughts

for a few minutes. The shore drew nearer, and she could make out the outline of the house in the moonlight.

A shadow flitted by the front porch, and she put her hand to her throat and leaned in closer to see. Someone was out there. Abby? Maybe her mother had slipped outside without being seen? But something about the figure seemed to be male, and Elin remembered the other night when she thought she'd seen someone walking along the beach.

Her throat tightened, and she wanted to call out a warning as the man paused in front of the large front window. The light filtering through the curtains revealed his shape a bit better, and something in the slant of his neck terrified her.

It's him!

She pressed down the fear as illogical, but her terror only escalated. What if he was watching Abby and Josie, trying to decide how to break in and harm them? She whirled and ran for the wheelhouse to tell Marc to hurry. As she reached the door, she looked behind for one last glimpse. No one was there. Only a tree moving in the stiff wind.

Had that been all she'd seen? Or was there more?

Every nerve was strung tight enough to twang. Marc strode the grounds looking for a possible intruder, even though Elin hadn't been certain of what she'd seen. The night breeze blew the scent of the sea into his nostrils, and the recent rain left the ground mushy under his Nike flip-flops.

He swept the beam of his flashlight over the flower bed by the front window. It revealed no one lurking in the shadows, just the small tree with its branches moving in the wind. His high alert status began to ebb a bit. Maybe no one had been here.

"See anything?" Elin exited the front door and came down the steps to join him by the plantings. She wore a white robe over green pajamas and was barefoot.

He gestured. "It might have been that tree."

"Oh, I pray so!"

The delicate scent of her perfume teased his nose, and he shifted to take in the sweetness a bit better. Though the vastness of the landscape surrounded them, it felt very intimate to be out here alone with her with the stars overhead and the sound of the surf in the background.

"Everyone else in bed?" He trained his flashlight on the ground again before moving on to the end of the house.

She followed closely. "I put Josie in my bed. I just couldn't face the thought of having her alone in a room in case someone is out here."

"And your mom and Abby?" As long as she

continued to follow him around, he could ask questions all night. What did that say about his level of attraction?

Elin grabbed his arm. "Marc, look at that."

He saw where she was pointing. Footprints. He focused the beam of light on the outline. "Looks like a man's sandal. Size twelve or thirteen. Big guy. And it's fresh." He knelt beside it. "Look here. No insect tracks through it, no collection of dew. The guy was past here in the last hour."

"I *did* see someone then."

He rose and stared down at her. "You sound relieved."

"Not relieved, exactly, but at least I know I'm not crazy. I–I was beginning to wonder. So many things have been happening to me."

He took her by the shoulders. "Elin, you are *not* crazy. I admit I had my doubts about cell memory, but you know details there's no other way to know."

The moonlight illuminated her face, and the relief there made his heart clench. She must have been worried about this more than he'd realized. He hadn't stopped to think of the stress she was under. How would he feel if he was experiencing things that had happened to another man? It would be hard to live with.

Her gaze, lit with vulnerability, searched his. "Do I seem different to you, Marc?"

What would she say if he told her he found

her immensely appealing? Being around her was messing with his peace of mind. He could conquer it, though, with a little willpower.

"Those are Laura's memories, not yours. Things will settle down once we have that guy behind bars." He forced himself to let go of her and sweep his flashlight over the ground again. "Looks like he went this way. Go on back inside and call the sheriff in Hope Beach. We probably ought to have him take a look out here since it's clear someone was trespassing."

"I think you should come back inside too. You don't have backup, and the guy could get the jump on you."

"I'll just poke around a little, then come in. I'll be careful."

She nodded, then retreated to the front door. "I'll be back out in a minute."

He watched her through the large window as she went to the portable phone and dialed. Her hair glimmered in the overhead light as she twirled a long curl of it around her finger and paced the floor while she spoke to the sheriff. Her trans-lucent skin held a flush of color, and it sounded as though she had raised her voice.

If he didn't move, she would come back out and find him gawking. He pointed his flashlight into the darkness and moved around the side of the house toward the back. His light illuminated the back deck and the fire pit in the yard. A small animal dashed across the grass and he flinched, then relaxed.

Then something pierced his arm, and sharp pain radiated up to his shoulder. He dropped to his knees—an arrow was in the fleshy part of his forearm. A warm trickle ran down his arm. He touched the sticky fluid. Blood. Someone had shot him with an arrow. His fingers closed around the arrow, but he didn't pull it out. Might cause more bleeding.

Gritting his teeth against the pain, he peered into the darkness near the edge of the tree line. The shadows made it too dark to see. Where was the guy? Adrenaline surged through him, and he breathed hard and fast through his mouth. He lifted his head, but there was no renewed attack.

An engine roared, and he staggered to his feet and looked toward the water. The lights of a small boat exited the small cove just down the beach, and the craft zoomed away.

The front door slammed, and Elin joined him a few seconds later.

"Did you hear the boat?" She inhaled sharply. "Marc, you're hurt."

"Yeah. The guy shot me with an arrow." The pain had ramped up, and he felt a little dizzy. "I think I'd better sit down."

She grabbed his arm and guided him to a chair on the deck near the porch light. She knelt and looked at his arm. "Sara, come quick!"

The back door banged, and his cousin came flying out of the house. Her eyes went to his arm. "Oh my gosh, is that an arrow?"

"Yeah," he said through gritted teeth. "I think I'm blacking out." That was all he knew as darkness rose to claim him.

When he came to, Elin was kneeling on one side of him and Sara on the other. Both women had wet cheeks. His gaze fastened on Elin, and he reached up to touch the tears on her face. "Don't cry." His voice sounded so weak, he closed his eyes a moment and tried to muster more strength.

"Don't talk." Sara put a blood pressure cuff on his arm. "I think you're in shock."

His vision swam and he tried to focus. Something white attached to the arrow fluttered in the breeze. "There's a paper attached to the arrow."

Elin leaned in close and studied the paper. "It's a note."

Her cologne wafted up his nose, and he struggled to speak. "A note? Can you read it?"

Her face was stricken when she raised her gaze to meet his. "It says, 'She's mine. And you're a dead man.'"

❧ Eighteen ❧

Sheriff Tom Bourne looked harried when Elin opened the door about ten that night. Her call had interrupted his investigation of a break-in at the school. "Thanks for coming out so quickly."

"Attempted murder is more serious than a little graffiti on a school fence." A big man, Tom's dark brown hair showed a few strands of gray at the temples. "Where is the arrow?" He carried a duffel bag in one hand and a flashlight in the other.

"This way." She led the sheriff to the living room, where Marc lay on the sofa.

Sara had managed to extricate the arrow and stop the bleeding. It had barely missed an artery. He would have some pain for a few days, but it could have been so much worse.

Marc's head lolled toward them. "Glad you could join the party, Sheriff." Pain strained his voice.

The sheriff walked a few feet and stared at the arrow on the coffee table in a plastic bag. "You use a latex glove to remove that?"

"I did," Sara said.

"Tell me what happened."

Elin shivered as she listened to Marc relay the events of the attack.

"There's a note here." Bourne peered closer. " 'She's mine. And you're a dead man.' " The sheriff shook his head. "Sounds like an irate boyfriend, Ms. Summerall. You have a messy breakup recently?"

She tensed. "Not at all. I'm a widow, and I haven't dated in five years." Was Marc remembering their one and only "date" when Josie was conceived?

Tom's brow furrowed. "Any recent admirers ask you out maybe?"

She started to shake her head, then remembered Isaac. Biting her lip, she tried to decide if she should mention him. It seemed a shame to pull him into something so messy.

"There is?" Tom probed.

She sighed and nodded. "There's a coworker who has asked me out a few times, but I've never dated him." She told him Isaac's name. "He's harmless though. Really, this is connected to Laura, not me. I'm just getting the fallout from whoever was after her. Maybe he's after me because he thinks part of Laura is in me, and he wants to eradicate everything about her."

Bourne didn't react for a moment, then he took off his hat and wiped his forehead. "Sounds right. So we should look into anyone Laura threw over. See if she had a disgruntled boyfriend."

"There's another wrinkle too." Marc told the sheriff about Lacy's death and how she was dressed.

Bourne's frown deepened the more he listened.

"It sounds like the guy is really fixated on you, Ms. Summerall. I'm not so sure this is about Laura. If he was focused on her, wouldn't he have dressed Lacy up to resemble her, not you? I think we need to keep an open mind about it and look at all the different angles."

He picked up the plastic bag containing the arrow and note. "I'll send this to the state boys and have them go over it. It might take some time for them to check for fingerprints and DNA. One of the disadvantages of living on an island with little resources."

"You might alert the police about this," Marc said. "It's probably tied in with their murder investigation of Lacy's death."

"I'd planned to do just that." Tom's tone implied his displeasure at being told how to do his job. He went down the steps into the yard with his bright flashlight. "I'll make a cast of the footprints. Can you show me where they are?"

Elin took a step toward the kitchen door. "Of course."

Marc held out a hand toward her. "You're looking a little stressed, Elin. You've been through a lot in the last few months. That virus, a heart transplant, and then the constant worry of a killer after you. You should get to bed. Sara can show the sheriff the crime scene."

His concern warmed her. "I'm no shrinking violet, Marc. If he's watching me, I don't want

169

him to think he's terrorizing me. I won't let that happen."

He struggled to sit up, his face contorted with the pain. "You don't have to be a pit bull all the time. There's no shame in getting some rest."

She tilted up her chin. "I'll rest later. Sara, watch him. I'll show the sheriff around."

She led the sheriff out the back door, although everything in her didn't want to venture into the darkness. An owl hooted in the woods, and a few moments later something shrieked.

"An owl got something, I think," Bourne said.

His impersonal tone made her shiver. Predator and prey, was that what the world was all about? Sometimes it seemed that way, but she was determined to get back to waking up every morning with anticipation for whatever blessing God might bring her way. She was tired of flinching at every shadow. In fact, she refused to let the stress affect her. If Marc had noticed, Josie probably had too.

Shouldn't every day be lived with anticipation? That maniac might succeed in taking her life someday, but he had no right to steal her joy. She'd let him until now, but no more.

Her head high, she marched around the side of the house. Only when the sheriff left did she head for bed, a place she was reluctant to go. The nightmares would be sure to come tonight, so she reached for Georgina's diary.

It just might keep the nightmares at bay. *For a while.*

August 21, 1907

Georgina ran her hands over her swollen stomach. This baby kicked so much that sometimes she didn't get a wink of sleep. A smile curved her lips. But she didn't mind. Another week or two and she would hold this little one in her arms. She fanned her face. The heat and humidity had grown unbearable in this past month, even though the servants opened every window.

She packed the last of Joshua's trunk and turned to find him staring at her. "What's wrong?"

He wore his captain's uniform and looked the picture of the handsome officer who had swept her off her feet a year ago. He planned to make a trip to Hope Beach to check on his ship. It would sail in another three weeks. They'd both prayed their baby would arrive before he had to leave.

He took a step closer to her. "Someone was outside last night."

Her gaze darted to the window, and she put her hand to her throat. "Someone was watching us?"

"Maybe. I was gone all evening." His eyes narrowed. "Did you have a visitor?"

She stared back at him, refusing to show any sign of guilt. "Of course not. I would have told you." She started to turn, but he caught at her arm and swung her around. "Let go of me. You're hurting my arm." She tore her arm from his grasp and rubbed it. "Your jealousy is ridiculous, Joshua."

"Oh, so now I'm ridiculous?" He raised his hand as if to strike her.

She tipped her chin up and stared him down. "You would *dare* lift your hand to me, your pregnant wife? Do not think I will cower inside and hide any bruises. The day you strike me is the day I leave. My father will welcome me back at a moment's notice."

He lowered his hand. "You have no money to leave."

She struggled to keep her tone level. "He would send me money as soon as I asked. I'm not your slave, Joshua."

He sank to the edge of the bed. "It maddens me to think of you with another man."

Pity stirred and she banished it. It did no good to sympathize with him. Another rage would strike him again. "Look at me." When he lifted red eyes her direction, she touched her belly again. "What man would look at me like this? I lumber like a beached whale, and I'm as fat as a toad. Your imagination takes you on ridiculous flights of fancy, Joshua. I am your wife. I would never betray you. Never."

They'd had this conversation before, and it never went anywhere, but she always hoped he would listen. She'd be able to breathe again out of his constant scrutiny. And she would have her baby to occupy her time.

"This isn't the first time you've seen tracks around the house. I must say, I'm rather worried. Who could be peering in our windows and checking out our property?"

At her question, his contrition vanished and he focused on the problem. "A thief perhaps?"

"Your money is safely stowed at the bank. We have nothing of real value here. Food, furniture. Nothing worth going to prison for."

He rose from the side of the bed. "I don't wish to make it seem an accusation, Georgina, but I found something in the yard."

He walked to his bureau and opened the bottom drawer. Under his socks he pulled out a krama. He held the scarf out to her. "Can you explain this?"

She picked it up in her hands, and the scent of curry permeating the fabric wafted to her nose. "It's Khmer."

"I know. Has Chann been in touch with you?"

She held his gaze. "He has not. I haven't heard from him since he was here four months ago."

Then who had left this outside if not Chann? Her thoughts flew to the leather pouch she'd hidden. Her friend had been panicked that it remain safe. Could someone be after that? Or was Chann back to reclaim his property?

"So you have kept track of the time since you saw him last."

She sighed. "Everything relates to my baby. I was about four months along. That is all, Joshua." She threw down the cloth and moved toward the door. "I'm quite tired of trying to reassure you. Believe what you like."

As she opened the bedroom door, a trickle of water between her legs became a sudden torrent. She stood staring at the puddle on the floor until she realized what it meant.

"The baby," she whispered. "The baby is coming. Fetch the midwife."

❧ Nineteen ☙

Elin shut the diary and smiled at her mother, who had curled up on the bed with her again. She'd been listening with rapt attention to Georgina's tale.

"I saw that pouch thing," her mother said. "It was folded and wrapped with leather ties."

Elin's smile faded. "That's not possible, Mom. I'm sure it's long gone. She hid it over a hundred years ago."

"I saw it. It's about this size." She measured about four inches by nine out with her hands. "I can't remember where I found it though. Or what I did with it. I think it's in the attic."

Hallucinations were common, and maybe

listening to the graphic story in the diary had made it seem real to Mom. Elin's eyes burned, and she wished she could bring her mother back from the fog.

Her mother's blue pajamas flapped when she leaped from the bed. "Let's go look upstairs. Maybe I'll remember where I hid it."

No amount of persuasion dissuaded her mother when she wore that expression of obstinacy. "All right." Elin dug the keys out of her bedside drawer.

Marc nearly mowed her down when she exited her room. His injured arm was in a sling, and his right hand shot out to steady her. The warm touch of his hand on her arm sent shivers up her back.

She didn't move away. "Sorry. I wasn't watching where I was going."

Her mother barely glanced at him and continued on down the hall to the stairway door. "Hurry up, Elin."

He finally dropped his hand. "Where's the fire?"

"Mom says she's seen the leather folder Georgina describes in the diary. She says she found it and hid it again, even though she doesn't remember where she found it or where she hid it. We were just going upstairs to look around." She shook her head. "I shouldn't have read her that diary."

"I'll help." He continued to look down at her with an amused expression.

"Bored, huh?"

He grinned. "Nothing to watch on TV except

175

home-improvement shows and a movie I've seen three times."

"You should rest. You lost a lot of blood."

"I'm fine. Knocked back three Advil and I'm good to go."

He touched her on the shoulder as they turned to join her mother. It was crazy how she felt around him. Where were these feelings coming from? Maybe she was going crazy. With all she had going on, the last thing she needed was a romantic entanglement, especially with Marc, who was a complication in her life in so many ways.

She went upstairs first. "There are some halogen lights over there." She pointed to the corner.

Marc went to drag them to the center of the space. The long cords reached the outlets, and Elin blinked when the bright lights flooded the room and pushed back the night shadows. The large room looked even bigger with the light reaching to all the corners.

She eyed him a moment. "I wanted to ask you something. Why didn't you tell the sheriff you'd take care of forensics? I bet you could get results faster than he could."

He hunched his shoulders. "It's kind of a problem right now. I, uh, I'm not supposed to be investigating this. My supervisor thinks I'm haring off on a wild-goose chase."

Her stomach plunged. "What do you mean? They don't believe me?"

He straightened and his gaze held hers. "I'm positive Laura's killer murdered my partner, but my boss thinks it was a mob hit. He told me to take some leave and let it alone."

"So you could get in trouble for poking into this?" Warmth spread through her when she realized how much he'd put on the line to help her. "Thank you."

His firm lips twisted into a wry grin. "Don't thank me yet. He's still out there."

"You'll find him."

"I will."

His confident tone gave her courage. "Thank you for telling me." She pointed out closed doors in two different walls. "There are more rooms than just this big room too. I hadn't realized. When I was up here before, I was looking for the way up to the widow's walk."

Her mother wore a faraway expression. Holding out her arms as though embracing someone, she began to dance to imaginary music. Elin remembered her dancing with Dad when she was a child. They would turn on "Unchained Melody" by The Righteous Brothers and slow dance on the living room rug. Did Mom hear that old tune in her head now?

Elin touched her arm. "Mom?"

Her mother danced on, oblivious to her daughter's presence.

Marc's eyes were warm with compassion, and

he touched Elin's arm again. "Let's look in the other rooms since you haven't seen them yet." He grabbed a halogen light in his good hand and carried it with him toward the first room.

She opened the door and flipped on the overhead light. The weak glow barely showed the floor right under it. Marc plugged in the halogen light and flipped it on. The bright light showed what was likely once a servant's room. About fifteen feet square, it held an old iron bed and a battered chest of drawers. A small closet held dresses draped on hooks.

"It's like a peek into another time." Elin touched a gray flapper-style dress in the closet and gazed at the T-strap shoes with their chunky heels so reminiscent of the early twenties. "The days of live-in help were pretty much over after World War I. I wonder who these belonged to?"

"And why didn't the family get rid of all these old things?" He moved to the dresser and pulled open one drawer after the other. "Old pictures in here. Doilies too and some old teacups. Doesn't look to be anything of value."

In slim-fitting jeans and a black T-shirt, Marc stood with his hands on his hips and surveyed the rest of the room. "What makes you think the pouch your mother has been talking about is the same one Georgina mentions in her diary?"

"I don't, not really. I think the diary has become vivid in her mind, but there is no way to distract her when she gets so obsessed with something. It's easier to just play along until she loses interest."

He nodded at the door to where the older woman still danced with an imaginary partner. "Like now. We could talk her into going to bed now, I think."

"Probably." Elin burrowed into the closet and began to pull out the long-dead servant's belongings. "I'll take her down in a minute."

"I think you're as obsessed as she is." Marc's voice revealed his amusement. "Here, hand some of that stuff to me."

She dumped shoes into his outstretched hand. "What if something is worth finding up here?"

"You mean like the leather-pouch thing?"

"No, I think that's long gone. But maybe there's an old van Gogh or Rembrandt up here. Or some fabulously valuable jewelry. Hidden treasure of some kind." She shot him an impish grin to show she was only joking. But was she? The bigger treasure to her mind was finding out about the people who had lived in Seagrass Pier.

She stumbled as she exited the closet. Marc caught her with his one arm and snatched her to his chest to steady her.

"Thanks," she mumbled through a mouth suddenly too dry.

His enticing masculine scent overpowered her reserve, and her hand stole up his chest. She stared into his face and willed him to kiss her.

His hands held her tight against him. His eyes darkened, and his head started a downward trajectory before he jerked back and released her as if her skin had burned him.

Her cheeks went hot, and she turned her back on him. "I think I'd better get Mom to bed."

The good scent of freshly turned dirt filled Marc's nostrils on Saturday morning, and he stretched out his back, then dusted off his hands. He'd taken off the sling this morning, though Elin had protested. His arm was a little sore, but not that bad. The roar of the sea was muffled here behind the house. "I think we're done. All the seeds are planted, and I'll water the tomatoes and peppers."

"You're a good son," Ruby said, her blue eyes vacant and watery.

His gaze locked with Elin's, and he wished he could erase the pain he saw in her face. He'd nearly kissed her last night. It would be stupid to go there, but he could at least look. The wind lifted her long curls and swirled them around her head like a halo. His fingers itched to plunge into that red hair.

Josie tugged at the hem of his knee-length shorts. "Look, Mr. Marc, I have my own tomato plant."

He touched her soft hair, marveling again at how much she looked like him. "I'm sure it will give you lots of tomatoes."

When was Elin going to agree to tell her who he was? He glanced at her and saw from her expression she'd read his mind. Her eyes narrowed, and she shook her head.

The screen door on the back entry banged, and he glanced over to see Kalianne heading their way with a tray of lemonade. She sent a smile his way that made him tense. He was decidedly *not* available to someone like her when he had a daughter to raise.

His gaze went back to Elin. And Kalianne definitely wasn't his type. He preferred the tall, willowy type with legs that went on forever and a giggle that made him smile.

Kalianne reached him. "Thirsty?" Her smile insinuated something other than lemonade.

"I could use a cold drink." He kept his tone light and avoided looking her in the face.

She moved to Elin and Ruby, and they both took a sweating glass of lemonade. There was a kid's cup with a straw for Josie. Kalianne set the tray down on a tree stump at the edge of the garden and took the last glass for herself.

"I noticed the third-floor stairway was unlocked," Kalianne said. "Tell me where to find the key, and I'll lock it up for you. We wouldn't want Ruby or Josie going up there by themselves."

Elin took a sip of her drink. "We were looking around up there last night. I'll lock it when I go back in. I've got the keys in my purse. I think Josie must have found them in my drawer because it was unlocked the other day."

"Looking around?" Kalianne's eyes still flirted with Marc.

"Mom was talking about having seen an old leather folder that rolls up. She insisted on going to the attic to look for it."

Kalianne straightened. "How interesting. Maybe she was just dreaming it."

"Probably, but we went up to explore."

"So you don't think she's actually seen something like that? She mentioned it to me too, and I told her I'd help her find it."

Elin lowered her voice. "Try to distract her. I'm sure there's nothing to her story."

"I'll do that, and if she won't be distracted, it won't hurt to look around with her like you did last night. Could you put the key somewhere I can find it?"

"I'd rather you didn't go up there at all if I'm not here. I'm happy to unlock it for you and go along if she wants up there. I'm just afraid she'll wander off and climb the stairs to the widow's walk. It's not safe for her. Or for Josie."

A look of displeasure flitted across Kalianne's face. She turned away to look at the garden. "Whatever you say."

Ruby moved closer to Marc. "My son here is a good gardener. Have you met him?"

Kalianne looked over and smiled. "I sure have. Though he's not your son."

Confusion filled Ruby's eyes, and Marc sent

182

Kalianne a warning frown. "She's just teasing you, Ruby." He patted the older lady's shoulder, then moved closer to Kalianne and spoke in an undertone. "Don't argue with her."

"I don't believe in lying to patients."

"She doesn't understand. You don't need to correct her when she's confused." When Kalianne shook her head and started to reply, he held up his hand. "Just do what you're told, Miss Adanete."

Her brows drew together. "I don't believe you're my employer."

Elin joined them. "Is there a problem?"

"I was just explaining to Kalianne that she shouldn't argue with your mother when she's confused. You don't do it. She doesn't think I have the authority to give her an order."

"No, the doctor said not to." Elin looked hard at Kalianne. "And Marc can give any orders he pleases. He's only looking out for Mom's best interests."

Kalianne's cheeks flushed, and her eyes sparked fire. "Whatever you say." She grabbed up the empty tray and stalked back toward the house.

"Sorry if I was out of line." Marc wasn't sure if she'd stood up for him because she believed it or because she wanted to save face in front of Kalianne.

"You weren't. I trust you, Marc."

Her words warmed him until he remembered she hadn't trusted him enough to tell him about Josie.

❧ Twenty ❧

"Mommy, we're home!" Josie's voice carried over the water as the boat docked. Abby had taken her and Mom to a festival at Kill Devil Hills right after they'd planted the garden.

Elin waved from the shore as her sister took Josie's hand and disembarked the ferry. Josie smiled hugely as she ran to her mother. Elin scooped up her daughter. "I missed you! Did you have a good time with Aunt Abby?"

Her daughter nodded and planted a kiss on her cheek. "We had a pedicure. I got five different colors." She pointed at her toes peeking from the ends of her sandals.

"Very nice." Elin put her down, and Josie ran to hug her grandmother, who was having a pretty good day from the clarity of her blue eyes.

Elin let her gaze sweep the passengers hurrying down the plank to shore. Could any of them be responsible for Lacy's death? Most seemed to be with families, but there were one or two men who ambled off by themselves.

She shivered and turned her attention back to her sister. "Thanks for taking her. She was very eager, and I just wasn't up to it."

Abby studied her. "You look a little pale. Have you heard anything else about the murder?"

Josie had dragged her grandmother over to the water to peer at a tide pool. They would be busy for at least a few minutes.

Abby looked over to where their mother crouched over the pool with Josie. "I think I should keep Josie for now. It's dangerous for her, Elin. Surely you can see that. Let me take her with me."

"I don't dare let her out of my sight. I know you love her, Abby, but I'd die before I'd let anything happen to her."

"So would I." Abby looked fierce.

Elin hadn't expected to be arguing with Abby over Josie. "Listen, let's not fight about this. We're safe. Marc is here. You have to admit he's quite capable of protecting all of us."

Abby's fists unclenched, and she gave a reluctant nod. "I always thought there was something between the two of you. You could cut the chemistry with a knife. Are you dating him?"

"What? Of course not." She would have to tell Abby the truth. "But he does have a vested interest in keeping Josie safe."

"I don't get it."

"He's Josie's father."

Abby's eyes went wide, then filled with certainty. "I knew it! Why on earth didn't you marry him? Did he leave you when he found out about Josie?"

"I never told him."

Abby gasped, and she shook her head. "I don't understand. You never looked at another man but Tim."

Elin looked down. "It's not something I'm proud of. The night Dad died, I kind of lost it. Drank too much. We both did. One thing led to another." Her face burned. "I ran out of there and wanted to forget it. He tried to talk to me a few times afterward, but I was so ashamed." The memory of that night still brought a lump to her throat.

Abby frowned. "You cried for days after the call came in about Tim's injury, and I thought it was because you were worried about him. It was because you were pregnant? Did you tell Tim?"

"Yes. He wanted to marry me anyway. I think he wanted to prove he could beat Marc. He never had a good thing to say about him after that." She shook her head. "I'm sorry if I sound critical of Tim. I don't mean to. He was good to Josie and me."

Abby's brow furrowed, and she shook her head. "I would disagree with that, Elin. You live in a rose-colored world, honey. Tim was demanding and short with you. He was often impatient with Josie. It was hard to bite my tongue."

Elin looked at her in surprise. "You've never said anything."

"Would it have done any good? I didn't want to make your life any harder than it was. You were

Tim's drudge. It was guilt, wasn't it? You let him treat you like that because you thought you deserved to be punished."

Elin couldn't hold her sister's gaze, and she looked down at the ground. "Maybe."

"I shouldn't say this, but I was glad when Tim died, Elin. I thought that finally you'd be free to be happy."

Elin bit her lip. She wasn't ready to admit she'd had a stab of relief herself. It wasn't something she was proud of. Her tears had mostly been for Josie, who would grow up fatherless. She hadn't minded the way Tim treated her. At least most of the time.

Abby took her arm and steered her to join their mother and Josie. "I bet Marc was livid. Most men would be."

"He was taken aback."

Abby studied her. "He's strong and driven. It's clear he wants to protect you and Josie."

"I wish he didn't have to." She rubbed her head. "If only I could remember that man's face. I get bits and pieces, then it fades into mist. I did remember the name Theo. Marc is checking it out."

"Don't wait on Marc to find it out. You're good at that kind of thing. I don't want you waiting around while the killer gets closer."

"Fair enough. I'll do some digging." She hugged her sister. "You're always good for me, Abby. Now let's get home."

• • •

The sunset threw gold and red colors over the sand. Marc leaped for the volleyball and spiked it over the net for the winning point. He raised a victorious fist at Curtis and Ben, who returned the gesture. They shook hands with the other team, all other Coasties.

Curtis slapped him on the back as they turned toward the parking lot. "You're a good player, Everton. It's all or nothing with you, isn't it?"

Marc grinned. "I don't like to lose. Ben didn't seem to either. Did you see how ripped that guy is? He must work out every day." He rubbed the towel over his perspiring face.

"He's big into martial arts. I wouldn't want to take him on in a dark alley."

"I'm pretty rusty with my training. I should get back to it." They reached the parking lot. "Thanks for inviting me. I needed to decompress."

"How's the investigation going? Learn anything new?"

"Not enough." Marc leaned on the hood of his Tahoe and told Curtis about trying to get Elin to remember the night of the murder.

"Man, that was extreme."

"Yeah. If my boss gets wind that the guy shot me with an arrow, he'll have my hide."

"Sara said your partner died while investigating this. I'm sorry, man."

188

"Me too. He was a good man. Left two little kids. I have to find his killer."

"Yeah, you're tenacious, Everton. I could see that just watching you play volleyball. That guy doesn't have a chance. But, dude, you seriously think your boss won't hear about this?"

"You're right. I probably ought to call and tell him." Marc didn't relish the reaming he was going to get. "It might actually convince him my partner's death wasn't an organized-crime hit." Or it might get him fired.

"Anything I can do?"

Marc shook his head. "Just have Amy keep feeding Elin those herbs. She has more color in her cheeks and more energy. She can't reject that heart. We need it to work a long, long time. Josie needs her."

He hadn't voiced his worry about that heart to anyone, especially not Elin. She had enough worries, but he bet this was one of the reasons for her nightmares too.

"Amy is confident she can keep it ticking along. She's a marvel."

Marc raised a hand. "See you next week, same time, same place."

"Tell Elin we're praying for her."

"Will do." Marc slid under the wheel and dug for his keys. As he slid it into the ignition, he spotted a yellow sticky note on the steering wheel. The block letters screamed at him. *IF YOU*

189

DON'T STAY AWAY, I WILL KILL YOU. Marc jumped from the SUV and looked around. The parking lot was deserted.

The glow of the computer lit the dark office. Elin had been so engrossed in her research she hadn't turned on the light. She rose and stretched out the cramps in her muscles, then went to open her window and smell the night scent of the sea on the breeze.

The moon glimmered on the peaks of the whitecaps. The only sound she heard was the lull of the waves. Nothing moved in the house either, so Marc had probably gone to bed too. The green glow of the clock blinked to midnight.

She turned and stared at the glowing computer through bleary eyes. She'd gotten a copy of the ship manifest and had looked up all the Barbaras. Only one was the right age, and she lived in Virginia Beach, close enough for her to pay a call. But Theo's face still eluded her. Was he the same as the killer? She wished she knew for sure.

Her cell phone chirped, and she picked it up, realizing it was connected to the wireless network in the house that allowed the text to come through. She swiped it to look at the message.

I can smell your fear. Shall I take Josie first?

The very thought that he knew her daughter's name took her breath away. She nearly dropped the phone, then tightened her grip on it. No, she wouldn't let him terrify her. He fed off her fear. The text had no cell number associated with it, so he must have used an online messaging service. Could she text him back? Would it go through?

She texted the message: You're smelling your own fear of being caught. And you will be.

With a defiant stab of her finger, she sent it on its way, but it bounced back almost immediately. Fueled by anger, she hunched over her laptop again and began to search. She would find him and bring him to justice. But a niggling of fear lifted the hair on the back of her neck. She couldn't let him hurt Josie. Would he really? Surely he was just trying to terrify her.

When a tap came on the door to her office, she straightened with a gasp, then curled her fingers into her palms. "Who is it?"

"It's just me." Marc's deep voice came from the other side of the door. "I saw the glow under the door when I got home and thought maybe you forgot to shut off the computer."

She threw open the door and flipped on the light, then blinked in the sudden glare. "I was just doing some research." He brushed past her close enough for her to smell the scent of sun and surf on him. She resisted the urge to reach out and touch him. "You've got Max."

He rubbed the little dog's head as he approached her laptop. "He was whining like a banshee at the back door." He must have felt her tense because he shook his head. "He heard a bunny or some other animal. I checked. All is quiet on the home front." He put Max on the floor, and the dog went to curl up under her desk. "See, he's not worried."

She smiled. "That's a relief."

He frowned. "What's wrong?"

"What makes you think something's wrong?"

"Your eyes are shadowed, and your lips are trembling a little."

She pressed her lips together to show him she was fine before giving up and reaching for her phone. "I got a text." She showed him the message. "I tried to text him back but it bounced." She lifted her chin. "But I'm not letting him terrify me. I'm going to track him down."

His jaw flexed, and a fire burned in his gaze. "I won't let him hurt you, Elin. Or Josie or Abby either. We'll find him." He reached out and gripped her arm.

The warmth in his touch brought heat to her cheeks. She could feel every whorl of his fingertips against her skin, and it took all her strength to keep from rushing into his arms. This unwanted emotion had to stop. The only reason he was here was because of Josie.

She shook off his grip and turned back to the computer. "I think I found our Bambi. The only Barbara young enough lives in Virginia Beach. She's thirty."

"Let me get into a confidential database." He

logged out of her screen and went to another site where he entered a username and password. "Here she is. Look familiar?"

He turned the laptop around to show her a young woman with blond hair. There was no other color on the tips in this picture, but she might have done the dye job just before the cruise.

Something lurched in Elin's chest. "That's her!" She leaned in closer. "I remember that birthmark by her eye too, now that I see it."

What were these emotions churning in her when she looked at Bambi's picture? It felt very much like jealousy. Elin rubbed her forehead. Oh, why couldn't she remember Theo's face? If only she could bring it into focus, it might help her know if he was the killer.

"Mommy?"

She turned to see Josie looking a little pale as she swayed in the doorway. "What's wrong, sweet girl?"

Josie clutched her midsection. "My tummy hurts." She folded over and vomited all over the gleaming wood floor.

Elin leaped forward, but Marc got there before she did. He scooped up Josie out of the mess and soothed her as she broke into noisy sobs. She vomited again, all down the front of him.

"I'll clean her up." He took her across the hall to the bathroom. "Can you grab her some other clothes?"

She rushed up the steps to her daughter's bedroom and yanked open her pajama drawer. When she got back to the bathroom, Josie had quit crying and was lying quietly on his bare shoulder with her eyes closed. Her soiled pajamas were at his feet along with his shirt. When he saw her, he sat on the toilet seat, and she helped him pull on the clean pjs.

"I think she's asleep." His hazel eyes held a shadow of worry. "Do we need to take her to the ER?"

"Children often get intestinal upsets." She touched her daughter's head. "She doesn't have a fever. I think she's fine. Just put her back to bed, if you would. I'll clean up the mess in the office."

"I'll do it when I come back down. I think I need to learn father-type things."

She gaped after him as he carried her daughter back to bed. She'd known he was a good man, but this was above and beyond the call of duty.

৶ Twenty-One ৶

After his shower on Saturday morning, Marc finally got the last trace of vomit odor out of his nose. He popped a mint as he poked his head into Josie's bedroom and saw Elin slipping flip-flops on Josie's small feet. The little Yorkie lay stretched out beside them. Beautiful mother, sweet daughter, and dog. All that was needed was the father to complete the picture of a perfect family.

"Mr. Marc!" Josie escaped her mother and ran to cling to his leg.

He hugged her tightly, her tiny form already so familiar. She'd taken complete possession of his heart. He picked her up, and she hugged his neck. "You feeling okay?" He looked to Elin for confirmation too.

She smiled and nodded, looking downright alluring in her close-fitting denim capris and green tee. Her feet were bare, the toes tipped in pale orange. "I slept with her, and there was nary a peep all night. Just a tummy upset."

He averted his gaze from the V where her T-shirt plunged. "Glad to hear it." She was too darned cute for his peace of mind. If he wasn't needed to protect his daughter, he'd be out of here so fast, he'd leave a wake behind the boat.

Josie wiggled to be put down, and he set her small feet on the floor. She ran for the door calling Abby. He started to follow her, but Elin spoke his name, and he turned with a lifted brow.

She took a step closer. "I just wanted to thank you for last night. Most people can't stomach cleaning up a sick kid, especially if they aren't used to it. You didn't even retch once."

He grinned. "I held it in, but I admit the stench about brought me to my knees."

She inhaled, and her gaze locked with his. "I think I'm about ready to tell her the truth."

He felt the impact deep in his gut. His little girl would know he was her father. How would she react? Was he even ready for it himself? The thought of disappointing his daughter caused him pain.

Elin's aqua eyes took on a shadow. "You have a funny expression. You don't want to tell her?"

He straightened. "Of course I do. I just hope she's not upset. She loved Tim."

"She doesn't really remember much about him. Only what she's been told. And she knows his picture, of course. She loves you already, Marc. You don't need to worry."

Abby's voice called down the hall. "Hey, you two, I could use some help out here."

Marc's pulse kicked. Was Josie throwing up again? He rushed down the stairs with Elin on his heels. In the kitchen, he found Abby with her hands in bread dough. Josie held out dough-coated hands to Max, who eagerly licked at them.

Elin scooped up the little dog. "He shouldn't be eating flour."

"Tell me about it." Abby swiped a lock of hair out of her eyes with her forearm. "After you get her cleaned up, could one of you get started on putting potatoes in the oven?"

When Abby looked at him, Marc realized this was going to be up to him. When was the last time he had more than pizza and takeout? It was about time he learned his way around the kitchen. When Josie came to stay with him, she needed more than breaded chicken strips and French fries.

He hooked Josie's waist with his arm and carted her toward the half bath off the entry. She smiled up at him, her dimple flashing, then planted a doughy hand on his cheek. "Hey, you did that on purpose."

She giggled and nodded. "I can make you look like a ghost." Her hand went toward his face again, and he flinched back. His instinctive movement made her giggle harder, and he had to grin. "You little scamp. I should dunk you in the bathtub."

"What's a scamp?"

"It's a playful little girl." He set her on the bathroom floor and turned on the water, then put her hands under the stream.

By the time they were done, he had more water on him and on the floor than he'd expected. He backed into the opposite wall and knocked off a vase sitting on a wall shelf behind him. It shattered on the tile floor, and he bent to pick up the pieces.

"Mr. Marc, what's that say?" Josie pointed to a decorative mirror above the shelf.

The smile on his face vanished when he saw words written in lipstick. The garish shade of red added to the ominous tone.

It's cold in the grave. He will soon find out.

Another threat, this one directed at him. Had the killer left it there Thursday night when he shot the arrow? This bathroom wasn't used often, and the vase might have covered up the message. "It's just lipstick." He dried her hands and hustled her out of the room.

When he headed through the living room, he saw Ruby knitting in her chair. "There's Grandma. Why don't you keep her company a little while? She could probably use some help holding the yarn."

Josie ran to her grandma and climbed onto the sofa beside her. Marc left them and went back to the kitchen. "Have either of you used the half bath under the stairs lately?"

"What's wrong? Is it a mess?" Elin started for the door, but he grabbed her arm. She stared at him with wide eyes. "What is it?"

"I broke a vase. The one on the shelf."

Relief lit her eyes. "That's fine. I'll get the broom and dustpan."

He released her arm and shook his head. "There was something written in lipstick on the mirror." He told her about the message.

Her eyes widened, and she gulped. "He was in here?"

"Looks like it. I'm praying he hasn't been here since the other night, that this isn't a new message."

"Max heard something last night," she reminded him.

He nodded. "I didn't see anything though. Unless one of you moved that vase when you dusted, I think it's safe to assume he was here on Thursday night and wrote that note."

"I haven't even been in that bathroom," Abby said. "This is scary though, Elin. I still think you should come stay with me when I leave this afternoon. I don't like you being out here alone."

"I'm not alone. And this threat seems to be against Marc, not me."

The concern in her eyes made his pulse stutter. But maybe Abby was right. What if he couldn't protect Elin and Josie? Being in town might be better, though home invasions happened even more often in cities. Still, someone might respond to a cry for help.

Or not.

He pulled out his cell phone. "I think I'll call and get some alarms on the doors and windows."

This skirt wouldn't do. It was much too short. Sara changed for the third time, this time pulling on a pair of black slacks that weren't too tight. The pink-and-white sleeveless top showed just a hint of cleavage, so maybe it should go too. She flung open her closet and surveyed her options. The white jacket over the top would hide her curves a little better.

She yanked it on and turned to survey herself in the full-length mirror on the door. Just the right touch in the nick of time since she heard footsteps on the walk outside. She quickly slashed on a bit of pink lip gloss and hurried to the living room as the doorbell pealed.

Ben smiled through the screen when she opened the entry door. "I'm five minutes early, but I couldn't wait any longer." He held up a bouquet of daisies. "These seemed the kind of flower you'd like. Not pretentious but with a beauty all their own."

Smooth, very smooth. She hid a smile as she pushed open the door. "Come in and let me put them in water." She took the flowers from him.

"You look very nice. I like your hair loose."

Maybe she should have put it up. "Thanks." He was eyeing her like he might lunge at any minute. "You look nice too." And he did. His khakis appeared new, and the light-blue shirt he wore was a good foil for his blond hair and blue eyes.

She led him down the entry hall to the living room on the right. "I'll be right back. There are chocolate-chip cookies on the coffee table."

"My favorite." He looked around. "Nice room. I like sea cottages. They make it feel like summer all the time. And this peach lets me know we're at the beach."

"This place was a wreck when I bought it. It's been fun to fix up." The old plantation cottage had been in bad disrepair. She'd refinished the maple floors and repaired the plaster walls. The last bathroom had just been redone too. "I'll be right back." She went down the hall to the kitchen, painted a pale yellow.

She put down the flowers and leaned against the counter, then inhaled. What was she doing? How could she blithely date another man when her heart still wanted only Josh? It wasn't really fair to Ben to get his hopes up. She could see this would end in heartache for him. He liked her way too much already. Could she ever feel anything for him? He was handsome enough.

But he wasn't Josh.

She was tempted to call Elin and ask her to call with an emergency. Shaking her head, she found a vase and filled it with water. She could handle one evening. Only time would tell if anything could come of this. She'd never expected to fall for Josh either. It just happened out of the blue. Lightning could strike again, couldn't it?

Carrying the vase of flowers, she went back to the living room where Ben perused the pictures on her shelves. He had a picture of her with the Coastie team in his hands. Josh had his arm draped casually around her shoulders in the photo. That had been a fun day. They went windsurfing and sat around a fire on the beach. An eternity ago when Josh hadn't been avoiding her like she was a man-o'-war who might sting at any moment.

He turned when she put the vase on the coffee table. His gaze was warm as it swept over her. "You've been with this team awhile?"

She nodded. "Three years. We work well together."

"You and Josh look pretty cozy. You ever date him?" His tone was too casual.

She bristled, then realized he had a right to wonder if she had any kind of relationship going on. What could she say, really? In spite of all her hopes and dreams, nothing had developed with Josh. She needed to accept the fact that nothing ever would.

She shrugged. "I'm good friends with all my team. We hang out, watch movies, and joke around. You know how it is."

"Yes, I sure do." He put the picture down.

Two could pry. She might as well find out about him too. "How about you? Any serious relationships?"

"I'm sure Elin filled you in. I was her brother-in-law once upon a time. And married to her friend Kerri." His grin widened. "You know how it is when you're in the military. You get shifted around too often to build a relationship if the spouse doesn't understand."

"Is that what happened with you and Kerri?"

He shrugged. "We just had different goals in life. She hated traveling, and I took every assignment I could. But I'm tired now, ready to settle down."

She inhaled and turned away at his admission he was ready to settle down. She'd thought she was too, but not with just anyone.

He came up behind her, and his breath stirred her hair. "Good job on that boat interception the other day. I hear one of the guys threw something overboard."

She turned to face him, then stepped back. He was a little too far into her personal space. "My friend and I found one of the boxes on the beach near her home. Heroin."

"No kidding. Our job of keeping out the drugs gets harder and harder. I heard we're looking for a drug lord out of Miami. I've been looking for him, but no luck so far."

"We haven't seen him either. He's pretty elusive from what I hear." She was bored with the conversation, but it was better than talking about Josh. Poor Ben's small talk proved he was just as nervous as she was.

She grabbed her purse. "I'm ready if you are."

His ready smile came back. "Sure thing. I'm ready for some seafood and Spock."

She smiled and followed him to the door. Maybe this evening wouldn't be so bad. He was a nice enough guy, right out there with how he felt. She didn't see him taking one step forward and two steps back in a relationship.

❧ Twenty-Two ❧

The SUV sped through the labyrinth of streets in Virginia Beach. Once Sunday lunch was over, they'd decided to make a quick run to try to catch Bambi. Abby and Josie had gone to town with them and would spend the afternoon at the festival again. Her mom and Kalianne were working in the garden.

Elin just *had* to figure this out. Then maybe the dreams would stop. Maybe then she could get her life back. She consulted her phone's GPS and pointed for Marc to turn right. He whipped the vehicle around the corner and slowed to stare at the numbers on the houses. "There it is."

The house was a neat beach bungalow with weathered gray shake shingles and white shutters. Honeysuckle rambled up the porch railing and spilled over the rock rim of the garden. The plant climbed so high, she could only see the movement of the swing and the dim outline of the people in it as it lazily swung back and forth.

Marc turned off the SUV. "Ready?"

She inhaled and nodded, then swung open her door. Would the woman recognize her from the newspaper article? And what about the man with her? Her head high, she walked up the flagstone path and mounted the front steps with Marc close on her heels. When she spied the woman's face, her flip-flops seemed rooted to the painted porch boards.

I know the woman staring at me from the swing.

She gulped and forced a smile. "Bambi. I hope we're not interrupting."

Bambi shot the man beside her a panicked glance, then rose and smiled. "I think you must have the wrong person. My name is Barbara." Her low, husky voice was the type that would attract men like bees to an empty soda bottle.

The man rose also. Dressed in a suit and tie, he appeared to be a wealthy businessman. Every blond hair was in order, and his shoes gleamed. "Who are you anyway? What a ridiculous name to call my wife." He gripped her waist protectively.

Elin glanced at Marc. Now what? Barbara's demeanor left no doubt she didn't want her husband to know anything about the cruise and what had gone on there.

Marc clasped Elin's arm and took a step back. "Sorry we disturbed you." He sent her a warning glance and led her down the steps to his SUV. She slid in, and he shut the door behind her.

When he got in the driver's side, she frowned and shook her head. "I wanted to talk to her."

"We will. I got the feeling her husband was about to leave. We'll drive down the street and wait a few minutes." He started the engine and pulled his vehicle away from the curb.

She glanced in the rearview mirror and saw the man kiss Bambi, then stride to the silver Corvette in the drive. "You're right. He's leaving."

Marc drove around the block. When they pulled up to the curb again, the sports car was nowhere in sight. Bambi wasn't on the porch any longer either.

"I hope she didn't leave too," Elin said.

Marc turned off the key and slid it into his pocket. "She wasn't dressed to go anywhere. She didn't even have shoes on. A woman like her would have on makeup before she even went to the grocery store."

Good insight. She swung open her door and waited for him to join her before heading back to the porch. They didn't even have to ring the doorbell. Bambi opened the bright-blue door before they could press the button.

"What do you want? Why are you tormenting me?" Tears hung on her lashes.

"May we come in? I'm sure you'd rather the neighbors didn't hear our questions." Marc's tone dared her to disagree.

Bambi bit her lip, then shoved open the screen door. "My husband will be back in an hour. I can't have you here."

"Our questions won't take long." Marc held open the door for Elin.

Inside, the cool gray walls mingled with yellow accents and gave a welcoming feel. The white linen furniture in the living room looked new. Whitewashed floors and white trim gave the room a modern look. It all appeared newly redecorated.

Bambi indicated the sofa before settling into an overstuffed yellow chair. "Have a seat and let's get this over with."

Elin perched on the edge of the sofa. "I want to know what happened on the cruise between you and Laura Watson."

Bambi folded her arms across her ample breasts. "I don't know what you're talking about."

"We can wait until your husband comes back to answer these questions if you'd rather." Marc's mild voice contrasted with his steely expression.

Bambi flushed. "Look, it was nothing, okay? She was all bent out of shape because we had a simple dance."

An image flashed into Elin's head. "You went back to his room, didn't you? And spent the night." She didn't know how she knew it, but when Bambi bit her lip and looked away, Elin knew the knowledge was true.

"It was just a shipboard fling. It meant nothing. It was only one night, but my husband wouldn't understand. You can't tell him!"

Marc leaned forward. "Your marriage is none of our business. But we need to know what Laura said to you. And how she acted."

"She was like a crazy woman! She caught us in the hall outside his room the next morning. She flew at me and would have scratched my face if Theo hadn't grabbed her. It made no sense. I mean, didn't she know he was just fooling around with her? That kind of man isn't the type to stay around more than a night or two."

"This Theo. What can you tell me about him?" Marc asked.

Her forehead furrowed. "Not much. I don't know his first name."

Elin felt a kick in her gut. "His first name is Ron." Marc hadn't told her that, but she somehow knew it.

"Do you think he could have murdered Laura Watson?"

Bambi laughed. "You've never met him, have you? He'd have to actually care about a woman to get mad enough to harm her. He had a bevy of women on that trip. Laura and I weren't the only ones." She twisted her wedding ring on her hand. "And don't tell my husband, but Theo was with me when the Watson woman died. He couldn't possibly be the murderer."

Now what? The death clearly had nothing to do with this love triangle. She glanced at Marc and recognized the furrow in his brow. The problem he was working out in his head was unpleasant.

"I'm in the kitchen," Sara called through the open window when Marc pressed the doorbell of her cottage. "The door's unlocked."

208

He stepped through the screen door and walked on the gleaming wood floors to the kitchen. "I smell coffee." The rich aroma teased his nose.

She was dressed in khaki shorts and a pink top that showed off her toned arms. "I put it on as soon as you called. You sounded serious. What's up?"

He accepted the cup of coffee she pressed into his hand. "Just some more questions."

She gestured for him to follow her to the back deck. "About Laura or Lacy?"

Hummingbirds fluttered at a feeder a few feet away from the chair he dropped into. "A little of both."

She frowned as she leaned back in her chair. "I'm not sure what that means."

Sara wasn't going to like the things he had to ask. He took a sip of his coffee. "How well do you know Josh? You've worked with him for three years, and I know you hoped a relationship would develop that hasn't."

She put down her coffee cup. "Why are you asking about Josh? I thought you wanted to talk about Laura and Lacy."

"He was there when both women died. I find that a little strange."

Her eyes widened, and she leaned forward. "That's ridiculous, Marc! Just because Josh is skittish about relationships doesn't mean he's some kind of killer."

"No, but it makes me wonder about him. I looked up his IQ. It's in the genius range. His father died in prison, and his mother was an alcoholic. Those are all characteristics on the list of things serial killers have in common." He inhaled. "And Josh and Laura went to the same high school. He even dated her a couple of times when he was a senior. Will's wife found some notes and scanned them for me last night. Will was looking at Josh too."

Her color high, she rose and paced the deck. "I can't believe you would even entertain a thought like this. Josh is a good man. He's had a hard life, yes, but that should be cause for compassion from you, not condemnation."

Her reaction almost made him question his suspicions. Almost. "When did he get to Elin's house in Virginia Beach?"

She stared at him. "Fine. I'll answer your questions, and you'll see how far off base you are. He got there about an hour after I called the police. He said he heard it on the scanner in his car."

"Many killers like to go back to the scene and see what's happening. Don't you find it odd he was so close? Clearly he was already in town."

She dropped back into her chair. "And that's a crime? Everyone on the island goes to Virginia Beach to shop. His mother lives here. I'm sure he was checking on her. As you said, she's an alcoholic. He worries about her. He often comes over on his days off."

"How did he seem when he came in?"

Her gray eyes held sorrow. "Elin and I both needed him. He came right in and made sure we were okay. The police seemed glad to have him too since we were both so upset. He helped calm us down enough to answer questions coherently."

He took a sip of his coffee, then set it on the patio table. "Does he play the guitar?"

She nodded slowly. "He has an old guitar that was his dad's that he strums on sometimes. He taught himself the chords. But anyone has access to a guitar string."

He gritted his teeth at her stubborn refusal to look at facts. "These things all add up, Sara. You are around him a lot. I'd like you to watch him, see if he reveals anything he shouldn't know about those murders."

She set her coffee down so hard it sloshed over the top of the cup. "I won't spy on him! You can't ask that of me. You know how I feel about him."

He looked at her steadily. "What if you're wrong about him, Sara?"

She didn't flinch away from his gaze. "What if *you* are? And then he finds out you suspected him of such a thing—and even worse—that I helped you? He would never forgive me."

"What about Elin? Are you willing to look the other way when she's in danger?"

Her color got even higher. "I'm not doing anything to harm her. And don't you dare suggest to her that she should distrust Josh. You have no evidence to base this on. It's not fair, Marc. I can't believe you could even entertain any suspicions toward a fine man like Josh. I mean, he puts his life on the line for other people all the time."

"Just because he's a Coastie doesn't mean he's incapable of murder."

"Well, I know Josh. You're on the wrong path here."

He shrugged. "No harm, no foul from looking into it."

"There's harm, all right! When you're looking at him, you're ignoring finding the real killer."

Darkness often hid inside the most innocuous face. She hadn't seen it as often as he had.

"Just keep your eyes open, okay? You can do that much for your best friend."

She stared at him. "Look somewhere else, okay? It's not Josh." She rose and scooped up their coffee cups. "You can let yourself out."

❧ Twenty-Three ❧

The old lady was driving her crazy. Kalianne wiped her muddy hands on her jeans. "We planted plenty of beans, Ruby. We don't need any more."

Dressed in red capris and an orange blouse,

Ruby looked the picture of a crazy old lady. She wore two different sandals, one brown and one white. Her graying blond hair hung limply under a straw hat.

When Ruby looked at her with a blank expression, Kalianne snatched the seeds out of her hands. "No more planting. We have enough."

Ruby whimpered and reached for the seeds. "But I want to plant more."

Kalianne slapped her hand away. "I said no more!" She tried to ignore the twinge of sympathy at the way Ruby's blue eyes filled with tears. "How about you water the seeds? There's a hose on the side of the house."

Ruby's expression cleared. "I'll get the hose." She trotted toward the house, moving fast for someone her age.

At last a bit of respite. Kalianne sat on a stone wall at the end of the garden and inhaled a breath of fresh air. She dug out her cell phone from the pocket of her cutoffs and called her brother. "Hey, it's me. They found a crate of heroin. Is there more for me to find?"

"I told you I'd call you tonight. I can't talk now."

"Just say yes or no. I've got a window of about an hour to look for more. Is one crate all there is?"

"Hang on a minute. Hey, guys, I need to run to my car a minute. I'll be right back."

She heard male voices in the background, then his footsteps sounded on tile. Traffic noise rumbled in the distance, and a door slammed.

"I'm here," he said. "They found just one crate? Who found it?"

"Coasties. They identified it as heroin and called the cops."

He swore. "Just what I didn't need."

"How many boxes?"

"One more. It's about a foot square brown box. Sealed up too and locked. Don't open it."

More drugs. How boring. "Okay. Anything else you want from me?"

"Have you found the pouch yet?"

She rolled her eyes. "No, but I've only started looking."

"Any way you can get those people out of the house for good?"

"Well, I could burn the house down, I guess." She was only half kidding. A constant dream of hers since childhood had been to burn down a house. She could only imagine the thrill of watching a consuming fire flare into the night.

"Don't be stupid."

She crossed her legs and glanced around for Ruby, who had been gone longer than she expected. "So I'll look for that box this afternoon. Anything you want from inside the house?" Maybe she could burn it down once she found that pouch.

"Just that pouch! I can't believe you let that old bat get the best of you."

The tension in his voice told her she'd pushed him as far as she should. "I'd better go check on that old lady. I'll let you know if I find anything."

"Okay, I'll call you tonight around nine. Thanks for doing this, Kalianne. You won't regret it. You'll be a Cambodian princess when this is all over."

The comment made her smile. "You'd better come through for me. I'm already sick of being buried out here. I'm not too keen on the thought of having to work here for even another day."

"Then find that pouch and that box and you can get out of there." A male voice shouted something indistinguishable in the distance. "Listen, I have to go. Keep me posted."

"I will." She ended the call. "Ruby?" Walking toward the side of the house, she wanted to scream with frustration. If there was one thing she hated, it was not knowing fully what was going on. She'd bet money her brother had only told her half the truth of all of this.

She rounded the corner. No Ruby. The hose lay uncoiled in the dirt with water running out the end. She shut off the faucet, then went to the front of the house calling her name. Elin was still gone, so she wouldn't have distracted Ruby. Kalianne looked over the landscape. A movement at the top of the cliff caught her eye.

Ruby stood at the very edge looking down into the waves crashing on the rocks below. She swayed as she stood. Kalianne's voice caught in her throat. She didn't dare shout for fear Ruby would be so startled she'd fall. She ran for the path and climbed the rocks. When she reached the top, she saw the old woman still standing at the edge. Taking care to move as noiselessly as possible, she hurried toward Ruby and grabbed her arm.

Ruby tried to pull her arm free to go back to the edge. "Owen is calling for me. I want to go to him."

"Elin and Josie need you. Let's go find them." When the woman continued to struggle, Kalianne slipped her hand into her pocket and grabbed a syringe. She uncapped it and plunged the needle into Ruby's arm, then pressed the plunger.

That should keep her under control for a while.

Elin pushed her windswept hair out of her eyes and crossed her legs. The Hope Beach sheriff's office was quiet, but then it was dinnertime. She jiggled her leg and looked out the window. Across the street Abby helped Josie with her ice-cream cone. Marc had picked them up in Kill Devil Hills on their way back from Virginia Beach.

"Nervous?" Marc went to the coffee service on a table along one wall. "I think this is probably coffee from yesterday." He felt the pot. "Yep, it's cold."

"I don't want any, thanks." She spared a peek at him.

Dressed in jeans and a pale-yellow shirt, he looked all male. His hair curled a bit at the collar, and his eyes were shadowed. His presence in her house had grown more disturbing with every passing day. She didn't want to feel this pull toward him.

The sheriff breezed in. Tom Bourne seemed to fill the room with his presence. He went to his desk and wasted no time in pleasantries. "I heard from the Virginia Beach police. I told them what you said about Josh Holman, and they're looking into his whereabouts during the time of the murder."

Elin gasped. "Josh? He couldn't be involved. He's a Coastie."

Both men stared at her. "Any profession has a few bad apples, Elin," Marc said.

She had to convince them. "You can't seriously be suspicious of him. He's a great guy. Just ask Sara."

"Sara is a little biased. I'm surprised to see you taking up for him though. You don't even know him that well."

"I know him through Sara. She's a good judge of people. If she loves him, he's worth it." She glanced at the sheriff. "What else did they say? Did they find any forensic evidence?"

He shrugged. "They found hair samples, but

those might belong to you or Lacy. They're checking out everything, but it's too soon to tell. And since you brought up forensics, I heard back from the state boys about the arrow. It was clean. They are heading this way to question Josh though. I'm supposed to have him here in a couple of hours."

"I think it's ridiculous. Whoever killed Lacy murdered Laura too. That couldn't have been Josh."

"He was onboard that ship too, Elin. And he dated Laura in high school."

At Marc's words, Elin sank back in her chair. Was it possible the killer could be Josh? She shook her head. "I have those memories, Marc. He doesn't have that signet ring. His build is all wrong too. Don't waste time looking at him. I'd be frightened of Josh if he were the killer."

"You don't know that for sure," Marc said. "Those memories might not be as accurate as we think. You might be experiencing emotions about him because of hearing Sara talk about him. There are lots of reasons why he might not cause alarm bells to go off for you. It could have been anyone on that ship, Elin."

She was getting nowhere with him. Maybe she would have to figure this out by herself. No one seemed to be listening. "Is that all?"

Tom nodded. "Not much to go on at the moment. The Virginia Beach police would like to talk to you again after they speak with Josh. You'll be around?"

She nodded. "I've told them all I know though. We didn't see anything that might tell them who did this."

"I'll send them your way." Tom rose and went around to open the door for them. "I'll let you know if I hear anything."

Elin strode down the hall, her heels clicking on the tile floor. She wanted to get far away from Marc. He was supposed to be helping her find the killer, not derailing law enforcement onto a useless rabbit trail.

"Wait up, Elin." Marc's steps sounded behind her.

She ignored his call and increased her steps until she burst through the exit door and out into the sunshine where she could breathe. His hand on her arm brought her up short. She jerked out of his grip and turned to face him.

"Don't shoot the messenger. We have to examine every possibility."

She pointed her finger at him. "No, we need to hone in on the real killer. Your obsession with Josh is going to get me murdered." She broke off, her voice choked.

"I'm going to protect you."

"Don't delude yourself. A determined killer can get to me unless we find him first. And it's *not* Josh."

He blinked at her vehemence. "You seem to feel strongly about this."

She put her hand to her heart. "I *know* it here, Marc. Josh isn't a killer. That murderer may be watching us even now, toying with us and waiting for his chance. We can't afford to get side-tracked."

His hazel eyes narrowed. "Okay. I'll look at the rest of the passenger manifest."

"What about that Theo guy? You didn't have a good feeling about him. I'd like to hear his voice myself and see if I have any reaction to it."

"Barbara cleared him. Or don't you believe her?"

"I'd rather doubt her word than suspect Josh." The tightness in her chest loosened. He was listening.

He finally nodded. "We'll see who else we can find. But there's something else I want to talk to you about."

She didn't like his somber expression. "What's wrong?"

"My parents are coming tomorrow to meet Josie. We need to tell her tonight who I am."

She bit her lip. She'd told him she was nearly ready, but now that the moment was here, she wasn't sure. "It's too soon, Marc. She needs time to get to know you."

"She already loves me, Elin. You know it as well as I do. We have to tell her."

She wanted to object again, but he was right.

She glanced across the street at her daughter, happily licking her Superman cone. "Let me think about how to do it."

A homeless man shuffled by with his shopping cart piled high. He looked at them as if he knew no one would help him. Marc pulled a twenty out of his pocket. "Would you like some dinner?"

The man blinked, and a bit of hope crept into his eyes. His dirty fingers closed around the bill Marc offered. "Thank you, sir. I haven't eaten in two days. You have a good heart." He turned toward the hot dog stand.

Elin gazed up at him. How many men noticed the homeless? "Why'd you do that?"

"I saw the way he looked at Josie's ice cream. He was hungry."

She couldn't look away from his earnest expression.

"What? You're looking at me funny."

"You're not all macho man, are you? You have a lovely soul, Marc."

A hint of color came to his face. "I'm nothing special that way, Elin."

She clamped her lips shut. She was liking everything about him these days. This was dangerous ground she treaded.

He crossed the street to join Abby and Josie, and she stared after him. She pressed her hand against her breastbone. Maybe she should lie down. Her lonely heart was yearning for him way too much.

❦ Twenty-Four ❦

Elin put the glasses of lemonade on the coffee table and smiled as she watched Marc frolic on the floor with Josie on his back. She loved horsey rides, and she clung to his shirt with both hands as she shrieked with delight. Max ran around them barking frantically. The little Yorkie had already become part of the family.

Josie kicked her small bare heels into Marc's ribs. "Again!"

He groaned and rolled over, snatching her off his back as he did. He cradled his daughter to his chest and breathed heavily. "You're making an old man out of me, kiddo."

Josie lay in his embrace for a few moments before she struggled to sit up. She straddled his chest, then bounced up and down, grinning when he let out a moan with every thump.

He finally sat up and ran his hand through his wild hair. "Your mommy and I want to talk to you." He thumbed a mint out of the roll in his hand.

Elin's smile vanished. Her pulse throbbed in her throat. How on earth did she explain something like this to a four-year-old? She needed to take the lead, though, or Marc would. And this should come from her. What did he know about small children?

She cleared her throat. "Sit up here by Mommy a minute, Josie. I have something very exciting to tell you."

Josie scrambled to her feet. "Are we going to the zoo?"

"No, it's even better than the zoo."

Josie climbed onto the sofa beside her. "Nothing is better than the zoo. Unless I'm getting a baby brother. Is that the special news?"

Elin couldn't meet Marc's amused gaze. "No, it's not a baby either. This is even better."

Josie frowned as if the very idea of something better than a baby was silly. "Did you buy me something?"

"No, it's not that. Just listen to me for a minute, honey." She glanced around for a prop. She spied Josie's picture on the end table and scooped it up. In the photo, Tim had her on his lap. They were both smiling into the camera. "This was you when you were one. See your dark hair?"

Josie touched her brown curls. "It's still dark. Not red like yours." Her tone indicated she was very displeased by that.

"No, it's not red like mine. It's not blond either. It's a beautiful shade of brown, the prettiest color there is. And your eyes are such a pretty color, part green and part gold. You look exactly like yourself, and I love everything about you."

Josie smiled and leaned in for a hug. "I love everything about you too, Mommy."

Elin held her close and pressed a kiss onto her daughter's soft hair, smelling of sunshine and coconut shampoo. This wasn't going to be easy. "Sometimes a little girl is lucky enough to have two daddies."

Josie pulled away and her brow furrowed. "Two daddies?"

"Uh-huh. One daddy brings her home and loves her, and the other daddy is where she gets her hair and eyes. He loves her too." Elin felt mired in topics too complex to explain to a small child. "You like Mr. Marc, don't you?"

Josie looked over at Marc. "I don't want him to ever go away."

His mouth softened into a smile. "I'm not planning on ever leaving you, Josie. I will always be around to help you."

Pain squeezed Elin's chest as she watched the two exchange a tender glance of devotion. What had she done? No wonder Marc had been enraged. If ever a man was meant to be a father, he was. The attachment between them could almost be touched.

Elin managed a smile. "Well, there is something special about Mr. Marc. He's the kind of daddy who gives a little girl her dark hair and pretty eyes. In fact, he's *your* daddy."

Josie had no reaction at first except to stare at him. Then she slid off the sofa and went to where he still sat on the floor. She fingered his hair, then ran a finger over his eyelid. "My hair is like yours. Your eyes have yellow spots in them too."

"That's right. I'm your daddy. I would have been with you before now, but I didn't know about you."

Elin tried not to feel hurt at his remark. Marc wouldn't try to turn Josie against her. At least she didn't think he would. She'd always thought him an honorable man. "There's another surprise, honey. Your daddy has a mommy and daddy too. They are your grandma and grandpa."

"I already have Grandma Ruby. And Grandma and Grandpa Summerall."

Though Josie hadn't seen Tim's parents much, she looked at their picture often and asked about them. They lived in California, and she'd only seen them twice in her lifetime. "I know, but you're a lucky little girl because Mr. Marc's parents are really nice. They don't live very far away, and they are going to come here tomorrow."

Josie absorbed the information. "They're nice?" She looked to Marc for confirmation.

"They are very nice."

"Should I still call you Mr. Marc? I'd rather call you Daddy."

Marc swallowed and his throat clicked. "I would like it very much if you wanted to call me Daddy."

"Okay. Can I go find Grandma Ruby and tell her?"

"She's napping," Elin said quickly. This news needed to come from her. She'd hoped to tell her mother when she got back from town, but Mom had been strangely sleepy all day and hadn't woken from her nap. "I'll go see if she's ready to wake up."

Heaven only knew how her mother would take this news. Or even if she could totally comprehend it.

Tuesday morning dawned with overcast skies. Rain showers should arrive by lunch. Marc threw a ball to little Max and kept an eye on the pier. His parents should be arriving anytime, hopefully ahead of the storm. Elin had been unable to rouse her mother last night, so Ruby still didn't know she would have to share Josie with another set of grandparents.

He gulped at the thought of telling his parents this news. He should have told them on the phone about Josie, but he wanted to break it to them in person. How would they react? They'd always been so proud of him, often telling their friends what a good Christian he was. Oh, he was a moral, upstanding citizen, all right. He hated disappointing them, but he'd wrestled his guilt to the ground with God, and that was all that really mattered. His parents would get over it.

The putter of a motor came to his ears. He tossed the ball one last time, then went down to the harbor dock to meet them. They thought they were just coming for a nice week at the island. He lifted a hand in greeting as the boat neared.

His father wore his old fishing hat, stained and floppy from many years of use. Lures circled the crown. No one would guess he'd been a well-known attorney with clients from all over the world. His grin appeared, and he rose to toss a line to Marc.

His mother waved gaily. She wore a pink sundress that strained a bit at the seams. She'd refused to go up the one size necessary since she'd hit menopause. Christine and Frank Everton had met in high school and married at nineteen. They were still the most loving couple Marc had ever seen. He'd always wanted to have a marriage like theirs someday, but that seemed a more and more unlikely dream.

Marc tied off the boat, then helped his mother step onto the dock. They looked younger than their early sixties. They'd stayed active over the years with golf and tennis. His father had recently retired from his law practice, and they both kept busy with charities and friends.

He hugged his mother and inhaled the familiar scent of her perfume, Chanel No. 5. "Glad you could come."

His father clapped a hand on his shoulder and squinted toward the house. "Nice place here, son. Where's Elin? We're looking forward to seeing her. And she has a little girl. Your mom will be in her glory spoiling her."

Marc managed a grin. "Yeah, well, I have something to tell you before we go find the others."

His mother hugged him. "You're getting married. I *knew* it." She released him and patted his arm. "You don't need to worry, son. We'll be happy to welcome any woman you choose into the family. You have good judgment."

Marc's neck heated, and he shook his head. "It's not that, Mom." He cleared his throat. "I shouldn't throw this at you so fast, but I didn't want to drop a bombshell on the phone." He gestured to the fishing pier to his right. "Let's sit down a minute." He led them along the shore to the pier, then sat on the edge of the boards and dangled his legs over the side. His mother joined him quickly, but it took his dad a minute to maneuver down with his bad knee.

"What's this all about, Marc?" His dad frowned. The frown that said, "Get to the point and make it quick." His attorney face.

"It's about Josie."

"Is something wrong with her? Oh, that poor little baby. Where is she?" His mother started to get up.

Marc stopped her with a hand on her arm. "She's perfect in every way, Mom. I'm sure you'll agree because . . . sh-she's my daughter."

An explosion couldn't have caused more of a

reaction. His mother blanched, and his father nearly fell into the ocean. Marc steadied his dad and kept his hand on his mom's arm. The situation could go either way, though he was betting on his mother's desire for grandchildren.

She stared into his face. She must have seen the truth in his eyes because she nodded. "She's four, right?"

"Yeah." He could see the wheels turning as she did the math, since she'd attended Elin's wedding. "I didn't know when she married Tim. You know me well enough to realize I would never have abandoned my baby. Elin had a bad time when her dad died and . . ." He looked away. "Anyway, I don't want you to think badly of her. She told Tim, and he wanted to marry her anyway. He never wanted me to know."

His mother shook off his grip and got up with difficulty in her tight dress and high-heeled sandals. "I think it's scandalous she never told you. And us. We had a right to know. I've longed for grandchildren forever, Marc. *Forever!* And you. You've missed years of your daughter's life. How dare she deny us the knowledge we had a little granddaughter?"

Marc scrambled to his feet too and stopped her before she could march toward the house. "Calm down, Mom. Tim made her promise to keep it to herself. He loved Josie and was good to her. I'm grateful for that." No reason to tell them about the killer just yet. They had enough to absorb with the news about Josie.

His dad struggled to his feet. "How are you handling this, son? Did she just tell you because she wants child support?"

Trust his dad to look at the legalities. "I was shocked. And Elin hasn't mentioned support." He made a mental note to start writing her a check every week. And there was no reason to tell them she wouldn't have admitted Josie was his if he hadn't guessed. It would make them think even more poorly of her. "I already love Josie. You will too. She looks just like me."

His mother's face crumbled at his words. "Like you?"

"Brown curls, hazel eyes. She has your chin, Mom." He offered her his roll of mints. "Here, have a mint."

She thrust them away. "A mint won't calm me like it does you." Her eyes swam with tears, and she clasped her hands together. "I can't wait to see her. What does she know?"

"She's only four, so all she knows is I'm the kind of daddy who gives a little girl her hair and eyes. It was hard to explain it to her last night. She's excited about having another grandma and grandpa though." He told them about Ruby's dementia.

"Poor little mite. We want to help in any way we can," his mother said. "Can we meet her now?"

He nodded toward the house as Elin and Josie headed their direction. "Here they come now. Take it easy on Elin. She's had a rough time."

But he was speaking to the wind because his mom was already flying toward her grand-daughter.

❧ Twenty-Five ❧

The sound of the chopper rotors faded into the distance as Sara walked toward her car. The bright-blue bowl of sky overhead did nothing to lift her mood. She hadn't been able to keep her gaze from Josh all day. Her cousin's insinuations —no, downright *accusations*—kept poking themselves into her thoughts.

But this was *Josh,* not some stranger lurking in the shadows. She knew him, knew his dedication to saving people, his concern for other people.

"Hey, Sara," Josh called from behind her.

She turned to wait for him and Curtis. They'd both changed into jeans and T-shirts. Josh wore a Dodgers one and his well-worn matching ball cap. They fell into step together and walked toward the parking lot. "I was just heading over for ice cream. Want to come?"

Curtis grinned. "Not today. Amy and I are meeting with the adoption agency. We got a call last night. They've got a little girl, two days old. I think we're going to get her today."

"Seriously?" Sara squealed and hugged him. "That is awesome news!"

"Amy couldn't sleep, and I found her painting the nursery this morning when I woke up. I told her she should have awakened me, and I would have gotten up to help."

"It was yellow, wasn't it? I bet she painted it pink."

Curtis grinned. "You're close. Lavender. I didn't even know we had lavender paint. She's been out gathering supplies all day. Stuff like diapers, powder, sleepers. I think she's texted me twenty times today with pictures."

"I don't blame her. It's super exciting. I want to meet the new baby as soon as you get her all settled."

"Libby plans to have a baby shower next week too. She arrived at the house this morning before I left."

They reached the parking lot, and Curtis headed for his truck. "Talk to you all later."

Josh leaned against her car. "I heard you had a date the other night."

She pressed her key fob to unlock the door. "Well, dinner at least. Just getting to know Ben a bit."

Was he jealous? She eyed his placid expression. He didn't seem upset or anything. Maybe he really didn't care. Or maybe he was relieved there wouldn't be any pressure on him to commit to something.

"Gonna go out again?"

Now there was an edge in the question. She considered her answer. While it might be telling to see if she could make him jealous, she didn't want to play games. Maybe it was a little naive of her to think their relationship was better than that.

"I don't know," she said finally. "He hasn't asked me, but we had a nice time. How did you know about it?"

"I overheard him telling someone he was going to marry you."

She blinked. "Whoa, that's a little extreme. We barely know each other."

"Sometimes a woman comes along who makes a guy reconsider his decisions in life."

Was he talking about himself? He'd never really responded to her confession the other day. She'd hoped he would tell her he loved her too, but that hadn't happened. Was this as close as she was going to get?

She put her hand on his arm. "What does that mean, Josh?"

He took off his Dodgers cap and raked his hand through his brown hair. "I don't know myself, Sara. I don't deserve a woman like you. I'm afraid I would fail you in the end. I want you to be happy. I'm not sure I could make you happy."

His expression tugged at her heart. "I don't know why you would say that. You're the first one to volunteer for dangerous missions. You do things for other people and never tell them about it. If I hear about someone finding a basket of food on her front porch or his lapsing insurance miraculously paid, I know you're the one who has done it. What has caused you to be so mistrusting of your own worth? You never talk about your past or your childhood. Something has hurt you, but you can let it go and move on if you want to."

He lifted tormented blue eyes to meet hers. "It's not that easy. I'm afraid of being like my father."

"You're not your father, Josh. I know the man inside you. You're a good man, the best. You can't look at your father's failings and take them on yourself."

"It's more than that."

At least he was opening up. "What do you mean?"

"He beat my mother and me. And I stood back and let him beat my brother to death." His face paled, and he dropped his gaze to the ground. "So much for being a good guy, huh?"

"How old were you?"

"Twelve."

She couldn't help stepping closer to hug him. He stood stiffly in her embrace, then sighed and dropped his head into the crook of her neck. His arms came around her, and he crushed her to his chest. She lifted her head, and he looked into her eyes. Her lids fluttered shut of their own accord. His lips came down on hers, and she tasted him outside of her dreams for the first time. Or maybe this *was* a dream. But no, her fingertips rested on the hard muscles of his chest. His hands fanned across her back as he pressed her closer.

If this was a dream, she wanted never to awaken.

He kissed her like a starving man, and she wrapped her arms around his neck and kissed him back with all the love welling in her heart, an emotion she'd never been able to express before. When he finally pulled away, she made a mewl of protest and tried to pull his head back down for another kiss.

His hands fell away and he stepped back. "I was trying to say good-bye, but you make it really hard, Sara."

"Good-bye?" She tried to clear her fuzzy thoughts.

"I told you—I can never make you happy. I know that about myself. And you deserve so much more." He turned and ran off toward his truck.

She didn't even try to go after him.

"Are those people my grandma and grandpa?" Josie asked in a loud whisper. She clung to her mother's hand.

Elin squeezed her daughter's small fingers. She was nervous too. Marc's mother had always terrified her. Christine Everton was one of those people with a personality bigger than life. She'd always been kind to Elin when she'd been at their house with Sara, but whenever Elin looked into her hazel eyes, she felt so inadequate. Christine did everything well.

She swallowed hard and pasted on a smile as Marc and his parents neared. "Welcome to Seagrass Cottage. It's a little remote, but your suite is very nice, and I think you'll like it."

Christine seemed not to hear. Her attention was fixed on Josie. Were those tears in her eyes? Elin felt horrible as she recognized the overwhelming love on the older woman's face. She'd thought she was doing the right thing in honoring Tim's wishes, but it seemed she was wrong about so many things.

Christine knelt in front of Josie. Her smile wobbled a bit. "You must be Josie. You look just like your daddy did when he was your age."

Josie looked from Christine to Marc. "My hair is brown."

"I know. And curly. You're beautiful." Her voice was choked.

In that moment, Elin opened her heart to Christine. Any woman who would show such unfettered love for her daughter was worthy of friendship and love. She looked up and met

Marc's gaze of approval. Something fluttered in her chest.

Josie hung on to Elin's leg, but she began to smile as Christine coaxed her forward with a piece of bubble gum she dug out of her purse. The older woman scooped up Josie as soon as she stepped forward. Surprisingly, the little girl didn't struggle. She stared at her new grandmother with wide eyes.

Frank stood close as well, and his big smile seemed to calm Josie. She hadn't been around a grandfather very often.

"Want to go find some seashells?" Frank suggested.

Josie looked uncertainly at her mother, then nodded. "Are you coming too, Mommy?"

"I'll be right here. Your new grammy and grandpa will take good care of you."

Josie's expression said she wasn't so sure about that, but she let Christine carry her toward the sand dunes. Elin exhaled. "That went better than I expected."

"I was afraid Mom might tear you limb from limb for depriving her of her granddaughter." Though he smiled, Marc's voice held a serious edge.

"Josie could use some extra loving. She doesn't understand the way Mom can change and ignore her."

"Where is Ruby today?"

"Napping. She's been extra tired the last few days. I probably ought to get her in to see the doctor. Something might be wrong." Elin didn't want to think about one more problem though. What if her mother had something seriously wrong? Though the time would come sooner or later, she wasn't ready to lose her mother. The dementia was bad enough.

"Is Kalianne with her?"

She shook her head. "I gave her the day off. I knew I'd be home all day." There was something in his manner she couldn't put her finger on. "Is something bothering you?" The breeze blew a long strand of hair into her eyes, and she swiped it away.

"They will want to see her often, Elin. Are you ready for that?"

At least he was being direct. "I think so. It did me a world of good to see the love on your mom's face. There's never too much love in a child's life."

"No." He continued to look at her with an unfathomable expression.

"What?"

"Elin, she needs a father in her life too."

"You're here, aren't you?" Her pulse sped up at his expression. Surely he wasn't going to ask for custody.

He took a step closer. "She needs two parents. All the time."

"That's not possible though. At some point we'll have that maniac behind bars. You'll go back to Norfolk to your job, and I'll go back to mine. But at least she can see you often. And your parents. I know it's not ideal, but it's how lots of kids live."

On one hand, his presence made her feel more secure, but it also left her unsettled. She couldn't decide if she was looking forward to him moving out or not.

"I don't want my daughter to live like that." He took a deep breath, then exhaled. "I think we should get married."

The breath left her lungs. She gaped but no words came. Studying his face, she saw he was serious. Or crazy. Or maybe she was the crazy one because her mind was conjuring up lovely images of a life spent with Marc. She couldn't love him, could she? Love didn't strike so fast, surely.

When she didn't answer, he rushed on. "Hear me out. I wouldn't expect anything from you, not a real marriage, of course. Too much water under the bridge for that. But we could buy a big place together where we each had our own space. Then we'd be there for Josie. Both of us." He turned and gestured at the big cottage. "Maybe even live in this place. I could get transferred out here maybe. You work from home anyway, so it doesn't matter where you live."

"B–But don't you think that's a little extreme?" She couldn't breathe, couldn't look away from his penetrating gaze. "Josie will be fine. She'll know she's loved. It warms my heart that you already care about her so much, but I think you're going a little overboard."

"I don't think so. Can you at least think about it, Elin? Josie deserves to be put first."

"I always put her first!"

He nodded. "I'm not saying you don't. But I'm willing to change my life for her. Can't you do the same?"

She turned her back on him and ran for the house. Because the one thing his proposal had shown her was that she was developing feelings for the infuriating man, and the thought of a loveless marriage left her cold.

≈ Twenty-Six ≈

Elin didn't know how she got through the rest of the day. All she wanted to do was think about Marc's proposal. It was like probing a toothache with her tongue. She couldn't seem to think about anything else. She got her guests situated for the night, then went to her bedroom.

The light was on, and she paused to take in the scene in her light-blue bedroom. Dressed in a light-blue nightgown, her mother lay curled up on her bed. "Mom, what are you doing in here?"

Her mother's blue eyes sharpened as she sat up and put down her book. "Elin, there you are. You should have been in bed at nine. I came to tuck you in. You should have sent your friends home long ago. Their parents will be worried."

If only she were ten again and could crawl into her mother's lap and tell her all her woes. Even if her mother understood what she was saying, she couldn't help. "They are Marc's parents, remember? They're here to see him." She'd tried to tell her mother Marc was Josie's father but had been unable to make her understand. "You should get to bed yourself, Mom. It's nearly mid-night."

"Is it? I'm wide-awake."

And her mother did look a little brighter and more alert than she'd seen her in a while, even if she did think Elin was a child. Elin joined her on the bed. It almost felt like when she was a teenager and would lie on her mother's bed and tell her about her day. Maybe her mother would understand tonight. She so needed someone to bounce around her thoughts with her. Just smelling the scent of her mother's cologne, a sandalwood she'd worn forever, took her back to her teen years.

Her mother brushed the long hair from Elin's face. "You look troubled, honey. What's wrong?"

Elin's eyes burned at the compassion in her voice. Every day it seemed she lost more of both herself and her mother. Why did life have to be so hard?

She swallowed the lump in her throat. "It's boy trouble."

The tips of her mother's mouth turned up into not quite a smile but an expression of commiseration. "Tell your mama all about it."

The familiar entreaty brought tears surging back to her eyes. "It's Marc. He wants to marry me."

"But isn't that a good thing?" Her mother caressed her cheek. "He *is* Josie's father."

Elin gasped. "You knew?" She hadn't thought her mother had understood.

"I'm not in my dotage yet, Elin." Her mother shook her head. "I knew the first time I saw Josie that Tim wasn't her father. You couldn't hide something that big from me. I know you too well. So what's the problem? Surely you told him yes."

"I ran away." Her voice wobbled. "All he wants is to be with Josie. I don't want to be just Josie's mother. What kind of marriage would that be?"

"You love him." Her mother smiled.

Did she? "I–I don't think it's love. Maybe it could be, but it's mostly that I realize now that I want a real family someday. Not some kind of sterile arrangement."

Her mom patted her hand. "Honey, it only takes seeing how he watches you to know he cares about you. He might have his guard up and not know it yet, but he'll figure it out."

"You really think so? I don't see it. Tim feared this would happen, you know. He hated Marc."

Even now, she could see the determination on Tim's face when he threw Marc out of the house that day. His jealousy had grown into downright hatred.

Her mother cupped her face in her hands. "Tim is dead, Elin. You're still a young woman. I would hate to see you lock yourself away from love and happiness because of a dead man's jealousy. That's just silly. You're more alive and fully yourself when you're around Marc. I see the old Elin then."

She blinked. "W-What do you mean, the old Elin?"

Her mother dropped her hands away. "You haven't been as open and transparent as usual for a while. Coming so close to dying did something, I think. It made you more serious, more guarded. He's good for you. And you're good for him."

Elin relaxed a bit. Her mother wasn't talking about personality changes, just the trauma of the illness. She looked her mother fully in the eyes. "What makes up who we are, really? What we like or dislike? How we walk, talk?"

"It's how we love, honey. And you love with your whole heart. God shines through you. Don't ever let that change."

"How do I stop it?" she whispered.

But her mother's blue eyes were clouding up,

obscuring the loving woman who had guided Elin for all her thirty years. Where did Mom go when she left? And was there any way to bring her back, or would she go away forever? This was worse than losing her to death, and it mirrored what Elin felt was happening to her.

She helped her mother to bed. When she got back to her room, she looked out at the dark night. The nightmares seemed close tonight. She picked up Georgina's diary.

December 5, 1907

The three-month-old twins slept peacefully in their cradles in Georgina's lavish bedroom. *Twins.* She still couldn't believe it. A son and a daughter. Joshua had paid little attention to his daughter, but he nearly burst with pride when he saw his son. He'd almost delayed his departure at their early arrival, but he'd had little choice. Two months had stretched into three, and he was overdue by a good month now.

She left her children in the care of the nurse while she went up to the widow's walk. Joshua was due in anytime, and he would be quite tiresome if he didn't see her wave from the parapet. She'd been watching for him for weeks, and though it was too soon to worry, she had felt dread curling in the pit of her stomach with each passing day.

Some sailors never came home.

She couldn't imagine Joshua allowing anything to keep him from his destination. He wrapped his power and determination around him like an impenetrable cloak. Not even the sea would dare to contradict his will.

She reached the parapet and rested her hands on the iron railing. Black storm clouds roiled on the horizon, and the wind freshened. She lifted her face and inhaled the scent of the approaching rain. The heavy surf pounded the sand dunes and rolled back for a fresh attack.

No white sail marred the sea's blue perfection. Tension uncoiled in her neck. Maybe she had a few hours before he arrived. She lived with the constant hope he would return and be the man she'd thought she married. One who cared more about her than about his image in society.

A sound startled her and she whirled. A man exited the door to the walkway around the top of the house. She'd never seen him before, but she instantly recognized him as Khmer. About her own height, he had glossy black hair and almond-shaped eyes that reminded her of Chann. He wore a bright-red krama around his neck.

Even as a smile formed on her lips, the menacing expression on his face penetrated. She took a step back, but the railing prevented her from moving more than a few inches. "Who are you?"

"It is where?" His heavily accented English was difficult to make out.

"What is it you want?"

He stopped a foot away and glared at her. "The pouch, woman. Given to you by Chann. I want it."

How did she get rid of him without lying? "My husband will be here anytime. You need to leave."

In a movement as quick as a mongoose after a snake, he grabbed her by the shoulders and shook her so hard, her head flopped back and forth. His roughness left her dizzy. He didn't release her, and she winced as his fingers tightened, then he thrust her back until she was hanging partially over the railing.

The sound of the sea mingled with the roar of the blood in her ears. She fought to get away from him before he could throw her off the parapet. He bent her back so far, she was nearly upside down. The spikes on the railing bit into her waist. Her hands flailed, then she dug her fingernails into his face. He winced, but his expression grew more determined.

He intended to throw her over the side with as little thought as a fisherman tossing a fish back into the sea.

Then he reeled away, and the pressure on her shoulders was gone. She staggered to an upright position and realized Chann had pulled the man off her. The two struggled in a deadly two-step near the edge of the railing. One wrong move, and they'd both go over the end.

Gusts of wind shook the house as the storm intensified. Chann's face twisted in fierce determination, and the other man growled and fought back. He was bigger and heavier than Chann and had nearly pushed her friend over the railing. Georgina twisted her hands together in a futile desire to do something to help. If only she had a weapon.

Her hair! She dove her fingers into her updo. The wind teased her hair loose when she extracted a hairpin. She quickly rushed to the struggling men and plunged the point of her hairpin into the back of the assailant's neck. It wouldn't kill him, but it would distract him like a bee sting.

He released his grip on Chann and slapped his hand on his neck. Chann launched forward and seized his arm, then hurled him over the side of the railing. The man plummeted to the ground without a sound. Nausea roiled in Georgina's stomach, and she bent over, retching.

Instantly, Chann was by her side. He didn't touch her but stood back respectfully and offered his hanky when she finally lifted her head. "I am so sorry, little sister. You are hurt?"

She pressed his hanky against her lips and shook her head. "No, no, I am unharmed. Who was he?"

"A very bad man. I cannot stay. Others will come for what you have hidden. Do not let anyone take it. Someday the world will be ready to see this treasure, but not now. Not when greedy men would seek it for their own gain."

"I don't understand."

His gentle smile came. "You will do what I ask?" When she nodded, his face grew more sober. "Even if you hear of my death, do not tell anyone, little sister. What you hide is a map to a great treasure, an ancient city of wonder in Cambodia. It must not be discovered in my lifetime. Maybe never. Guard it well."

"I do not wish to keep this from my husband. May I tell him?"

His dark eyes grew shadowed. "I am sorry to tell you this news. I heard in town that his ship sank. All aboard were lost."

Spots danced in front of Georgina's eyes, and she swayed where she stood. "H-He's dead? Joshua is dead?" Chann caught her as she crumpled.

What did she care about hidden cities? She would have to raise her children alone.

☙ Twenty-Seven ☙

Marc kept glancing at Elin from the corner of his eye as they drove to Norfolk on Thursday morning. She hadn't said much the entire trip. Ignoring his proposal wouldn't fix anything, but every time he opened his mouth to bring it up, he shut it again. What more could he say to convince her? He didn't know what her problem was. Any logical look at their conundrum would arrive at the same answer: marriage.

"Anything new in the diary?" he asked.

She straightened, and a hint of color came to her cheeks. "I know what it was she hid. Her friend had discovered an ancient city full of treasure somewhere in Cambodia. Others were after the map to its location, but he said she was never to turn it over. So it might actually still be in the house."

"You think your mother found it?"

"Maybe." Then she shook her head. "I think it's all a little far-fetched to think it could still be there. I mean, that was over a hundred years ago. Surely someone would have found it."

"Has any Cambodian city been discovered in the past hundred years?"

"Well, there was Angkor Wat. But I don't think that was the one from her description in the diary."

"Maybe there really was no city. We have all those satellites now to find missing structures."

"Maybe. But if I find the pouch, I'm going to hide it again."

They entered the city limits, and he slowed the vehicle.

"Josie has taken to your parents," she said, still staring out the window as they entered the

Norfolk traffic. "We should pick up a little gift to thank them for keeping her while we investigate."

"Spending time with her is all they need. They're eating it up." Maybe this was his opening. "Have you thought about what I said Tuesday night?"

"There hasn't been much time."

"Surely you can see how much sense it makes, Elin. Josie will thrive in a stable home."

Her jaw set, she shook her head. "You would regret it someday, Marc. What if you found another woman you could love? Then where would we be? Right now you're a novelty to her. If you become an integral part of her life and then leave, it would crush her. She's lost one father. I don't want her to lose another."

"I'm not going anywhere. It's not like I'm going to date if we're married. What kind of man do you think I am?" Maybe he didn't want to know because the thought she believed him capable of such a lack of integrity stung.

Something stirred in his heart as he looked at her. Her face was set and strained. What was holding her back?

She looked at the paper in her hand. "We can talk about it once we get the killer behind bars." She gestured to the stop sign at the next street. "We turn here. The Watson house is the third one on the left. It has red shutters and a red front door."

"You've been here before?"

"No." She turned to look at him. "I don't know how I know it, but I do."

This whole cell-memory thing had him a little off center. "Okay." He saw her slight shudder and realized she was as disoriented by this as he was. Probably more.

He turned and drove down the street slowly. There it was, just as she had described it. A two-story with neat shutters and a red door. The yard was well kept, and the grass freshly mowed. A swing set sat in the backyard. "There it is."

He pulled the SUV into the driveway and opened his door to the pungent odor of asphalt. "Smells like the driveway was just resealed. Maybe I shouldn't park here."

As if on cue, a man exited the house waving his hands. "Park in the street!"

Marc spared a glance at the guy. Tall and thin with a balding head and small, neat ears. He wore khakis and a T-shirt proclaiming him the best dad in the world. Starting the car, Marc backed into the street and parked at the curb. "Is that her dad?"

Elin hadn't taken her eyes off the man. "Yes." Her voice was barely audible. "I–I'm frightened of him, Marc. I don't want to get out of the car."

"Sit here. I can handle questioning him."

She turned a pale face toward him. "No, I want to go too. Just stay close to me."

He nodded, and they got out of the car. He took her arm at the curb and approached the house.

The man didn't return his smile but stared at them with obvious suspicion. "If you're selling something, just get back in your fancy Tahoe and head on out of here."

"We're not selling anything. I'm a special agent with the FBI. We have a few questions about your daughter." He'd thought mentioning Laura would cause the man to put down his guard, but Mr. Watson continued to glare at them. With Watson's obvious hostility, Marc didn't want to reveal Elin's identity.

"What do you want? I already answered a ton of questions." He turned back toward the house.

A woman stepped through the screen door. In her fifties like the man, her hunched shoulders and downcast eyes told a story of submission. Were those bruises on her arms? She wore cutoffs and a red V-neck top. Her feet were bare.

"I need to talk to you both. I'm investigating your daughter's death." Marc's fingers curled into his palms. A man who would hurt a woman was pure scum. He hadn't liked Watson's attitude, but now he actively disliked the man.

"Is everything okay, Jerry?" The woman's voice was timid. "This man is with the FBI. Maybe they've found Laura's killer."

"Get back in the house, Judy. This doesn't concern you."

She cowered back against the door and turned to go back inside.

"You'll answer more questions for me here, or I'll haul you in for questioning." Marc didn't rein in his sharp tone. "You can answer them in your living room or in a locked room of my choosing. Your choice."

The man glared at him, then shrugged. "Suit yourself." He turned and stomped back toward the house.

Marc raised his brows at Elin, then took her arm and followed Watson inside. It took a moment for his eyes to adjust to the dim interior. Foil covered every window, and only a few lamps illuminated the interior. The place was neat, but a pungent odor permeated the air. Marijuana.

He didn't like how white Elin looked, and the way she pressed against his side told him she'd rather be anywhere but here.

She couldn't stop shivering. Elin sat beside Marc on a sofa that was much too familiar. The house reeked of pot, just like usual. Her father—no, *Laura's father*—had been smoking it most of the day, evidenced by his red-rimmed eyes and dilated pupils. Had Marc noticed? She glanced up at him. He'd noticed all right. If his jaw got any harder, it would crack.

"Let's get this over with." Watson plopped into his worn leather recliner. "Judy, get started on lunch. I'll handle this."

When Mrs. Watson turned toward the kitchen door, Marc shook his head. "You can eat later. I need to speak to both of you."

To Elin's surprise, Watson scowled and allowed his wife to sidle over to the rocking chair where her knitting lay on the floor. She eased into the chair and picked up her yarn. The material appeared to be a pink baby blanket. Who was having a baby? Laura's little sister? Her name hovered on the edge of Elin's memory. Sammie. And she was sixteen.

"Where's Sammie?" she blurted out. "We need to talk to her too."

Watson scowled again. "Samantha isn't feeling well. She doesn't know anything anyway."

"Not well?" Elin rose and turned toward the stairs when she heard a creak. "Sammie, are you up there?"

A figure moved down the steps. A young brunette stood on the bottom step. Dressed in pink capris and a sleeveless white top that stretched over a bulging belly, she stared at Marc and Elin.

"Samantha, this is none of your concern. Go on up to your room," her father barked.

Samantha didn't budge, though her hand drifted along the smooth surface of the oak banister. "I–I thought I heard Laura's voice. Just now." She rubbed her eyes. "Maybe I was dreaming, but I heard her say, 'Sammie.' No one else ever calls me Sammie anymore."

Heat flooded Elin's face. What would this family do if she revealed she had Laura's heart? That she heard things, saw things that only Laura could know? She thought Sammie would rush to embrace her, but Watson might just throw her out the door.

A lock of hair fell into her face, and she brushed it back without thinking. Sammie's eyes widened. She stepped down the final step and came toward Elin as if in a trance. When the young girl stopped in front of her and continued to stare, Elin couldn't look away. What did Sammie see in her face? Was Laura in there somewhere looking back?

"Who are you?" Sammie whispered.

"They're here to ask questions about your sister," Watson said. "That's all you need to know. Get on back upstairs."

"I'd like to speak to the whole family," Marc said. "Do you have any other children? Any other members of the family who live with you, like a grandparent?"

"We just had the two girls. No one else. Look, what's all this about? And Samantha, you will make them think you are some kind of weirdo with the way you're staring. Sit down. You're making a fool of yourself."

"Who are you?" Sammie asked again. "You remind me of Laura somehow. Did you know my sister?" Her voice broke. "I miss her every day. I told her he'd kill her."

Marc shot to his feet. "Who? Do you know who might have targeted your sister?"

Watson jumped up too. "Now you've done it, you stupid girl. I told you never to talk about that. He had nothing to do with Laura's murder."

Elin felt such pity for the young woman. A terrible grief crouched in Sammie's eyes. The two sisters had been close, and her heart clenched with a reciprocal love. How could she not give Laura's sister some assurance? Yet she wasn't convinced it would help the situation.

Sammie didn't move. "You knew her, didn't you? That's why you called me Sammie with her same inflection."

Elin nodded. "I knew her a little." A confession hovered behind her lips, but she managed to hold it back when Marc's hand slid across the sofa and covered hers with a warming squeeze.

The tension in Sammie's shoulders eased, and she moved to lower herself awkwardly by her mother's feet. Judy put down her knitting and rested her hand on her younger daughter's shoulder as if to bring a measure of comfort.

Elin could almost feel that touch on her own shoulder. She knew the weight of it, the touch of the work-roughened hands on her skin. The scent of the woman's shampoo and lotion. This was like some kind of time warp, and she needed to get away. To breathe fresh air and not look into the grief-ravaged faces of the other two women.

But with Marc's hand on hers, she managed to compose herself. They had to know whom Sammie referred to. Whom her father wanted to protect.

Marc leaned forward. "Samantha, who frightened Laura?" He held up a warning hand to Watson, who was practically snarling from his recliner.

Sammie leaned her head against her mother's knee. "Dad's business partner, Ryan Mosely." She shot a defiant glare at her father. "He was obsessed with her. Always asking her out and stuff. And he was *old*. In his forties. He should have known she was too young for him. Dad encouraged it though. He wanted Laura to marry the pervert. And when she finally told Ryan she didn't ever want him to even call her, he went ballistic."

"In what way?" Marc asked.

"He sent her nasty e-mails and stuff. He even left a dead rat at the back door." Sammie shuddered. "Laura asked Dad to call him off, but he wouldn't. He said she should wake up and realize what side her bread was buttered on. So Laura decided to work for the cruise line to get away for a while. She hoped Ryan would move on to someone else."

"But he didn't?"

Sammie shook her head. "He booked a cabin on her first cruise. I tried to get Laura to quit her new job and stay home, but she thought he wouldn't be able to do much onboard the ship. She was wrong. He killed her. I know it." She burst into tears, then turned and buried her face against her mother.

"D-Did he frighten her with music from *The Phantom of the Opera*?" Elin asked.

Sammie rolled her eyes. "He wouldn't be caught dead listening to something like that. He's a redneck all the way."

Something in what she said rang true to Elin. Chills skittered down her spine. Laura had been afraid of this Ryan Mosely.

❧ Twenty-Eight ☙

Marc exhaled and put the SUV in gear. The vehicle rolled away from the Watson residence. He couldn't get out of there fast enough as Watson had hustled them out. Marc had asked Samantha if she wanted him to find her a shelter, but she refused. He feared she was in for a tongue-lashing with her father. Or worse. What a family. He braked at the stoplight, then turned to head back to Hope Beach.

"You okay?" he asked Elin, who hadn't said a word since they got in the Tahoe.

When she didn't answer, he glanced over at her and saw sobs shuddering through her. He pulled the Tahoe to the side of the road and unbuckled his seat belt so he could slide across the bench seat and embrace her. He slipped his arm around her and pulled her close. The faint scent of her sweet perfume slipped up his nose. Having her in his arms again felt like coming home. Resting his chin on her hair, he patted her back while she sobbed against his shirt. She fit exactly right in his arms.

He pressed a kiss on her hair. "Hey, you did great. I know it had to be hard, but you held it together. We got some good information today."

She stiffened and pulled back. "You don't know what it cost me."

His hand stilled on her back. "The memories were bad in there."

She nodded. "They're so vivid, Marc. I knew just how Judy Watson's hands would feel. I knew that odor in there was marijuana. You smelled it too, didn't you?"

He nodded. "He smoked pot a lot?"

"Every night, I think. And did you see the bruises on Judy's arms? He hits her all the time. I hate him, and I don't even know him."

"I saw the bruises. I'd call the cops, but I think she would say they happened in another way. It's sad. But I saw enough today to hate him myself. It's not just what you remember from Laura."

"It *is*. I just felt the hate rising up. And I don't

like to feel that way. I want to like people and extend them the benefit of the doubt. I was unable to do that with him. He's an evil, evil man."

"I could feel that too." How did he even go about reassuring her? "In this case, it was a good thing you knew Sammie's nickname. I don't think we would have gotten anything out of them if she hadn't heard you call her that."

She pulled out of his embrace. "Marc, you don't get it!" She thumped her chest. "I even said Sammie's name the way her sister did. I'm afraid, so afraid. I don't want to be someone else. I want to be me. What if someday I wake up and look in the mirror and Elin Summerall isn't there anymore? What if I forget who I am?"

He heard the desperation in her voice, but he didn't know how to alleviate it. "I've seen some changes in you, Elin, but they aren't important to the core of who you are. I mean, identity changes all the time. You've been a daughter, a wife, a mother. You've been an employee. Now you're a somewhat-notorious figure in the news with your memories of the murder." He grinned but she didn't smile back. "You're still you."

"In what way?" She was listening now, the tears in her eyes drying up.

"Tastes aren't who you are. Memories aren't who you are. Roles aren't either, for that matter. Your personality is made up of how you think and react. How you treat people. How you interact with strangers and family. Those things haven't changed, Elin. You always think of other people before yourself. Was Laura like that? With a father like Watson, I doubt it. I bet all she thought about was escape, no matter who it hurt."

She bit her lip and pushed her hair behind her ears. She scrubbed the last traces of tears from her cheeks with the back of her hand. "I'm afraid of suddenly not loving Josie. Or Mom or . . ." She looked away.

Who else was she afraid of not loving? Tim? But he was gone. Something stirred in Marc. Jealousy? Ridiculous. Tim was never coming back from the grave. Marc examined her face, the sweet curve of her cheek and her large, expressive eyes. She had no idea how beautiful she was. Exactly how did he plan to live with her and not feel the desire welling even now? Not want to touch her petal-soft skin? Not remember the way her lips tasted and how she felt in his arms?

He jerked his thoughts away from the danger zone. Maybe his idea of a marriage of convenience between them really *was* a pipe dream. He might not be able to keep his hands off her.

His office was quiet as Marc navigated around the computer screen. Elin could have been beside him, but she feared getting too close to him would cause her to give away her feelings. He could tell her what he found.

She walked to the window and looked down onto the busy street. The virus hadn't killed her. This problem could be overcome too. God had made her who she was, and she intended to keep herself. But how? How did she protect herself from Laura's influence?

Marc glanced at her. "Shut the door, would you? If my boss sees us poking around, I'm in trouble. He's not supposed to be in today, but you never know."

She stepped across the room and shut the door. "Lock it?"

"Yeah, good idea." He leaned back in the office chair. "Aha."

She turned and went to look at the computer with him. "What did you find?"

"First off, Josh is in the clear. He got a delivery of food about the time Laura was murdered. And he called to complain about a noisy party in the next room fifteen minutes later. I think we can rule him out."

"Oh, good! Sara will be so relieved. What else?"

He popped a mint. "Ryan Mosely and Jerry Watson own a mechanic's shop. They've been in business together for twenty years. Mosely must have started working there in his twenties. And they are solvent. Not raking in a ton of money but a nice, steady income."

"Has he ever been arrested?"

"That's the interesting thing. Look here." He

clicked to another screen. "When he was eighteen, he was arrested for peeping in windows. Got probation. Then when he was twenty, he was arrested for battery. A girlfriend claimed he was stalking her, and when she ordered him to leave, he hit her with his fist. Spent a night in jail, then she dropped the charges. We should talk to her." He pulled his iPad toward him and jotted down her name and address, then rose and took her arm.

She fell into step beside him, and they headed for the exit. "Do you think we should go see Mosely too?"

"Let's get some evidence first about his past behavior. We can bring it up to him and see how he reacts."

She blinked in the bright sunshine as they headed to the Tahoe. "Do you remember seeing his name on the passenger manifest?"

"He's there. I'm going to take a look at the logs and see if she registered a complaint about harassment."

He slid under the steering wheel, and she went around to the passenger side. The traffic was heavy on the street, so she waited a moment before opening the door. Before she could slide in, she heard the squeal of tires. Her head jerked up to see a dirty brown car speeding right at her. She stood frozen as the vehicle seemed to deliberately take aim at her.

She felt a tug on her arm as Marc yanked her

inside. The car crashed into the door and tore it partially from its hinges. She sat stunned as the vehicle raced away and disappeared around the corner. Her pulse thudded in her chest. If Marc hadn't intervened, the driver would have hit her.

"That appeared deliberate." His breath was harsh in her ear, and his hand, still on her arm, trembled a little.

Elin nodded. "And he didn't stop. I didn't see the license number, did you?" She should move away, but his presence helped still the tremors rippling along her skin.

He shook his head. "It all happened so fast." He finally dropped his hand away and scooted back under the steering wheel. "I didn't even see the driver, did you?"

"I caught a glimpse of a figure wearing a fedora. I couldn't tell if it was male or female. Or any details, really." Her hands trembled as she fastened her seat belt. "Marc, could it have been Mosely? What if Watson called him and told him we'd been informed of his unwanted attention to Laura?"

"Maybe." His lips flattened. "But it might have been Laura's killer too."

She shuddered. "It didn't seem his style. He seems much more inclined to terrorize me before he strikes."

"Maybe. Or he could just be done playing cat

and mouse. Maybe we're getting too close so he planned to finish it." He started the Tahoe and pulled out into traffic. "It could have been Mosely. That makes a lot of sense." He turned at the light.

"How far to the old girlfriend's house? What's her name?"

"Kimberly Bussey. She's on this side of Norfolk, about ten minutes away."

Elin twisted in her seat and looked behind them. No sign of the brown car. She wanted all this to be over. What if he'd killed her today? She had no provisions for Josie other than her sister taking custody. Marc would not want Abby to have his daughter. He would want to raise her himself. And really, he should. He was her father. Josie was growing to love him more and more every day.

Was she being selfish by refusing to consider his proposal? She wanted only the best for her daughter, and there wasn't a finer man around than Marc Everton.

He glanced at her, then flipped on the turn signal. "You're awfully quiet. You okay?"

What would he say if she told him she was actually considering his offer? She exhaled. "Fine. I–I was just thinking about what would have happened to Josie if that car had hit me."

He braked, then turned left. "I would take care of her. I don't want you worrying about that. You're thinking about marrying me?"

She wasn't quite ready to go that far. "Well, at least you should probably adopt her legally. Right now she's Tim's daughter by law."

"I'm willing to do that." He sounded eager. "What about Tim's parents? Will you have to tell them?"

"Yes, but I don't think they'll care. They haven't shown that much interest in her. I suspect Tim may have told them Josie wasn't his biological child."

He braked. "Here we are. Let's pray she's home and will talk."

❧ Twenty-Nine ❧

The search for the missing contraband hadn't turned up anything. Sara redid her ponytail and surveyed the landscape off the point at Seagrass Pier. She turned to Josh and shrugged. "I think this is a waste of time."

They'd been instructed to make one more pass looking for the other crate thrown overboard in the rescue two weeks ago. It seemed a lost cause. She didn't think there were more drugs to find.

"Yeah, I think so too," Josh said.

Since their discussion on Tuesday, he hadn't strung more than two sentences together to her. Two could play that game though, and Sara was trying to act as though he meant nothing to her.

Her attempt to be honest hadn't gotten her anywhere. Maybe because it was hopeless.

"I think I'll check over on the other side of the forest. There's an area behind the house we haven't searched. You guys go on back to Hope Beach, and I'll talk to you tomorrow. I promised Elin I'd hang around tonight at the house and make sure there were no problems with her mother."

"Fine." He turned to go.

She couldn't bear another minute of his distance. "Josh, your brother's death wasn't your fault. Besides, you were only twelve years old! What could you have done to stop it? Don't you think he would want you to be happy? He wouldn't want you punishing yourself for your whole life."

He stilled. "I don't know. You deserve someone better than me. I wouldn't want to disappoint you."

"What do you think your rejection is doing?" She took a step closer and touched his arm. "I know you love me. Why can't you just say it?"

"Once I say it, I–I . . ." He gulped and took a step back so her hand fell from his arm. "I'm an all-or-nothing guy."

"So give it your all," she said softly. "That's all any of us can do."

He shook his head. "I don't know. I love you too much to . . ." His eyes widened as he realized what he'd said.

The words were like a balm to her sore heart. Her smile burst out, and she threw her arms around his neck. "That's all I wanted to hear."

His arms came around her, then just as quickly released. He grabbed her wrists and tugged them down from his neck. "I'm sorry I said that, Sara. It solves nothing. I'd better go search. Talk to you later." He turned and ran in the opposite direction.

Her smile faded as she watched him rush down the sand dunes toward the other boat. This time it was one step closer and five steps back. But at least he'd *said* it. She had no idea how to get through his fear of failure, but she would figure it out. Now that she knew he loved her. Maybe Marc could throw some light on a guy's thinking with this problem. She'd ask him.

The last place for her to search lay through a thick maritime forest of gum trees and loblolly pine interspersed with grasses and holly bushes. A glimpse of southern twayblade drew her deeper into the cool woods. She decided to relax and enjoy the walk even if she found nothing. It was a beautiful July day, and the sound of birds twittering in the trees drained all her tension away. She inhaled the fragrant scent of forest. Maybe she could even forget about Josh's hurtful behavior for a few minutes.

She wound through the trees and stood at the edge of a small clearing. A movement on the other side caught her eye. The figure was half hidden in the shadows, but something about the other person struck her as furtive.

Sara moved as quietly as she could to the left to circle around to see what was going on. The glimpse of a red top kept her oriented as to where to head. Twenty feet away, she stopped behind a large oak tree and peered around.

Kalianne. What was Elin's new aide doing out here alone? Sara stepped a bit closer and saw her bending over a crate. One very much like the one tossed overboard in the drug boat rescue. Kalianne lugged it toward a small cave in a rock face. She shoved it into the space, then heaped leaves in front of it.

Why would she be hiding it? Sara watched her a moment longer, then stepped out from the shelter of the trees. "Looks like you found what we were looking for."

Kalianne whirled around and stepped in front of the opening. "What are you talking about? I was just out for a walk." Her walking shoes were worn and caked with mud.

Really? Did she think Sara hadn't seen what she'd just hidden? She pointed to the cave. "That crate. The Coast Guard is combing the area looking for it. It's probably drugs from a boat we rescued last week. We knew there was another one out here."

Kalianne shook her head. "It's just some stuff

Ruby asked me to hide for her. You know how old people can be."

"Let me just take a look, okay?" Sara walked toward her.

Kalianne stayed put in front of the crate. "I can't let you look at it. It would be a breach of Ruby's privacy."

"I know Ruby much better than you do, and I know she wouldn't mind." Sara tried to walk around the other woman, but Kalianne stepped to the left to block her again. "Kalianne, you will not stop me from looking at that crate. If you resist, I'll call for assistance. I'm not the only Coastie out here looking for this evidence. Now let me pass."

Kalianne's eyes were desperate, but she stepped aside. "Suit yourself."

Sara was bending toward the crate when something in the woman's deceptively mild tone warned her. She turned and started to stand, but she was too late. Kalianne brought up a large rock in her hand and smashed it into the side of Sara's head.

Bright flashes of color and light exploded in Sara's vision, and she crumpled to the ground, smelling the scent of mud and leaves as darkness claimed her.

Kimberly Bussey's house sat in the middle of a block of well-manicured lawns and stately, sweeping driveways. Marc parked in front of a porch with massive white pillars. "I don't know what I was expecting, but I hadn't thought she came from money."

Elin released her seat belt. "I guess it's because the Watsons are middle class so we assumed Ryan was as well." She opened her door and got out.

Marc did the same and joined her at the bottom of the wide stone steps to the front porch. "There's a Corvette in front of the garage. A new one. Wonder if it's hers."

"She might live here with her parents."

"I doubt it. She has to be forty by now or near there. You wouldn't think she'd be living with her parents at that age." He mounted the steps and pressed the doorbell. Elin stood close enough behind him he could feel her breath stir the back of his neck. He moved a fraction of an inch closer to the door. He refused to let his thoughts wander.

The door opened, and a woman in her late thirties or early forties peered at them. Her blond hair, cut in a stylish bob, looked freshly highlighted. She wore a short white skirt and a sleeveless pink top. Pretty in a way that looked like any enhancements had cost the earth. "Can I help you?"

"Are you Kimberly Bussey?"

She frowned. "I am. Who are you two?"

"I'm a special agent with the FBI and am investigating a murder aboard a ship a couple of months ago. Could we come in and speak with you?"

"I haven't been on a cruise in years. What's this all about?" She didn't wait for his answer but opened the door wider and stepped out of the way. "This way."

Her high-heeled sandals clicked on the polished wood floors as she led them to a large living room dominated by a massive stone fireplace. The white leather furniture was so pristine, he was half afraid to sit on it.

She gestured to two upholstered chairs flanking the fireplace. "Have a seat and tell me what you want." She went to the sofa and sat gingerly on the edge of the cushion.

Elin held out her hand. "I'm Elin Summerall."

Kimberly looked startled, but she shook her hand. "Pleased to meet you." Her expression sharpened. "Elin Summerall. The woman with the memories of a murder? I saw the article in the newspaper a few weeks ago. I thought you were a crackpot, but you seem to be sane."

The woman was outspoken, so maybe she would be just as candid about Ryan Mosely. Marc settled into the comfortable chair and waited until Elin sat down. "In our investigation, we ran across a complaint you made against an old boyfriend, Ryan Mosely."

Her gray eyes widened. "You think Ryan might have something to do with this murder?

Honestly, it wouldn't surprise me. He's a scary, scary guy."

Marc took out his iPad. "In what way? What was your relationship with him?"

"We went out a few times. He seemed to think it was more than that when I told him I didn't think we were compatible."

"How did you meet him?"

"I took my car in for repair. I was young and impressionable, and he was a handsome devil who had a way with words. That proverbial bad boy who is always irresistible to women." Her bark of laughter held no levity. "Luckily for me, I caught him peeping in my bedroom window and realized what a sleazeball he was. The problem was, he wouldn't leave me alone. I came home one night and found him in my kitchen." She gave a delicate shudder.

"What happened?"

"He tried to kiss me, but I wrenched away and grabbed a knife. I told him to leave. He knocked the knife from my hand, then smashed his fist into my face." She fingered her jaw. "Right here. I had a bruise for weeks. I'm lucky he didn't break it."

"He didn't . . . harm you?" Elin put in.

Kimberly wrinkled her nose. "Not in the way you mean. I screamed at him, then grabbed a pan and threw it at him. He finally left, and I called the police, who took a statement."

"Why did you drop the charges?"

She swallowed hard. "He told me if I didn't, my little sister would be next."

"You believed him?" Marc asked.

"Not at first. But a week later my sister came home bubbling about this really gorgeous guy named Ryan who walked her home from school. I had a sick feeling in the pit of my stomach. I knew it was him."

"And it was?"

She nodded, her face pale. "I parked by school the next day, and he was there waiting for her. He saw me and saluted with a smirk that turned my stomach. I drove straight to the police station and dropped the charges."

"Did he bother you or your sister again?" Elin asked.

"No. And you can be sure I went to another place for auto repair." She shivered and hugged herself.

"Have you ever run into him?"

"I saw him once in a department store. He grinned and started my way, but I boogied out of there before he could get to me. I hope never to hear his voice again. Why are you looking at him for this murder?"

Marc itched to get his hands on this Mosely. "He was stalking the young woman who died. She was the daughter of his partner. Even though she told him she didn't want to date him, he booked a cabin on a ship she worked on. Do you think he's capable of murder?"

"Absolutely. I think he's capable of anything. I hope you throw his butt in jail. I'd be happy to know I'd never run into him again."

Marc rose and closed the cover of his iPad. "We'll check him out. Thanks for your cooperation."

ঌ Thirty ঌ

They were stalled in traffic, and the stink of exhaust made Elin feel half sick. Her tummy rumbled, and she realized they hadn't eaten lunch. She glanced at her watch. Nearly five. They had a three-hour drive ahead of them, plus a ferry ride out to the island. The last ferry left at seven. "We aren't going to make the ferry. I had no idea it was so late."

Marc braked to miss a car cutting in front of him. "I didn't either. Sorry, I should have paid better attention. We can drive to Nags Head and charter a boat home, then come back tomorrow to get my Tahoe, or we can stay here and talk to Mosely. What do you want to do?"

She considered it. "Your parents are there with Josie. Do you think they'd mind if we don't come back tonight? And I could call Sara and have her make sure Mom is doing okay. Kalianne is off tomorrow. We can stay in a hotel."

"My parents are in their element. They won't mind at all." He frowned. "I have a spare room at my place if you don't mind staying there. And Sara left some things in the spare room. I think you're about the same size."

"We are." The thought of being alone with him made her pulse race. She wasn't sure how she could handle it, but she didn't want to spend the night in a hotel either. "Okay." Surely she could keep her distance. She'd be mortified if he figured out how she was beginning to feel about him. He'd made it clear he had no romantic interest in her.

She hadn't been at his place since *that night*. And she wasn't sure she was up to it tonight, but it was the logical choice. They were only friends, focused on the common goals of finding a killer and raising their daughter. That was all.

"Let's grab some food, then track down Mosely." He glanced at her. "Let's go to Los Fiesta."

"Okay." He'd gone after food from there that night, but she'd never been there.

She shut up and looked out the window. Traffic was finally moving again. A car followed very close on their bumper. She moved in her seat so she could see better. "What's that car behind us? It kind of looks like the car that hit us."

He looked into the rearview mirror and frowned. "It's a brown Chevy just like that one. Let's see what he does."

He looked to the right and left, then whipped the car into the right lane and made a quick exit off the interstate. The other car tried to follow them but missed the exit and rolled to a stop along the side of the highway. The car started to roll back-ward, but the vehicle approaching in the closest lane honked.

She clenched her fingers in her palms. "I think it was him!"

"Looks like it. Let's see if we can follow him." Marc gunned the Tahoe onto the freeway entrance. "There it is in the right lane."

"Don't get too close. We don't want him to see us."

Marc nodded. Two cars were between them and the brown car. "Write down the plate number."

She grabbed her phone and notated the number. The car ahead of them moved to the left lane, and Marc eased the vehicle a little closer to the brown car. The red pickup between them and the brown car rolled off the freeway at the next exit.

"I think I'd better hang back," Marc said.

But the driver must have realized he'd been spotted. Black smoke roiled from the tailpipe, and the brown car darted into the left lane.

Elin leaned forward. "Don't let him get away!"

Marc whipped the steering wheel to the left and

jammed the Tahoe in between a white Honda and a black SUV, but the brown car accelerated again and zoomed around the three cars in front of it, then darted into the right lane and exited the freeway.

Marc smacked the steering wheel. "I can't get over."

Elin watched the brown car race to the stop sign, then make a left. It disappeared over the hill. "We tried. We can call in the license-plate number."

Marc reached for his phone and nodded. Elin turned her head and looked out the window at the passing buildings. It looked like he was heading toward the restaurant now. Her pulse still raced from the chase, and she didn't feel like eating anymore.

He put his phone on the console. "The plate was reported stolen."

She groaned. "Great. So we have no idea who it was."

"Nope. Let's go eat and forget this for a while." He pulled into the parking lot of the restaurant.

Marc parked the Tahoe, and she quickly climbed out and stood looking at the bright-blue building with its garish orange lettering.

Marc came around the front of the vehicle and touched her arm. "Looks like it pays to be a bit on the early side for dinner. We might even get a table."

They walked inside, and some of Elin's discomfort faded at the rich scent of spicy tacos and fajitas. The orange walls and comfy booths made her smile. They placed their order for chipotle chicken tacos with an order of guacamole to share.

Elin glanced across the table at him. "Nice place."

"Yeah." He stared at her intently. "I don't bring people here much. I don't like to share it. I've only been here with Sara and my partner."

His words left her tongue-tied. Was it some kind of tacit admission that he felt something for her? "Will. Have you checked in with his wife lately?"

He nodded. "She requested Will's cell phone records for me. I've been looking through them for any unusual numbers. I asked her if he ever mentioned the mechanic shop or Ryan. She thought he took his vehicle in for work there a couple of days before he was killed."

"So we might be on the right track."

"Maybe."

The server brought their chips, dip, and guacamole. Marc thanked her and salted the chips. His gaze collided with hers in a way that made her cheeks warm. She searched for some hint of how he was feeling. His mouth was relaxed, and his hazel eyes stared straight into hers. She might have seen a flicker of heat in their depths, but she wasn't quite sure.

•••

Sara's head pulsed and throbbed with a pain that seemed to be centered above her left ear. She struggled to open her eyes, knowing the agony would intensify once she was fully awake. Her shoulders hurt, and something chafed at her wrists.

She moaned and realized a rag prevented her from speaking. She forced her lids open to a mere slit. Instead of brilliant sunlight, she found darkness had fallen while she was out. Her hands were tied behind her, which was why her shoulders felt out of joint. Leaves covered her legs, and the darkness above her was complete. She saw only a glimmer of light in front of her. She struggled to a sitting position but could not get any leverage to stand. Her head bumped something.

A cave, she was in a cave.

It all came back to her then. Kalianne and the crate. The rock in her hand and the crushing blow. Where was the woman? And why had she left her here?

Panic struggled to gain control, but she fought it back. *Breathe.* In and out, in and out. The tightness in her chest eased, and she rolled to her stomach, then wriggled toward the mouth of the cave where the small amount of light beckoned. Leaves crunched under her, and the strong, damp odor of detritus and mud filled her nose.

When she reached the exit of the cave, a pair of boots blocked the opening. Someone walked back and forth. She couldn't reach out, couldn't speak. Grunts and moans came from behind the gag, but she wasn't sure she was being heard. Her gaze traveled up the bare legs extending from shorts as the person strode past.

Kalianne.

What was the woman up to? She paced the front of the opening, waving her hands and muttering to herself. Sara struggled to hear past her own harsh breathing.

"Sends me out here and leaves me to figure out what to do by myself!" A kick at a shrub nearly sent Kalianne sprawling. "How dare he leave me to handle this by myself? He should have been here over an hour ago. I'm tempted to get in my boat and head out of the country. I don't know what I'm supposed to do about this." Another kick.

Kalianne whirled, and the moonlight struck her face. Her eyes widened. "You're awake." She offered up an uneasy smile. "Sorry I had to do that. Your head hurt?"

It hurt so badly Sara was afraid she was going to be sick. She swallowed down the bile in her throat and managed to nod.

Kalianne knelt beside her. "I'll remove the gag if you promise not to yell. The Coasties were all over this place looking for you. They're gone now, so yelling won't do you a bit of good. Promise?"

A wave of dizziness assaulted Sara when she nodded again. All she wanted was a sip of water.

Kalianne reached around and untied the cloth. "I've got a canteen of water. Here you go." She held the cold metal lip up to Sara's lips.

Sara sipped greedily, then coughed. The nausea passed more quickly with the brackish water calming her roughened throat. "Thanks." Her voice was a hoarse croak. "Can you untie me?"

Kalianne stepped back and shook her head. "Sorry, I can't go that far. My brother should be here any minute, and he'll figure out what to do with you."

"W-Who's your brother? Devi Long?"

Kalianne inhaled sharply. "How'd you know? Do you know Devi?"

"No, but I heard he was behind this drug shipment." Dread curled in her stomach. The man wasn't known for his mercy. He was likely to dump her overboard for the sharks. "He's going to kill me, Kalianne. You know that. Then where will you be? An accessory to murder. Do you want that on your conscience? Let me go. Please."

Kalianne stared down at her. "H-He wouldn't kill you."

Sara flexed her arms against her bonds. Were they just a trifle looser? "He's murdered other people."

"That's just what the news says. It's not true. Yeah, he's a drug smuggler. I wish he weren't, but it pays the bills." She must have seen Sara's wince because she shrugged. "You'd be surprised at how many people don't really care how he makes his money. He spends it freely on others, and he's quite popular with people whose names you would know."

Sara turned her head when a twig snapped. More rustling noises came from her right. Whoever headed this way walked with assurance as though he knew where he was going. The breeze lifted her hair, and the faint aroma of a cigar came to her.

Kalianne sniffed. "Here he comes now. He's never without his cigar." She looked down at Sara. "I'm really sorry you got messed up with this. You should have left it alone." She moved away in the darkness, and her thrashing through the under-brush grew fainter.

Sara heard her greet someone, then she made out the deeper tones of a male voice. Her pulse ratcheted up, and she strained harder at her bonds. There was no question they had to kill her. If they let her go, they knew she'd go straight to the authorities. She had to get away.

The rope at her wrists gave a bit, and she felt something wet run along the skin. A coppery scent wafted to her, but she didn't care if she was bleeding. He'd do a lot worse to her than rub the skin off in a small place. She worked the knots until finally her left hand slipped free. Bringing both arms around in front of her, she tore the remaining piece of rope from her right hand, then untied her ankles. She couldn't feel her feet, but she stumbled up anyway.

Her legs wouldn't hold her, and she fell to her knees just as a dark figure loomed in the moonlight.

❧ Thirty-One ☙

Marc rested his hand on Elin's shoulder as he escorted her back to his SUV. "I shouldn't have eaten so much." He patted his belly. This had been almost like a real date.

"You might have to roll me to the Tahoe." She moved so his hand fell away.

Had she done it deliberately? She'd been skittish all day, probably from his proposal. Yet he could have sworn she was thinking about it. The thought of living with her and Josie forever made him want to push harder, but he didn't want to scare her.

"Mosely doesn't live far from my place, only about five minutes." He started the engine and pulled into the street. She still hadn't spoken, so he glanced at her from the corner of his eye. "You're quiet."

"Just contented." She leaned her head against the seat. "It's been a crazy day, and I'm tired."

He wanted to ask what she was thinking, but she'd already let him know she didn't want to talk about his proposal. "There's his place." He pulled to the curb and turned off the car.

The house was a ranch, probably about twenty years old, with tan vinyl siding and a small porch. The weeds and grass were a good eight inches tall. The shingles showed some wear and would need to be replaced in the next year.

He glanced at her in the dim twilight. "Wait here. I'll just check and see if he's home. It kind of looks deserted. I bet the yard hasn't been mowed in three weeks."

She shoved open her door. "I'm coming too. I don't trust that guy. He might be waiting to ambush you."

Though he appreciated the way she sprang to his defense, he didn't need protection. He came around the front of the vehicle and caught her arm. "Let me go first in case he's the one who's after you."

He stepped in front of her and advanced to the front porch. Spiderwebs clung to the siding around the door. Another web sparkled in a corner between a porch railing and the ceiling. Several newspapers, their print blurry from rain, lay piled near the door.

A cat darted from under the swing and leaped

down toward them. Elin gave a startled scream, then leaped to his other side. "Keep that thing away from me."

He grinned and pushed the cat away with his foot. "Shoo, cat. I forgot you were so afraid of them."

She shuddered, her eyes fixed on the cat as it sprang into the overgrown bushes. "They're so sneaky."

"I think we should get Josie a kitty." It was all he could do not to grin.

"Over my dead body." She peered up at the darkened window. "I don't think anyone is here."

"Doesn't look like it." He mounted the steps, then pressed the doorbell.

It echoed eerily inside. There was no other sound, so he went to the picture window and cupped his hands around his eyes to look inside. The furnishings consisted of a sofa and love seat plus a couple of chairs. There was no movement in the shadowy interior.

"Let's look in the garage," Elin said.

He followed her down the steps and around to the attached garage. The grimy windows obscured much of the view, but he rubbed at the glass, then peered inside. "There's only a lawn mower and tools inside. No vehicle."

A male voice spoke behind them. "You looking for Mosely?"

He turned to see a white-haired man in shorts

holding a pit bull by a leash. The man's skinny legs ended in white socks and black shoes. "We are. You a neighbor?"

The man waved to his left. "I live next door. Haven't seen him in a while. I called the police a couple of days ago to have them check inside. I was afraid he'd fallen or something."

"There's no vehicle. You know what he drives?"

The man's eyes narrowed. "Seems a personal question. Who are you?"

"FBI. I have a few questions for him."

The man's frown eased. "He in trouble?"

Marc ignored the question. "He didn't mention any trips to you?"

"Nope. Which is why I called the cops. They checked in at the mechanic shop he owns. They hadn't seen him either, but according to the other owner, Mosely takes off like this on occasion. I don't know though. I've been living here five years, and this is the first time he's vanished."

It sounded like Watson knew more than he'd let on. They might need to pay him another visit.

"About that vehicle?" Marc prompted.

"He drives a brown Chevy to work."

Mosely *had* been driving the brown car. Watson had to have warned him he was being investigated. "Thanks for your help." Marc took Elin's arm and led her toward the Tahoe. He could feel the older man's gaze on them until they pulled away from the curb.

Elin twisted in her seat to stare at him. "So it was Mosely who tried to hit us?"

"Looks like it. Let's go back over there and talk to Watson." Marc glanced through the window. It was after eight and would be dark soon. "I think that guy is a powder keg waiting to go off. I'd rather not have you around when he does, so I think we'd better wait until morning."

"I'm not afraid of him." Her quivering voice betrayed her true feelings.

"We're almost home. We can stop by in the morning. Hopefully he won't have started smoking his pot by the time we get there."

"Okay."

He pulled into his driveway and shut off the engine. Marc's house was on a quiet cul-de-sac. Painted in a cool blue-gray, its white shutters and red door gave it a restful air he'd always loved. What would Elin think about his remodel inside? He hadn't been able to figure her out ever since he'd suggested marriage.

Marc flipped on the lights, and the soft glow of the lamps illuminated the interior of gleaming wood floors, white trim, and warm gray walls. He tried to dispel his grumpy mood and forced a smile when she joined him in the kitchen, which thankfully was clean. He'd put all the dishes in the stainless steel dishwasher before he left.

He gestured toward the island. "I redid the

kitchen two months ago. Granite counters, cherry cabinets. Cost the earth, but I like it."

"I do too." She was a little pale, and her voice seemed strained.

"I could use something to drink. How about you?" He moved past her to the fridge. "I've got Pepsi, iced tea, and bottled water. Or I could make coffee."

"Toomers?" Her tone picked up.

"Of course. My favorite Hope Beach blend."

"I'll have some of that."

He moved to the Cuisinart coffeepot. "It won't keep you awake?" He ground the coffee and made a full pot. The aroma began to fill the kitchen.

"It might, but it will be worth it. Besides, I'm not sleepy. We need to go over what we know so far."

The unspoken question hung between them, and he turned to pull down cups from the cupboard. She reached past him for a cup.

He resisted the urge to draw in her scent. Being alone here screamed danger. "Mosely's probably getting notices from the city about his grass. Looks like he's been gone awhile."

"Or too busy to cut his grass. Should we ask the police to help track him down?"

"Maybe. But they didn't seem concerned enough when the neighbor called them in. I'd guess Watson dispelled any worries when they questioned him about his partner." The coffee was done, so he poured two cups of it. "Heavy whipping cream?" He handed her the cup, and their fingers touched. The jolt of electricity made him pull his hand back hastily. When she nodded at his question, he went to the fridge and got out the carton of cream.

"Thanks."

She poured a liberal amount into her coffee. The tension between them was palpable, and he swallowed. Maybe this hadn't been such a good idea. His mind kept returning to that other night. He was honest enough to admit to himself he felt a powerful attraction to her. She seemed different now. So warm and caring. Or maybe he was just getting to know the real person.

She carried her coffee back to the living room, then curled up on his tan leather sofa. "What next?"

He dropped into his favorite chair and set down his coffee. "This is maybe a crazy thought, but let's verify that he owns a brown Chevy."

"Good idea."

He leaned over and grabbed his laptop from the tabletop. He navigated to the DMV site and entered his authorization code. "Hmm, he owns a pickup truck. A 2013 Ford. And a '95 brown Chevy Lumina. Bingo."

He closed the lid of his laptop and put it back on the table. An awkward silence filled the room. He grabbed his coffee and swallowed down the tepid drink, then set down his cup. "Well, I might as well show you to your room. We can watch a movie or something, if you like. It's only nine fifteen. Unless you'd like some alone time. There are girl books Sara has left."

She smiled. "Girl books?"

"Romance." He grinned back at her, relieved the tension seemed to be easing.

"And guys aren't into romance?"

"Well, not that kind of starry-eyed stuff. It pays to be practical when you think about who you're spending your life with." He leaned forward. "Like us raising Josie together. It makes sense. We're friends and we get along. There shouldn't be any real surprises. We like a lot of the same things, and we know each other pretty well."

"You're pushing again." Her voice was quiet.

"I'm just passing the pressure along that I'm going to get when we get back to Seagrass Pier." He sent a cajoling smile her way. "My parents will want to know what I'm going to do about providing for their granddaughter. That reminds me. I have a check for you." He dug into his wallet and pulled out a check for two thousand dollars. "Here you go."

She didn't smile back, and she didn't take the check from him. "I don't need any help in providing for her. As long as I'm alive. That's not why I told you about her, Marc."

What was her beef? Why couldn't she see past

their troubled history to the logical answer? "I know that, but she *is* my daughter. Don't you feel even a little guilty you deprived me of her for five years? I had a right to know."

The edge of anger in his voice shocked him. He'd thought he'd moved beyond recriminations. Getting angry about it wouldn't change the past. "Sorry."

"And I'm sorry for what happened too." Her voice was nearly inaudible. "Don't you think I've agonized over it all this time? If I could change it, I would."

Getting up, he gestured to the hall. "Let me show you your room."

❧ Thirty-Two ❧

The house felt close and airless, but Elin knew it was just her mental state. The realization she had feelings for Marc threw her. She wasn't ready for something like that, not after Tim. What if Marc changed like Tim had? Tim had been loving and supportive too, in the beginning.

Marc gestured to the first bedroom on the right of the hall. "This is where Sara stays when she visits. There's an attached bathroom, and it's already stocked with bubble bath, toothpaste, and everything else she uses."

The large room felt even bigger with the

cathedral ceiling and the pale lavender paint. Crisp white linens covered an enormous four-poster bed. Brightly colored pillows added a punch of color. The white carpet was spotless.

She stepped into the room. "Nice. I think I even catch a scent of her perfume." She stepped to the dressing table and picked up a spray bottle of violet water. "That reminds me, she was supposed to call tonight after she checked on Mom and Josie."

A sense of unease gripped her. Sara was the most responsible person she knew, and she'd promised to stop by after work. "I hope everything is okay."

"Maybe her phone died, and she had to wait to get back home to call. She might still be there. My parents love her, and they'd make it hard for her to leave."

"Maybe. I think I'll call." She dug her phone out of her bag and called her friend. The call rang four times, then went to voice mail. "No answer. Maybe you're right. Her phone won't work on the point unless she's in the house."

"I'm sure it's nothing to worry about. Want me to call Mom at the house?"

"I hate to bother her. She'll think I'm neurotic." She managed a smile. "And maybe I am. I'm not used to being away from Josie so much, but I know we have to find the killer before he comes back."

A horrible thought assailed her. Maybe he'd already come back—and murdered everyone in the house. "Actually, yes. I do want you to call and make sure everything is okay. She logs on to the Wi-Fi, right?"

He nodded and dug his phone out from his pocket. After a few punches on the phone, he put it to his ear. "Hey, Mom. Just checking in. Everything okay?" He listened a moment, then gave Elin a thumbs-up. "No sign of anyone hanging around the place, right? Okay, great. Listen, have you seen Sara? Hello? Are you there? I seem to have lost you."

He pulled the phone back from his ear and looked at it. "I have full bars."

"Wi-Fi service comes and goes out there, especially in a storm." She pointed to the window where flashes of lightning lit up the western sky. "It might have taken out the power, even temporarily, and the Wi-Fi would have gone down."

He put away his phone. "Maybe she'll call back when she gets a signal again. But she said all was well. She and Dad are playing Candy Land with Josie. I could hear her giggling in the background."

"That's great. What about Mom? Did Christine mention how she'd been today?"

He shook his head. "I didn't get a chance to ask her." He stepped past her and pulled open the top drawer. "Sara left nightgowns and some other clothing in here. There's a dress or two in the closet too. If you can think of anything you need, just let me know. I'll let you get settled. I think I'll shower, then go watch a movie. Feel free to join me or stay here. Your call."

He closed the door behind him, and she stared at it. Her presence here seemed to cause him no discomfort, but it had given her a taste of the torture she would experience if they were married in name only. How could she even think about it? And yet she *was* thinking about it. A lot.

She went to the bathroom and turned on the shower, then disrobed and stepped into the steaming spray. He was right—it made a lot of sense for Josie's sake. Elin had mourned the thought of her daughter being raised by a single mother. A child needed a father around too, and seeing him only on the weekends wasn't the same thing at all. Plus, Marc's parents would be doting grand-parents. Mom tried, but she was retreating further and further into the mists of time.

She sudsed her hair, then rinsed it. Marc would be a dutiful husband. He'd be home on time and would let her know where he was. He'd take Josie to the park and out to dinner on a father-daughter "date." At every school function, he'd be there with her cheering on their daughter. If she played volleyball or ran in track, he'd be out there coaching her. When the boys started calling, he'd vet every male who walked through the door.

Maybe that would be enough. It was more than Tim had done.

What would happen once Josie went off to college? It would be just the two of them then. Divorce? She didn't believe in divorce, and neither did he. They were both believers, and they would take marriage vows seriously. The long, lonely years of an empty bed stretched ahead of her. What kind of life would that be? And did God expect her to bury all the longings of her heart for Josie's happiness?

She wasn't the first mother to wrestle with these questions. Maybe Marc had the answers she didn't. She turned off the tap and wrapped a fluffy white towel around her, then padded into the bedroom where she found blue cotton pajamas. There would be no seduction in these baggy things.

Not that she intended there to be. She'd wrestled with enough guilt over the first time, and she wasn't about to repeat it. She dried her hair, then left it down on her shoulders and went to find Marc.

Standing in the moonlight, the man in front of Sara was as sleek and muscular as a sea otter with hair just as black and shiny. He wore close-fitting designer jeans and a green polo. With a pencil-thin cigar clenched between his teeth, he stared at her without speaking. He appeared to be in his late forties and was at least part Asian. Women would find his magnetism attractive.

Sara swallowed and rubbed her tingling legs. She wobbled to her feet and stood to face him. There was no emotion in his eyes. He could kill her as easily as he'd stomp on a bug.

Kalianne plucked at his shirtsleeve. "She didn't really see anything. I say we just take her out to one of the outer islands and leave her. A passing ship will find her in a few days, and we'll be long gone."

Sara cast a furtive glance into the shadows. This man would have no mercy. She needed to get away from him and find help.

He never looked away from Sara. "Don't be ridiculous, Kalianne. She's seen you and me. She can identify both of us. I'll handle this. You go on back to town."

His dark eyes were mesmerizing, and it took great effort for Sara to pull away her gaze and send an imploring glance at Kalianne. "Don't let him pull you into murder, Kalianne. I don't think you want my death on your conscience."

He took a step closer. "Shut up."

Something glittered as his hand came up. A gun. Sara stared down the deadly bore. If she could just leap into the shadows and escape him. Seagrass Cottage was not that far. But if she headed to the house, she'd be putting everyone there in danger. What should she do?

Kalianne stepped between her brother and Sara. "I don't like it, Devi. Smuggling drugs is one thing, but I won't be a party to murder. Sara has been good to me."

"Get out of the way, you idiot," he snarled.

Sara took advantage of Kalianne's distraction to dive for the cave. There might not be a way out in there, but at least it was dark, and he'd be at a disadvantage too. His gun barked, and a bullet spit rock shards inches from her face. She felt along the cave face for the small opening she'd noticed earlier. It might only be an indentation, but it might also be a way out of here.

There it was! She moved farther into the darkness, feeling her way. The tunnel widened until she was able to stand up. She stood and turned the other direction, listening to him swear and order Kalianne to find a flashlight. Sara heard a slap and winced. He was taking out his rage on Kalianne, but she couldn't worry about that. She had to get out of here.

She moved deeper into the cave, keeping her fingertips in contact with the rock surface to orient herself. What if she ended up lost in here? She had a tiny flashlight attached to her keys, but she didn't dare use it. Not when she could still hear the two arguing outside.

Pressure seemed to build in her ears, but she wasn't sure if it was because she was descending or if it was panic building from the claustrophobic darkness. She paused and concentrated on her breathing. In and out, in and out. The pressure around her eased, and she listened to Devi and Kalianne again. Their voices were fainter now, barely distinguishable. Were they moving away? She strained to make out what they were saying.

"I'll stay here and guard the entrance. Go back to my boat and get a flashlight." His voice was faint.

Sara stared behind her. There was not even a glimmer of moonlight. Maybe he wouldn't be able to see her flashlight if she flipped it on. For good measure, she shuffled another ten steps into the cave, then turned and looked and listened. Nothing. Her hand dove for the keys in her pocket, and she pulled them out, fumbling for the tiny flashlight. Her trembling hand found the switch, and she turned it on.

Nothing.

Panic closed her throat. She would be stuck in here forever waiting for him to come find her and shoot her. She fought down the fear and felt along the length of her tiny light. The end seemed a little loose. She tightened it, and a small beam of light rewarded her. Even though the illumination was minute, it comforted her. She listened to deter-mine if Devi had seen it, but no sound was behind her. Shining the light ahead of her, she moved deeper into the cave.

It branched in two different directions, and she

stared at her options. Which way should she go? Instinct told her the one on the right might lead back to the main cave, and she started to the left, then heard running water. She stopped and shone her light into the distance. A trickle of water ran from the ceiling. Would it take her to the ocean? She might get into a dangerous spot that way too.

Which way, Lord? Something still nudged her to the left, so she listened and walked toward the sound of the dripping water. It was cooler and danker here. She almost turned back then, but an imperceptible nudge moved her forward.

She walked on until she came to a passage that turned back to the right again. It was beginning to feel like a labyrinth. She would need to remember which way she went at every branch of the passage. She went right, though it felt less out of true knowledge than panic.

She wanted to put as much distance between her and her pursuers as possible. But she was beginning to feel there might not be an end to this cave.

❧ Thirty-Three ❧

Marc turned at a soft footfall and saw Elin with her damp hair on her shoulders. The soft blue pajamas intensified the color of her eyes. She had no idea how beautiful she looked in those shapeless pajamas with her feet bare.

He averted his eyes and gestured to the chair. "Have a seat." Best to have her as far away as possible. He fast-forwarded the movie through the beginning credits and paused it. "Want to play Trivia instead?"

She groaned. "You're still playing that? Sara and I always thought you had the cards memorized. I'm no challenge for you." She padded across the gleaming wood floor and settled beside him. "But before you get it out, could we talk?"

He put down the remote. "Sure." Her serious tone made him wonder what she was thinking.

She pulled her knees to her chest. "It's about this whole marriage thing."

"Okay." Was she going to say no? Her eyes seemed to indicate her answer wasn't going to be the one he wanted.

"Have you really thought about what this would mean? Neither of us believes in divorce. What kind of life are we going to have if we get married only for Josie's sake? In fifteen years she'll be off to college, and it will be just the two of us. Then what?"

He stumbled over the question. "I hadn't thought about that."

"Do you want a loveless life?"

Her soft question made him blink. Loveless? "Was that what you had with Tim?" When she winced, he knew he'd struck a nerve. "Tell me."

She swallowed hard. "Tim was so different before he was injured. Kind, strong, a take-charge kind of guy."

"I figured that never changed. The injury changed him?"

She shook her head. "My sin changed him." She focused on her hands. "He *said* it wouldn't matter, that he could love the child because she was mine. And he tried, but I broke his trust. He grew suspicious, hostile if I came home late from work. By the time he died, he was a bitter, angry man. At least he tried to love Josie. He gave up on me."

"It wasn't your fault, Elin. He chose to let the bitterness grow. You asked for his forgiveness, right?"

She gave the barest nod of her head. "More than once."

"Yet he never let go of it. That was a sin he chose."

"Maybe." She raised anguished eyes to his. "You might change too, Marc. I a-admire you now. I have no doubts you want to take care of Josie and me, that you want to do what's right. But you might grow bitter at being denied a real marriage."

He examined his heart, then shook his head. "I'm not that kind of man. I don't hold on to slights. I deal with them and move on."

She stared at him, then nodded. "I can see that

about you. But what about Josie? Is it fair to make her grow up without any siblings? I'd always thought I'd have more children, a houseful, really."

"So you're saying you want to remarry and have kids with someone else?" The thought of that left him feeling like he'd just been hit by a tank. The thought of her with another man made him curl his fingers into his palms.

She shook her head. "Maybe you want to marry someone and have kids with her. Josie would have siblings that way. We need to think this through carefully."

He frowned. "I thought about it before I asked you, Elin. I want to do what's best for Josie. I know you do too. A-And I think it's best for us too. I'll be a good husband to you."

She wet her lips and looked down. Something was going on in her head that he couldn't figure out.

She finally lifted her head and looked him in the eye. "What's best for Josie is to grow up in a happy home. For her to feel loved and treasured. For her to know her home won't be torn apart by divorce or bickering."

"I don't intend to bicker with you. Or to ever divorce. I put high regard on my word, and I won't break it." Did she think he would enter into marriage lightly? He thought she knew him better than that.

She nodded. "I feel the same, but have you thought about the day-to-day business of being married?"

"You think I'll make it hard on you? I won't. We can have separate suites, and you can do what you like. I won't make any demands on you. I'll even do my share of the cooking and cleaning." He grinned to try to defuse the tension.

She wet her lips again. "We can't just ignore the chemistry between us. Can you deny it still exists? I feel it every time you look at me."

He'd thought he was doing a better job of hiding his attraction. "What difference does it make? I won't act on it."

"Why not?" she asked, her voice soft. "Because you don't trust me? Trust is pretty important in a marriage."

He exhaled and leaned back, unsure where she was going with this. Did he trust her? Maybe not.

"What are you thinking? Your silence is making me nervous," she said. "Talk to me."

"Thought that's what I was doing. I'm thinking about trust and what it means. You didn't tell me about Josie, and that was wrong. Part of me understands why you did it, but maybe I'm afraid you won't be honest with me."

She winced, and her eyes grew luminous. "You don't understand the pressure I was under."

"He's been dead for two years."

"I didn't want to open a can of worms. And I

wanted to forget that night. I assumed you did too. It was so out of character for us."

"We have to quit beating ourselves up over it."

She nodded. "I haven't forgiven myself even now. And I'm sure Tim never did." Her voice lowered to a whisper and wobbled on the last two words.

"God has and that's all that matters." Against his will, he saw where her decision had come from.

She inhaled. "What do you want from a marriage, Marc? Can you tell me honestly?"

He stared into her face, seeing the vulnerability she laid bare. How did he feel? He hadn't let himself look too deeply for fear of what he'd see. He wasn't aware he'd reached for her until his fingertips traced the curve of her cheek and sank into her thick, damp hair. He stared into her eyes and felt something rising in his chest, a powerful emotion he'd never thought to experience.

Her eyes fluttered shut as she drifted toward him. His gaze went to her lips, so soft and kissable. He leaned closer, nearly dying for the taste of her, the feel of her in his arms. He brushed his lips across hers. The sweet scent of her breath made him pull her closer and sink in for a deeper kiss. He'd forgotten how wonderful it felt to hold her.

His cell phone rang, and he blinked. He didn't want to open his eyes, didn't want to let the world intrude on this moment.

"Marc?" she muttered against his lips. "Your phone. It might be important."

He opened his eyes and smiled down into her face. "Slave driver." He reached for his phone. The screen read *Josh Holman*. Why would he be calling? He thumbed it on. "Marc here."

"Have you heard from Sara?" Josh's voice was worried. "She never came back from Seagrass Pier. I called the house, and they haven't seen her. I'm there now, and her boat is still here, but there's no sign of her."

"We haven't heard from her." Marc glanced at the clock above the fireplace. It was ten. She should have been back hours ago. "On our way."

The moon illuminated her brother as he knelt over his bag. Kalianne didn't like his quick, furtive movements or the way he flexed his jaw and muttered under his breath. She inhaled when she caught sight of the long cylinder in his hand. "What are you doing?"

He glanced up. "Thanks to your ineptitude, I must ensure the Coastie never talks."

He puffed on his cigar, then held the tip to the stick of dynamite in his hand. The fuse began to sputter, and he tossed it into the cave, then turned and walked away.

Her chest burning with the desire to stop this, Kalianne followed him, and they stopped a safe distance away. The *whump* that came a few

306

seconds later made her cry out and clap her hands over her ears. A cascade of rocks and debris rained into the space that had once been the opening. She sank to her knees and moaned.

She'd participated in a murder. Her stomach revolted and she fought nausea.

Her brother jerked on her arm. "You are weak, Kalianne. We did what had to be done."

She didn't resist as he dragged her to her feet. "You mean, *you* did what you wanted." Tears coated her lashes and blurred her vision. She was just as guilty as he was.

"Now you must get back into the house and find the pouch. It is most unfortunate you let the old woman take it away from you. We were so close."

"At least we know it's there. Are you *sure* it's the map?"

"I'm positive. Chann Seng never gave up its hiding place, and that golden city still exists somewhere in the jungles of Cambodia. I mean to find it. We will be kings and queens, Kalianne. There are riches there beyond imagination."

"Why do you care so much? You don't need the money."

His teeth gleamed in the moonlight. "Power, Kalianne. The money I have now is but a drop in the bucket to what I will have. Plus, I can shed the persona of a smuggler and take my rightful place as an explorer. The world will open at my feet. No one would dare seek to arrest me."

He propelled her away from the murder site. She tried not to think about poor Sara, crushed and buried under tons of rock. Really, it was the woman's own fault. She shouldn't have interfered. To distract herself, Kalianne imagined finding that ancient Khmer Empire city. Gold, precious jewels, vast statues worth millions. Such wealth was beyond her imagination, though Devi had expounded on it at great length for years. He'd sought that pouch for over ten years, and when he'd found Chann's diary in a shack in Cambodia, he'd known it would soon be in his hands.

He'd sent her in here with the promise of all the money she could imagine. If only she could find that pouch with the map. That stupid old lady.

They exited the forest, and she looked toward the house. Lights shone from several of the windows. "I'll find it if I have to shake the truth out of her."

"There will be a great search for the woman tomorrow. Go tonight. Find it now while there is still time."

"People are in the house. An attorney and his wife. Also the old woman and the little girl."

"Drug them." He reached into his bag and handed over a vial of pale liquid. "One drop of this in their drinks, and not even a hurricane will wake them."

"Okay." Her fingers closed around the vial. She

wasn't about to drug the little girl. The old lady, yeah. And the other couple. But not the kid.

"Don't leave until you have the map. I want it found tonight." He took the path toward the pier.

She took a deep breath, squared her shoulders, then walked briskly to the back of the house. The Evertons sat at the table on the deck.

Mr. Everton waved when she got nearer. "I thought you were gone for the day. What brings you back?"

"I forgot to give Ruby some medicine."

Mrs. Everton lifted a brow. "You could have called. We would have done it."

"I tried, but the phone was out. It's probably not a big deal since it doesn't seem to be helping her memory, but I want to do everything I can for her. Is Ruby in the living room?"

Mrs. Everton nodded. "She's reading Josie a story."

"I brought some new tea I found and thought I'd make some before I go. You want some too?"

"That would be lovely. You're a sweet girl, Kalianne. I'm so glad you're taking such good care of Ruby."

Kalianne smiled and thanked her. Inside the kitchen, she shut the door behind her and exhaled. This was working out better than she'd hoped. When she peeked into the living room, she saw Ruby holding Josie. The little girl was already asleep.

"Here, Ruby, let me take her to bed. She's out."

Ruby's eyes were vague, but she didn't protest when Kalianne lifted Josie out of her lap and carried her toward the stairs. "This kid is heavy."

It was all she could do to carry Josie up the stairs and deposit her in bed. She pulled the covers over her, then went back to the living room. "Ruby, do you remember where you put my leather pouch? You know, the tan one? It's old and about this big." She measured the width with her hands. "I want you to help me look for it."

"Okay." Ruby started to get up.

"Not now. I'm going to fix some tea, but I'll be back. Maybe you can show me where the pouch is, okay?" She waited a moment, but Ruby didn't respond.

Kalianne pressed her lips together and went to make the tea. Checking to make sure the Evertons weren't looking through the window, she put a drop of the pale liquid into each cup. When the water was hot, she brewed the tea, then carried out a tray of cups and the teapot.

"Here we go." She placed it on the table, then poured the tea, taking care they got the right cups.

In fifteen minutes, they yawned and excused themselves for bed. Now to find the map.

◈ Thirty-Four ◈

Elin glanced at the house as they hovered in for a landing on the front of the beach by the pier. The windows were dark, so everyone was asleep. It was nearly midnight. The moon, bright and golden above them, lit the scene as well as a streetlight.

Marc took her arm, and they bent over and ran under the rotating blades to meet Josh and Curtis on the beach.

"Any sign of her?" Marc asked when they reached the two men.

Josh shook his head. "Just her boat." He pointed out the dinghy bobbing at the pier. "We were searching for another crate that had been tossed overboard from that drug-boat rescue a couple of weeks ago. We'd searched most of the area, but she was going to look over there." He pointed to the area behind the house that backed up to the maritime forest. "Then she planned to hang out at the house."

"How did you know there was a problem?" Elin wanted to grab a flashlight and go looking now herself.

"I tried to call her a bunch of times, thinking she was at her house." His voice was pinched. "When I kept getting voice mail, I found Mr. Everton's cell number and called him. He said they hadn't seen Sara. I had him come down to see if her boat was still here. When he called back and said it was, I knew something was wrong. I shouldn't have left her to search alone."

"Has anyone gone into the forest to look for her?" Marc asked.

Curtis nodded. "Your dad went back there with a flashlight, but he didn't see any sign of her." He gestured toward the pile of equipment on the sand. "So we gathered lights and com units, then took the chopper to Kill Devil Hills to get you so we could do an organized search by grids."

"Let's go."

From Marc's clipped tone, Elin knew he was worried about his cousin. She was too. This wasn't like Sara. She could have fallen down a hole or something. Or she'd run into the drug smugglers, and they'd shot her.

She shuddered and turned toward the path to the forest. "Let's get going. We have to find her." She grabbed a bright halogen light and headed away from the ocean. The others seized equipment and followed her.

Marc jogged to catch up with her. "I tried to call her too, and it dumped me right into voice mail."

"If she's here, there is no cell service. It's going to be hard looking in the forest at night, even with lights."

"I know."

Elin reached the tree line and flipped on the light. She cupped her other hand to her mouth. "Sara!" She paused and listened. Nothing but the rustle of the wind in the trees.

Josh moved off to her left. "I'm going this way. Curtis, you fan out to the east."

The halogen lights put out more light than Elin had imagined. With four lights glaring into the darkness, it was almost as bright as dusk.

Marc shone his light along the path. "I want to see if she's dropped anything, or if there's a sign of other people tracking through here. You ever been back here?"

"No. We always go to the beach."

The smell of the forest, fecund and earthy, added to her sense of unease. She stopped and called often for Sara, but there was no response.

Shining his light on the ground, Marc strode a couple of feet ahead of her. She kept her light glaring higher, at face level, hoping to catch a glimpse of Sara running to meet them.

They reached a small clearing and walked through it to an area where rocks protruded from the earth. Stopping, Elin called again. The search felt hopeless.

"Whoa, what's this?" Marc stooped and picked up something. "Is this Sara's cell phone?" He held up a white iPhone.

She stepped closer to see. "Looks like it. Turn it on."

"You found her cell phone?" Josh spoke from behind them.

"I think it's hers." Marc turned it on, then went to recent calls. "Yep, there's a call from me last night. And a couple from you, Josh. She has to have been here." His beam scanned the area slowly, lingering on every bit of ground.

"Is that rope?" Josh stepped close to the rock face and knelt, then turned with a hank of rope in his hands. "Looks like it was tied. Could she have been restrained with this?" His voice held an edge of fear.

Elin swallowed and touched the rope. "Maybe." She didn't want to believe some criminal might be doing harm to her best friend. Turning away, she shone her light around the area. "Looks like something was dragged here."

Marc stooped. "I see it. That crate maybe."

She swept her light up the rock face. A tiny sliver of an opening peeked out at the top of a pile of rocks. "Do you think this is a recent cave-in?" She prodded the rock pile with her foot and small pebbles rolled off. "Look up there. Could this have been a cave?"

Josh began to climb the rocks, but he kept sliding back down. "I think it's recent. Call Curtis, and let's try to remove the rocks."

"You don't think she's in there, do you?" The thought of finding Sara's crushed and broken body under this pile made her shake.

Marc grunted. "I hope not, but there's evidence she's been here. I think we have to consider that she might be inside."

Her hands shook as she tried to raise Curtis on the walkie-talkie. When he answered, she spoke quickly. "Curtis, it's Elin. We need you right away. We have clues to Sara." She told him where they were.

"On my way," he said.

Marc paused to wipe the dust and sweat from his face. The same dust coated his throat and mouth. They'd made little headway on the cave-in. Had it been done deliberately? He didn't want to find Sara's body on the other side.

The moon had gone behind some clouds, but their lights lit up the place and illuminated the graffiti on the rocks.

Josh worked tirelessly at the pile, not pausing or even showing any signs of weariness. Marc took his arm. "Have some water, Josh."

"Sara has none." He didn't look up and renewed his efforts.

"I think we need to regroup and think about this. It might take days to get through this by hand. Maybe we should call for some equipment."

Josh finally paused and wiped the back of his hand across his forehead. He looked from Marc to the rock pile. "Maybe. This thing seems to go on forever. We have to find her. She has to be all right." His shoulders slumped as he joined the rest of them by the backpack of water and snacks.

"We'll find her. I'm sure she's fine." Marc wished he felt as confident as he sounded.

Elin came from the other side of the pile. Her face and hands were black with dirt. "I'll take some water." Her voice was hoarse.

He handed her a bottle of water, and their hands touched. If only she didn't have to be working out here so hard. She appeared so fragile in the glare of the halogen lights. He wanted to protect her from what they might find in that cave. With every minute that passed, he grew more concerned.

Josh accepted the bottle of water Curtis offered. "Let's mobilize some assistance."

"I'll call it in." Curtis walked a few feet away, out from under the tree cover. His low voice echoed back to them.

Josh glanced around. "I used to come out here when I was a kid with my dad. He liked hunting deer. Something keeps bugging me. I have this memory of playing in a cave, but it wasn't here." He gestured to the north. "It was that way, I think. I wish he were still alive so I could ask him about it."

Marc capped his water. "Think, Josh. It might be a branch off this one. If you can find it, we might be able to use the lights and wind through the passages to find her." He couldn't help the leap of hope he felt, even though it was a long shot.

Josh rubbed his head. "I'm thinking. It was a long time ago, and it's hard to remember."

Curtis jogged back to join them. "Ben is sending out some equipment, but it will be daylight before they get here. I say we keep working in the meantime. We might get through."

"Yeah, I agree." Marc set down the bottle of water and started for the rock pile.

"Wait a second." Josh turned and looked to the north. "I seem to remember it being by a waterfall. Anyone know of a waterfall around here?"

Elin frowned. "I haven't explored this area, but Sara said something about a waterfall. She said it was at the head of Larson Creek."

"I know where that is!" Josh ran off to the north, his light bobbing ahead of him.

"Wait for me!" Marc grabbed his light. "You two want to come or stay here and keep working on moving the rocks?"

Elin grabbed a light and stepped toward him. "I'm going with you."

"Let's split up and maximize our chances," Curtis said. "I'll keep working here. Ben was going to see about sending out some manual labor in the meantime too, and I'll need to guide them here."

Marc took Elin's hand. "Stay close. Curtis, call us if you break through."

"Will do." He bent over the rocks again.

Marc kept hold of Elin's hand as they chased the bobbing, weaving light ahead of them. "Josh seems to know where he's going."

"I just pray it's a passageway that will lead us to Sara." She sounded out of breath.

The chances of that were slim. Marc was beginning to lose hope altogether. They crossed a stream and climbed up a hillside covered with clover that filled his nose with its scent when they stepped on it. Josh's light had stopped at the top of it, and they found him bending over a small opening.

Marc stooped and stared. "That's it? It hardly looks big enough to crawl though."

Josh kicked a clump of dirt out of the way. "It's bigger inside than it looks out here. Of course, I was a kid then, so even this opening seemed bigger than what I'm seeing now."

"I think I can fit through if you men can't," Elin said.

Josh laid on his belly and shoved the light through, then poked his head in. "The room is still there. Looks to be about five feet high, and it branches off to the south. I'm going in." His voice was muffled.

"I'll be right behind you."

Josh's head emerged, and he looked up at Marc. "I don't know what we'll find in there. It may be very unsafe. No sense in both of us getting killed. Let me go, and you stay here and guard this entrance. Whoever caved in the other opening might try to do the same here."

The man made sense. Marc nodded. "If you haven't found anything in an hour, come back. We need to get those rocks moved if this doesn't lead to her."

"I'm not coming back without her. This is the answer. I just know it." Josh wriggled through the opening and was gone.

Marc glanced down and saw tears in Elin's eyes. "You okay?"

She nodded. "We have to find her."

The leather pouch was important. Ruby clutched it to her chest and huddled in the corner of the attic. The darkness outside frightened her, but she had to do this. Elin had told her the story of Georgina's pouch. It must never be found. She must guard it with her life.

For a moment, she saw a girl with long brown hair standing on the parapet with this pouch in her hands. Where would Georgina want her to hide this? Ruby didn't like her new aide anymore. She'd been so insistent on having this treasure, but it was not for her. Not ever.

Ruby's gaze fell on a space under the stairs to the roof. Would there be a hiding place under there? She rose and examined the wall encased in oak paneling. There was a screwdriver around here somewhere. She put down the leather pouch, then found it in an old toolbox. She used the tool to pry a corner of the paneling loose to reveal the cavity under the stairs, then she opened the pouch and withdrew the old map inside.

It didn't look that important. Hand drawn, it looked old and faded. She stuffed the map behind the paneling, then tapped the nail back into place. No one would ever find it unless she told them where it was.

This secret would go to the grave with her. Owen would be so proud of her. Smiling, she carried the pouch to the chest and put it in the hidden compartment in the bottom.

❧ Thirty-Five ❧

Kalianne checked on the guests, but they didn't stir when she spoke their names loudly. Mr. Everton's breathing was loud and labored, so she hoped she hadn't harmed him. She didn't want another murder on her conscience.

Maybe she should search this room while they slept so soundly. She hurried to the living room and took Ruby by the hand. "Let's go find my pouch now, okay? It wasn't very nice of you to hide it. It's mine, Ruby."

Ruby blinked, and tears filled her eyes. "I didn't take anything, Kalianne. I'm sleepy. I want to go to bed now."

"You can't go to bed until we find my pouch." She jerked on Ruby's arm and led her up the stairs. "Let's look here first."

Ruby dug in her heels. "That's Christine's room. I'm not supposed to go in there."

"They're sleeping and won't notice." Kalianne opened the door and dragged Ruby inside the bedroom.

The old woman huddled in the corner and wouldn't budge. She was going to be more trouble than she was worth. Gritting her teeth, Kalianne went to the closet and flipped on the light, then went through every bit of the closet. Nothing. She pressed and tugged on anything that might be a hidden panel, but she didn't find the pouch. She checked every inch of the room and attached bathroom.

When she came out of the bathroom, she saw Ruby sitting in the corner with her eyes closed. Kalianne shook her, then pulled her up. "Let's go to the attic, Ruby. Maybe you'll remember where you hid it."

She'd been certain the old woman had put it up there initially, but after searching when she could, she'd thought maybe Ruby had moved it. But it was likely still up there. She flipped off the light, then urged the old woman up the steep stairway to the third floor. Even with the light on, there were too many shadows to be able to perform a good search. This was never going to work.

And she was tired, emotionally exhausted from what had happened in the forest. Maybe she should just go home tonight.

"I remember where it is."

Kalianne whirled and saw her heading to a chest against the wall. Joining the old woman, she watched as Ruby lifted everything out of the chest, then opened a hidden compartment in the bottom.

"The pouch!" She snatched it from Ruby's hands and clutched it to her chest. Finally.

"What are you doing?" said a tiny voice to her right.

She turned to see Josie standing near the top stair. Dressed in white pjs, she held her pink bunny in one arm. "What are you doing out of bed, honey?"

"I heard Grandma crying. Why is she crying?"

"She just cries sometimes. You know that."

Josie nodded and climbed the last step. "Why are you up here? It's dark."

Kalianne did her best to hide the leather pouch behind her. "I like to come up here and imagine watching for a ship." She needed to get that kid out of here and back to bed. Maybe she should drug her after all.

"Mommy likes to read the diary up here."

Diary.

"What diary?"

"You know, the lady who used to live here a

long, long time ago. Mommy likes to read about her. She had twins. Mommy read it to me." Josie lowered her voice and leaned forward. "She hid a leather pouch here."

"Your mother did?"

"No, silly. The lady who lived here. Mommy read me that part the other day. A friend asked her to hide it forever, to never let anyone find it. I think she hid it really, really good."

Kalianne gave her best smile. "Where did your mommy put the diary?" Maybe it would be helpful for Devi as well.

Josie shook her head. "I don't know where it is."

All she had to do was come back when Elin was here and grab the diary. Kalianne took Josie's hand. "We'd better get to bed. Your mommy will be upset that you're still up."

Josie's fingers curled around Kalianne's. "Where is Mommy? She always tucks me in. And I want a horsey ride with my daddy. I'm not sleepy." Her lower lip trembled.

"How about if I read you a story? Then when Mommy and Daddy come, I'll send them to tuck you in. Okay?"

She breathed a sigh when Josie nodded and didn't object to moving toward the stairs. Finding the pouch was a jolt of adrenaline. Devi would be so happy with her.

"Come along, Ruby." When she turned to look, Kalianne felt a cool breeze on her face. Ruby had opened the door to the outside. "Josie, I'll be along in a minute. You go pick out the book you want, okay?"

" 'Kay." Holding on to the railing, Josie went back down the stairs.

Kalianne hurried up the steep rooftop access. When she stepped out into the sea breeze, she saw Ruby with one foot half over the railing. Kalianne rushed to grab the old woman's arm and got there as the other leg swung toward the railing. If she hadn't been here, Ruby would have fallen from the parapet.

Kalianne dragged her back to safety. "Ruby, what were you doing up here?"

The old woman cried noiselessly, the tears leaving tracks on her face that gleamed in the moonlight. "I want to be with Owen. I miss him."

"It's not time yet. Come to bed." She led Ruby toward safety.

That had been a close call. The last thing she needed was to get the police out here.

Sara's light was beginning to flicker, and she fought back the rising panic. She was going to die in this inky blackness. No one would ever find her bones. She slid to the ground and turned off her light, plunging the cramped space into utter darkness.

She pulled her knees to her chest and buried her face as she tried to pray. The words wouldn't come, but she felt God's presence, and her panic began to edge into peace. She and Josh were not to be. She'd never hear him finally tell her he loved her. She'd never rest in his arms.

The hard rock bit into her head as she leaned back and tried to think of what to do. Her flashlight wouldn't last much longer. Should she try to go back the way she'd come and see if she could dig out of the cave-in, or would that be futile? Should she press on, hoping she'd find another tunnel out? There was no easy answer. She sat in the inky blackness and listened to her shallow breathing. It was the only sound.

She couldn't curl into a ball and die here. If she was about to step into eternity, she would do it on her feet, still fighting. Her fingers curled around the tiny flashlight, but she resisted the impulse to flip it on. She would turn it on every few minutes, just to orient herself. Sidling along the cold rock face, she shuffled forward a few feet. Her feet struck something in the way, and she flipped on her flashlight.

It was another branch in the trail. Which way now?

She stared to the right, but it was too dark beyond three feet. The left passageway went only two feet, then stopped at an impassable wall. Or was it? The wall was only six feet high. Was that a glimmer of light from above it? She shut off her flashlight to make sure. Yes, it was! She moved to the wall in her path and ran her fingers along its surface to see if she could find indentations to use to climb it. The dim light gave her courage.

She found several likely spots and fitted her right foot in the first one, then reached above her head for the tiny sliver of a grip she'd found. Grunting, she hoisted herself off the floor, then reached for the next hold. Her fingers began to cramp, and she paused a moment to try to fit her toe into a better spot. There it was. Little by little, she crept up the wall until she could peek over it. The faint light didn't show her much, just more rock.

Her fingers lost their purchase, and she slid down a few inches below the top of the wall. Resting a moment, she leaned her head against the cold rock, then tipped her head at a sound she couldn't place. It seemed to emanate from the other side of the wall. A kind of shuffling sound. Her heart seemed to stop as she realized it was probably Devi coming to kill her.

Where could she hide? Or would he even look on this side of the passage? Maybe he would come to the wall and stop. The opening at the top might be too small for a man. She didn't want to slide down the wall for fear he would hear her, so she waited with her face pressed against the rock.

Someone coughed, a short bark, then more shuffling came to her ears. She waited, barely breathing, to see what he might do.

"Great, just great," came a barely discernible mutter.

Her eyes widened. It sounded like Josh, but it couldn't be. Could it? The Coasties would have put up a hue and cry when she didn't return, but why would any of them be in this cave? Cautiously, she stretched onto her toes so she could peek over the top of the wall.

A familiar Dodgers ball cap was right below her. Josh leaned against the wall and wiped his forehead with his forearm.

"Josh?" Her voice was barely a squeak.

His head jerked up, and he brought up the flashlight. The beam hit her full in the face and blinded her after being in the dark so long.

"Sara!" He dropped the flashlight and began to climb the wall.

She reached for the top and pulled herself up, her toes scrambling for purchase in her urgency to reach him. His fingers touched hers as she struggled up the final few inches. Both panting from exertion, they faced one another at the top.

"Josh, I can't believe you're here. How did you find me?"

He leaned forward, and his lips found hers. She struggled to stay glued to the wall as the press of his lips brought tears coursing down her cheeks. She thought she'd never see him again, never smell his cologne or feel the roughness of his evening whiskers. Her fingers itched to plunge into his hair, but all she could do was hang on to the wall for dear life.

He lifted his head. "I thought you were dead." His voice was choked. "We saw the cave-in, and we thought we'd find your broken body inside. I couldn't stand it." His gaze bored into hers. "I love you, Sara. I've always loved you. My life has no meaning without you. Forget everything I said earlier. It was fear talking."

"I know." She could barely whisper past the lump in her throat. "I'm going to try to get through this opening."

"I'll catch you." His feet thudded back onto the cave floor.

She sought another toehold and found it, then pushed with her left leg and swung her right onto the top of the wall. With her last bit of strength, she hoisted herself atop the wall. It wasn't as wide as she expected, and she couldn't stop herself from hurtling right on over. Then she was falling.

A pair of strong arms caught her and held her close. She looked into Josh's blue eyes. Safe.

❧ Thirty-Six ❧

Elin wrapped a blanket around her friend, who looked a little shocky with pale skin and blue lips. Sara's teeth chattered, even though it was seventy-five outside and about the same here in the living room. The big windows showed the sun beginning to peek over the water.

Elin thrust a cup of hot tea in her hands. "Here, drink this."

Sara wrapped both hands around the cup. "I d-don't know why I'm s-so cold."

Josh sat close to her on the sofa. "You're having a reaction. Are you hurt at all?"

Sara sipped the tea, then shook her head. "I don't think so."

"What happened?" Marc sat in an armchair on the other side of the area rug. His hazel eyes were alert, and he didn't look like a man who had been up all night.

Sara stared up at Elin. "You're not going to like this, Elin. Kalianne was part of this."

Elin lowered herself to the chair. "K-Kalianne? Mom's aide? I don't understand."

"She's Devi Long's sister. I came upon her with a crate, and when I insisted on seeing inside, she knocked me out." Sara shook her head. "I'm ashamed I let her get the upper hand."

Josh took her hand. "She didn't seem the type to get violent." He laced his fingers with hers.

Elin looked at their linked hands. Something good had come out of this awful night. "She tried to kill you?"

"No, that was Devi, I'm sure. She called him, and he came to take care of their 'little problem.' She objected and tried to protect me. When she stepped in front of me, I ran into the cave. I found the deeper passage, and the next thing I knew, I heard the cave-in."

Elin shuddered. "I have always thought I was a good judge of character. I guess that's not true." She looked at Marc. "Can we get her picked up?"

"We can try, but I'd guess Devi took her away before she could give away any more information about him." He pulled out his cell phone and placed a call.

A sense of dread curled in Elin's belly. "Mom's been sleeping a lot. I thought it was part of her dementia. What if it wasn't? What if Kalianne's been drugging her so she could go out and search for those drugs?" Her fingers curled into fists. "I've been so stupid!"

"We all trusted her. I gave her those tops and capris. I liked her." Sara took another sip of her tea. "She was good at her masquerade."

Marc ended his call. "I think they have a lead on her and her brother. A Coast Guard cutter stopped a speedboat offshore a few hours ago. There was a couple aboard who sounds like those two. The Coasties didn't find anything amiss, so they let them go, but they told the patrol they were headed to Kill Devil Hills. We've got the description of the boat and its identification number. A patrol boat is headed that way to see if their boat is in the harbor."

"I doubt they'll be there." Josh still hadn't let go of Sara.

"I should check on Mom." Elin started to get up, but Marc shook his head.

"Let her sleep. I don't think Kalianne did her any real harm."

"I'm so glad I never had her watch Josie." She glanced at Josh and Sara. "There must have been a lot of money in the drugs for them to go so far."

"A crate that size could contain millions of dollars in heroin," Sara said. "I wish I'd gotten a chance to see inside it."

Marc yawned. "There's time for a little shut-eye if you all want to head to bed. Everyone will be up in a couple of hours."

A secret smile hovering on her lips, Sara glanced at Josh. "I'm not really tired. I think I'd like a walk along the beach."

"I'm game." Still holding on to her hand, he rose and helped her up. "We'll be back in time for breakfast."

Elin watched them go. "Something happened between them."

Marc grinned. "You think?" His smiled faded when their gazes locked. "We got a little interrupted in our own discussion. Want to go back to it, or are you too tired?"

What was he saying? That kiss had shattered her last bit of resistance. She loved him so much. Had he been about to admit he had feelings for her? She'd asked him how he felt, and he hadn't answered.

She feigned a yawn. "We can talk about it another time. I'm pretty tired." She rose and headed for the stairs.

Elin had gone off to rest awhile ago, and Marc sat with his parents on the back deck with the birds singing from the trees lining the back of the property. Saturday morning cartoons playing on TV would keep Josie and Ruby occupied for a few minutes while he discussed things with them.

His mother looked about to burst. She still wore her blue robe, but his father was dressed in jeans and a red T-shirt. His fishing hat perched on one side of his chair. They both looked tired, probably from keeping up with a four-year-old.

Marc stirred nuts into his oatmeal. "What do you think of your granddaughter?"

His mother handed him the cinnamon. "Oh, Marc, she is darling! But I'm so worried Elin is going to yank her away from us."

"Elin wouldn't do that."

His mother shifted in her chair. "We have no rights to her. I'm sure her birth certificate lists Tim as her father. What if you and Elin get into a spat, and she refuses to let us see her? We'll have no recourse."

"Elin wouldn't do that."

His father gave a slow nod. "She doesn't seem the vindictive type."

"What are you going to do to ensure you get to see Josie? That we all do?"

His mother would worry that bone into shards. "I'm working on it."

"What does that mean? Have you gotten a lawyer? Your father could help with that. I think we should get Elin to agree to give us grand-parent rights."

"Things are fragile right now, Mom. Don't rock the boat. Let me handle this. I don't need a lawyer." It took everything in him to keep his voice from rising. He wasn't four.

She bit her lip. "I'm just worried, honey. We love Josie already."

"So do I. And Elin is thankful we love her daughter. A child never has too much love."

"You know how your father and I feel about a child growing up without a father. You'll need to take extra steps to ensure Josie always knows you'll be there for her."

"I intend to." He choked down another bite of oatmeal.

Feeling so helpless in this situation wasn't something he relished. Elin held all the cards. He had to dance to her tune. For the first time, he wondered if he *should* talk to his dad about the legalities. How many fathers had found them-selves standing on the outside of their children's lives? He didn't want to be one of them. And the killer closing in made things even more difficult.

"You know exactly what you want to do," his father observed. "Let's hear your plan."

Trust his father to recognize the intent on his face. "I want to marry Elin."

His mother gasped and half rose until his father grabbed her arm. "I knew you had feelings for her! I can see it whenever you look at her." She toyed with her spoon, twirling it around on the table. "I was beginning to think you didn't believe in a lasting love and marriage."

He had to shake his head and look away from his mother's penetrating gaze. "I only have to look at you and Dad to know real love exists. That kind of love is hard to find."

"Does she love you?"

He made a face. "I doubt it." Though that kiss last night had shattered his certainty about a marriage of convenience only. But if she loved him, why was she avoiding talking more about marriage?

His father leaned forward. "Marriage takes work. It's not about luck or just love either. It's about commitment. When you're in the thick of the battle with raising kids, juggling busy careers, and finding time to mow the grass, a couple can look at each other and wonder where love went. It's still there though, if you look for it and nurture it. You don't enter into a commitment like that for convenience sake."

"You against it, Dad?"

His father shook his head. "I didn't say that. You are not the kind of man who makes a promise lightly. How do you feel about Elin? You skirted your mom's question pretty well, but that speaks volumes too. You love her."

Marc exhaled and sat back in his chair. The bald statement was a stone pressing against his heart. It was so much easier to convince himself he only wanted this for Josie. The truth was so much more complex.

"No rebuttal?" His father was in full attorney mode now as if he were arguing a case.

Marc shook his head. "I don't want to love her."

His mother's eyes softened. "Love isn't something you can turn off and on like a water spigot."

He exhaled. "Yeah. Kind of inconvenient though. I don't think she feels the same."

"You're afraid to talk to her about it?"

"She'd run away if she knew I loved her, and things would be strained between us. I don't want that. I thought it was better if we had a common goal. We could at least be friends, and maybe in time she'd come to feel something for me."

His dad gave that sound he often made in court —something between a chuckle and a clearing of his throat. "Son, you need to take a good look at her. Love is written all over her face."

"I've only seen distance and wariness." But that was a lie. There had been something she wanted to say last night, but he'd been too afraid to let her close.

❧ Thirty-Seven ❧

Sunday morning Elin slept in until eight, and by the time she showered, Christine had everyone fed and ready to head out for church, followed by an afternoon at the beach. Elin hated that she'd overslept and would miss church.

Christine hailed her when she came down the stairs. "I can't get your mother out of the garden. She thinks she has to pull every weed before church."

"I'll see what I can do." Christine followed her out the back door. Mom was standing in the mud in her bare feet, and she didn't stop when Elin called to her.

Her mother plunged the hoe into the dirt, displacing a tomato plant. "I need to find it."

Elin touched her arm. "What are you looking for, Mom?"

"The pouch. That leather pouch. It has to be here. Kalianne took it."

Elin frowned and looked at Christine. "What's Kalianne got to do with this? Have you seen her lately?" She hadn't told them about Kalianne's involvement. There hadn't been time.

Christine frowned. "I don't know. We haven't seen her since late Friday night."

"Friday night?" Elin's pulse sped up. "I thought she left early."

"She did, but she came back, saying she forgot to give your mother her medicine. She fixed us some tea, and we went off to bed while she was still here." Christine rubbed her eyes. "Neither of us have felt very well this weekend. I'm tempted to stay home from church today myself, but I don't want to disappoint Josie."

"She'll be fine if you don't feel up to going." She studied the circles under Christine's eyes. "But about Kalianne. What time was this?"

"Oh, after dark. Maybe nine?"

After her attack on Sara. "Did she give Mom her medicine then?"

"I think so. I didn't watch her. She went inside for a little while, then came out with some new tea. It had a funny taste, and I wondered if I was allergic to it. Maybe that's why I haven't felt well." Christine shook her head. "But Frank feels the same. Maybe it's a bug."

"Maybe she drugged you." Elin launched into what Kalianne had done. Christine's eyes got bigger and bigger. "So she came here after she thought Sara was dead. What does she want here? That's what I don't understand." She glanced at her mother again, who was still digging in the dirt.

That leather pouch. Could her mother have mentioned the diary to Kalianne? Maybe that's what she was looking for. Elin kicked off her flip-flops and stepped into the garden. "Mom, come with me for a minute. I need to talk to you."

"I can't find it." Tears hung on her mother's lashes. "It's not here."

"I don't think you put the leather pouch in the garden. You went to the attic, remember?"

The clouds in her mother's eyes lifted, and she nodded. "We found it though, me and Kalianne. I told her to leave it here, but I can't find it."

"Kalianne wants the leather pouch?"

Her mother nodded again. "It belongs to her."

"It doesn't belong to her. If she comes here asking for it again, tell me, okay?" Though her mother nodded, Elin knew she'd never remember. "Did Kalianne give you tea the other night? Or did she give Josie anything?"

"Josie." Her mother looked toward the house. "Josie couldn't find it either. Kalianne made her go to bed." Tears ran down her cheeks. "I don't like Kalianne anymore. She yells at me."

"She's not coming back," Elin assured her. "Let's get you cleaned up."

She led her mother out of the mud and over to the hose where she washed the mud from her bare feet. "You're going to miss church if you don't hurry."

Her mother brightened. "I like the songs." She shuffled toward the house at a slightly faster pace.

Christine leaned down and turned off the spigot. "I think we should take Josie and your mother back to our house, Elin. Surely you can't want them here with so much danger."

"You're right." Elin hadn't wanted to let go of her little girl, but the danger wasn't over. And there wasn't anyone to watch Mom either. Kalianne and her brother would be back. Laura's killer too. "Take them home with you after church. Call me every day though, okay?"

Christine embraced her, and Elin clung to her solid figure. "I'll take good care of her, honey. We already love her. Frank knows a lot of policemen. We'll hire someone to watch the house too, just in case."

"Thank you," she choked out. "We'll get through this. Thank you for loving my little girl in spite of everything."

"Thank you for letting us into her life. And yours." Christine released her with a final pat.

Elin watched her go. What would Marc think of this turn of events?

With the house quiet, Elin went to her office to do a little work. She heard the shower running in Marc's bedroom, so he was up too. She rubbed bleary eyes as she fired up her program. She'd gotten a text message a few minutes ago about a new donor she needed to work on ASAP. She studied the middle-aged woman's stats. Good lungs, bad heart, good corneas, kidneys, and liver. The work would get her mind off what was happening here.

She pulled up her list of recipients and began running through her matching procedure. She pulled out her phone and scrolled to the first recipient, a man in his midthirties who needed a liver transplant. Before she could place the call, a bar filled the screen of her computer.

YOU WILL NEVER MARRY HIM. YOU LOOK GOOD IN BLACK.

She gasped and rocked back in her chair. Looking around wildly, she tried to think of how someone could have taken over her computer. This was a highly secure website. It would be no easy matter to hack into it.

Marc appeared in the doorway with no shirt and his hair still wet. "What's wrong?"

She pointed to the screen. "Look."

He moved around behind her, and she caught a whiff of his clean-smelling skin. She handed the laptop to him so she could move to a safer distance.

"He knows a lot about computers. And I think he's obsessed with you, wants you for himself. It would explain why he hasn't just killed you the way he did Laura."

She shuddered and clasped her arms around herself. "I'm beginning to think so too."

He stared at the screen a moment. "What if he's another OPO representative?"

Her eyes widened. "Oh, I hope not. That seems wrong—that someone who is dedicated to bringing life from death would parcel out such pain to people."

"Evil can lurk in any heart. Let me get my computer too." He handed her the laptop, then headed for the door. "Can you get me a list of all the OPO representatives in this area?"

She nodded and went into an even more secure area where she downloaded a list of names. The thought of one of her coworkers being involved made her shudder. "Before you go, I need to tell you something. I told your mom she could take Josie home with her today. I'm worried about her being in the middle of this mess." She told him about Kalianne coming over after the attack on Sara.

"I was going to do my best to convince you to do that today. My parents will take good care of her. I want her out of here too. Glad you agreed." He stepped into the hall. "I'll be right back with my computer."

That had gone better than expected. Now to get this mess figured out.

Marc returned and sat in a chair with his computer on his lap. "I'm going to export the manifest. Send me the list, and I'll run a comparison to see if there were any OPO representatives on that boat the night Laura died."

She nodded. "Give me your e-mail address." She typed it in as he rattled it off, then attached the file to it. "You realize I'm not supposed to share this information?"

"You can trust me with anything." He bent over his computer keyboard. "It's here. Let's see what I can find out."

Warmth spread through her at his words. She knew she could trust him.

The ominous message on her screen vanished, and she eased back into her chair and exhaled. The doorbell rang, and she glanced out the front window of the office to see Sara standing outside. "I'll be right back."

She went to the door and hugged her friend. "You're okay?"

"Yep." Her smile was brilliant. She wore a sleeveless white top over a full skirt that swirled around her knees.

"I want to hear everything." She gestured to the hall. "Marc is in the office. We might be on to something." She led Sara to the office and pulled a chair up for her beside the desk.

Marc barely looked up. "Hey, Sara."

She smiled. "Is that the best you can do when I nearly died Friday night?"

He looked up then, and his slow smile emphasized the dimple in his right cheek. "Sorry. Distracted. Did Elin tell you what happened?"

"No, just that you might be on to something. What's up?"

"I had a threatening message come up on my computer. It was when I was in a secure OPO website, so Marc thought maybe the killer is another representative."

Sara's levity vanished. "How bizarre. I hope he's wrong."

Marc looked up. "I'm not. There was one on the ship."

"You're kidding! Who was it?" This wasn't something Elin really wanted to hear. Work would never be the same again.

"Kerri Summerall. Know her?"

Elin nodded. "Quite well. But she's the nicest person you'd ever meet." She turned to Sara. "You know Kerri. She was instrumental in getting me the new heart."

"And we know the killer is a man, so this is a dead end," Sara said.

"It wouldn't hurt to at least talk to her," Marc said. "Maybe she saw something." But his voice held little enthusiasm.

"I'll talk to her." Elin looked at her computer screen. "So we're back to a master hacker. Can we research the people on the manifest and see if there are any computer experts on it?"

"It will take time, but yeah, I can work on that. I'll get my assistant to start running checks."

Sara rose and walked to the window. "I

wondered if the two of you would like to have a celebratory dinner with Josh and me tonight." When she turned back toward them, her smile beamed.

"Only if you tell me what you're celebrating." Elin wanted to hear the whole story from her friend. "I bet I can guess though. The idiot finally came to his senses."

"Hey, that's my future husband you're talking about." Sara's smile grew wider. "We're getting married in a month."

Elin leaped up to hug her. "A month! Isn't that a little fast?"

Sara's smile was bright enough to light the room. "Neither of us want a big wedding, and I've waited on him for way too long as it is. I want to nab him before he changes his mind."

Marc hugged her too. "I hope I get to give you away."

She clung to him. "I wouldn't have it any other way. And Elin will be my maid of honor."

At least the horrible evening had brought something good with it.

◈ Thirty-Eight ◈

The moon glimmered on the waves as they rolled to shore. Elin's flip-flops smacked on the old boards as she and Marc walked out to the end of the pier. Marc kicked off his flip-flops and dangled his feet off the end of the pier. She lifted her face to the fresh sea scent as she settled beside him. A dolphin leaped out of the water and splashed back down a few feet to their west.

A good omen for what she intended to tell Marc.

Her heart thumped in her chest. Maybe it was too soon for this decision. Maybe it was the wrong decision, and she would regret it.

She turned her head and looked at the lights gleaming out through the house. "I wonder what this place looked like in Georgina's day. I think it was about the same size. I haven't seen any obvious additions. Of course, she probably didn't have electric lights out here for a long time. Maybe when she was older, electricity made its way this far."

"Still no sign of the leather pouch you're looking for?"

She shook her head. "I wanted to hope Mom really found it, but I think it was just a halluci-nation. I'm sure it's long gone."

"She said Kalianne found it. When the police

pick them up, hopefully we can get it back. If it even exists. The city hasn't been found though, so maybe it does."

"True." She lay back on the grayed boards with her legs still dangling over the edge of the pier and stared into the night sky. A million stars twinkled down on her, and the moon looked as big as a hot-air balloon.

"Gorgeous night."

"It is." What was she doing making small talk when she'd suggested this walk for a specific purpose? Her cowardice disgusted her.

Marc lay back too, then rolled on his side to stare at her. "Okay, Elin, what gives? It's not like you to suggest a romantic walk on the beach, so you must have something up your sleeve. You remembered something about the killer?"

She rolled to her side too, and they lay nose to nose about a foot apart on the cool boards. His spicy cologne mingled with the salt air. It felt way too intimate for what she wanted to say, but she wasn't backing out now.

She propped her head on her hand. "It's not about the murderer. I've been thinking about what you said about raising Josie together."

His eyes widened, and he propped his head on his hand too. "You've made a decision?"

"Sort of." She wet her lips. "I'll accept your suggestion."

"That's great!"

A little stunned at the light in his eyes, she shook her head. "Don't agree too quickly. I have one caveat."

"Name it." No regret lingered in his eyes, no trepidation.

Now came the difficult part. She could already feel the heat building in her cheeks. What kind of woman said what she intended to say?

"You look frightened." His words were soft. "You can tell me anything."

He was much too close and much too enticing. Unable to look into his eyes, she sat up and drew her knees to her chest. "What do you think of me, Marc?"

He sat up too. "I think you're strong and courageous. You see a glass half full no matter what is going on in your life. I love the way you think about other people first."

"I didn't phrase that right. How do you *feel* about me?" She wasn't sure she'd even be able to hear his answer over the pulsing blood in her veins. Surely that kiss meant something. Marc wasn't like some men. He wouldn't have kissed her like that unless he felt something.

The moonlight illuminated his face as he turned toward her. "I don't want to tell you because it might change your mind."

Her chest hitched, and pressure built behind her eyes. She would *not* cry. "I see. You feel nothing for me but friendship?"

He frowned. "I didn't say that. Heck, I might as well get it all out in the open." Reaching over, he twisted a long lock of her red hair around his finger. "I love you, Elin. I didn't want to, but when I'm around you, I feel somehow bigger and more capable. More whole."

Her throat closed, and her mouth went dry. Was he saying what she thought he was? She was afraid to look away in case the warm light in his eyes would disappear when she looked again.

"Nothing to say?" His rueful smile wobbled a little. "You going to change your mind now that you know I'm crazy about you?"

Moisture gathered on her lashes, and she shook her head. "I love you, Marc. Everything about you—your tenderness for Josie—did me in. When I saw how much love you were capable of, I began to want a piece for myself. My caveat was that I wanted us to at least have a date once a week and see if there was any spark left on your side."

His hand plunged into her hair, and he pulled her into his arms. His familiar male scent made her burrow closer. She could feel his heart thudding under her ear.

He touched her chin and tipped her face up, then his lips claimed hers. Warm and persuasive, the sweet pressure of his mouth made her wrap her arms around his neck. He loved her! Wonder filled her, and she returned the passion in his kiss with all the pent-up loneliness of the last five years.

He ran his thumb over the tears on her cheek and then passed the back of his hand over the other side of her face. "Why are you crying?" A shadow hunkered in his eyes.

"I'm happy, so happy," she whispered. "I never thought you would say you loved me. I never dared hope for it."

"I looked up that verse last night, the one in Corinthians about love." He fumbled in his pocket with one hand. "I wrote it out and was going to give it to you when I proposed with a ring, but you derailed my plans." He pressed the paper into her hand. "Love is always supposed to protect, trust, hope, and persevere. I want to show that kind of love to you and Josie."

More tears spilled from her eyes. "What do you think Josie will say?"

His tender smile beamed. "She'll ask if she can be the flower girl. But enough of Josie. Kiss me again, woman."

So she obliged. The taste of him wasn't anything she was going to get tired of.

Marc put down his suspense novel and wished he could go to sleep. He kept replaying the evening with Elin. They were going to be a family. He wanted to shout it from the rooftop.

He wasn't a warm milk kind of guy, but maybe a bowl of cereal would help. The kitchen was quiet, and he fixed his cereal, then carried it to the table by the window. He glanced down on the moonlit backyard. Silvery light bathed the flowers and trees all the way to the line of live oaks. He sat down and lifted the spoon to his mouth.

The glass shattered, and wood splinters flew from the chair he was sitting in. That was a gunshot. He dove under the table as things exploded around him again. His gun was in his room. He had to get his gun before Elin became a target. Reaching up, he flipped off the light and crawled into the living room and down the hall to his room. He grabbed his Glock from the top shelf in the closet and raced to Elin's room.

She was in the doorway when he got there. "I thought I heard gunshots." Her eyes were wide and frightened.

"You did. Go to your room and lock the door. Call the sheriff too. I'll go after the shooter."

She grabbed his arm. "Be careful, Marc. If he hurts you . . ." Her eyes swam with tears.

He squeezed her hand. "I will. You won't get rid of me so easily."

He raced down the stairs, then paused at the bottom and listened. The only sound that came to his ears was the wind. He dropped to his knees, crawled to the living room window, and looked out toward the water. Nothing moved but the waves and the trees.

After checking to make sure the front door was

secure, he crawled to the dining area. The breeze came through the broken glass and lifted his hair. The hammock on the deck creaked in the wind too. He went to the kitchen and cautiously peered out the window. Nothing out of order.

The roar of a motor caught his attention, and he went to the living room again in time to see boat lights heading away from shore.

On Tuesday morning Elin hurried along to Oyster Café in Hope Beach. Kerri waved to her from a table in the courtyard. She wore her auburn hair up in a ponytail, and the turquoise top she wore enhanced the green in her hazel eyes.

Elin hugged her. "You got here early."

Kerri released her and sat back down. "You're buying. And besides, I could hear the excitement in your voice when you called. You're really going to marry Marc?"

Elin couldn't hold back the smile. "I am. I still can't believe it. I can't even tell you how happy I am."

"Where is the bridegroom today?"

Elin told her about the attack the night before. "He took the bullets to the FBI office to check ballistics." She rubbed her head. "I just want this over so we can get on with our lives."

"Me too. This is so scary. I'm glad you have Marc. But you said you had something else to talk to me about. What's up?"

Elin held up one finger as the server, a middle-aged woman dressed in shorts and a tank top, approached. They ordered coffee and she-crab soup. Once they were alone again, she pulled her chair closer to her friend. "Were you on the *Seawind* cruise? You never mentioned it."

Kerri went red, then white. She nodded. "I should have told you, but I didn't want you to know how stupid I was."

"I don't understand."

Her friend slumped back in her chair. "Ben had been calling, asking if we might stand a chance of getting back together. At first I told him no, but he told me he'd booked us on that cruise. I thought, what the heck? It's worth a try, especially if I got a free cruise out of it. Boy, was I wrong."

"What happened?"

"He'd gotten us two separate cabins, but I found it almost impossible to get him out of mine. But not for the reason you might think. He only wanted to talk about you. He asked how you were since the transplant, if you were seeing anyone. I think he only wanted me to go so he could grill me about you. He never so much as tried to kiss me." She blinked rapidly.

"I'm sorry, Kerri."

She nodded and twisted the napkin in her fingers. "I should have known better. And it's not your fault. He's just a freak."

The server brought their coffee. Elin thanked

her and stirred in the cream as her thoughts raced. Could Ben still be attracted to her? But no, he'd gone out with Sara and seemed very interested. And he hadn't been by to see her, though she'd suspected he would.

"Did you meet Laura at all? She worked in the medical facility. You probably wouldn't have needed that, but I thought she might have been around for meals or something."

"I didn't, no. I would have told you I was there if there'd been the least bit of contact."

"I thought so, but I wanted to ask." Had Ben met Laura? Elin doubted Kerri would know.

"I didn't mean to upset you," Kerri said. "It's not a big deal. We tried and it didn't work. End of story."

"Ben is here, on Hope Island. Did you know that?"

Kerri shook her head. "But you know how he puts in for every fun assignment out there." She stopped and bit her lip. "Wait, are you saying he arrived after you did?"

When had he arrived on the island? Elin remembered back to what he had told her. "Actually, I think he got here before I did." The realization eased her trepidation. "A month or so before."

"Well, um, I think I might have mentioned to him that you were moving here. You put the offer on your house two months before you moved in. He called after we got home from the cruise. I think I might have said something."

She pushed away her unease. "At least he hasn't bothered me. It's no big deal."

"I hope not."

Elin stared at her friend. "What aren't you telling me, Kerri?"

"Haven't you ever wondered if he was a little obsessed with you?"

"Obsession seems a little strong."

"What happened when he showed up after Tim died? You didn't say."

Elin sipped her coffee to take away the chill she felt thinking about it. "He said in the Bible, the surviving brother took care of the widow, and he'd give me the children Tim couldn't."

Kerri shuddered. "Okay, that's seriously creepy. He tried to jump you?"

"Well, he tried to kiss me, but I shoved him away. He got really mad. I thought he was going to hit me, and I locked myself in the bathroom with my cell phone. I told him to leave or I'd call the police."

"And he did?"

She nodded. "I heard the door slam, then his truck started. I watched out the bathroom window until he pulled out of the driveway, then I ran to the front door and locked it."

"Did you see him after that?"

She put her coffee cup down. "I saw him a couple of times at his mother's. He acted like nothing had happened, so I did too. I chalked it up to distress over Tim's death. I think it was just grief talking. And when I saw him here, things weren't tense."

"That's probably it." Kerri looked unconvinced.

"Enough about this. All I have to do is stay out of his way. I think I need to warn Sara though. He may have transferred his obsession to her. Someone said he'd told him he intended to marry her. He won't be happy when he hears she's marrying Josh."

"Definitely warn her."

The server brought their soup, and Elin tucked into it. Sara was smart enough to handle someone like Ben.

Marc was getting coffee when his phone rang. He winced when he saw Harry's name on the display. His boss had already gotten wind of the bullets he'd brought in for analysis. His gut tightened at the thought of being fired.

He thumbed it on. "Everton."

"Well, you did it again, Marc."

Harry didn't sound mad. "Did what?"

"Ballistics of the bullets you brought in match the one that killed Will."

Marc's heart leaped. "Same gun?"

"Looks like it." Harry cleared his throat. "Looks like I owe you an apology. But you still disobeyed a direct order. I should fire you."

"But you won't."

"I'd be pretty stupid to fire my best agent. Find that guy, Marc. He murdered one of our own."

"I intend to. Thanks for letting me know personally, Harry."

"Least I could do. I'll send a couple more agents your way tomorrow. There will be nowhere for him to hide."

"Thanks. I'll touch base with you in the morning." He'd barely disconnected the call when his phone rang again. A Norfolk number. "Everton," he barked, expecting a sales call.

"Mr. Everton?" a female voice quavered, then gulped.

"Samantha?"

"Yes. I hope you don't mind me calling you."

He immediately remembered how pregnant she was. "Are you all right?"

"I'm fine." She inhaled. "I know where Ryan is. He just called Dad, and I overheard him say he was at the cabin."

"Cabin?"

"Yes, it's near Roanoke, out in the woods." She told him how to get there. "His family has owned it forever, and he's been holed up there. I forgot about it."

"Thank you for calling. I'm sure it wasn't easy."

"Don't tell my dad. He'd hit me if he knew."

"I won't. And if you ever want to get out of that house, I'll help you." He swung his

Tahoe around to head toward the Outer Banks.

"I'm going to get out of here. I'm leaving with my boyfriend in the morning. Find Laura's killer, Mr. Everton."

"I'll do my best, Samantha."

"What about the woman who was with you? I can't get her out of my mind. The way she said my name, the way she tucked her hair behind her ear."

The hopeful tone in her voice tugged at his heart. Didn't he owe her the truth? "She has Laura's heart, Sammie. And she has some of Laura's memories with it." Her quick inhalation echoed in his ear. "But she's not Laura, honey. Her memories of Laura's death are helping us track down the murderer."

"W-Will you call me when you arrest him? I just want to see justice for Laura."

"I'll do that. Will you still have this number?"

"I'll keep it. Thank you, Mr. Everton. For every-thing."

He ended the call and saved her number to his phone. Following Samantha's directions, he drove straight to the cabin. The drive was a narrow dirt track back to a small cabin with a green metal roof. A porch extended across the front of the structure. A green Ford pickup, only its bed showing, sat along the side of the cabin. Must be Mosely's. Assuming the man wouldn't answer the front door, Marc went around to the back door and tried the handle. It opened easily, and he stepped into a dimly lit kitchen smelling of bacon.

On the other side of the wall, someone hammered. A radio played country music in the distance, and he caught a whiff of strong male cologne. The same one they'd doused the red sweater with. The door opened noiselessly, and he peered into a square living room.

A man with shaggy blond hair appeared to be building bookcases. He sang in a low baritone along with the music, an old Willy Nelson tune.

"Ryan Mosely?"

The man jerked around and faced him with the hammer held up as if to strike. Marc tried a smile and held up his hand in a placating gesture. "Hey, I'm not a robber. I'm investigating the murder of Laura Watson."

Mosely's eyes went empty. "I don't know a thing about it. And you're trespassing. You didn't even knock."

"If you don't know anything about it, why did you follow us in your brown car and try to hit us?"

Mosely's face went red.

"I don't warn off easily." Marc advanced into the room. "You were aboard that ship too. I have the manifest. And I know you were stalking her. What happened? She rejected you one time too many and you strangled her?"

The man gripped the hammer hard, but at least he lowered it. "It wasn't me." His smile was way too easy and practiced.

Marc took another step toward him. "Then who did? You were stalking her. Don't tell me you didn't see something." Marc studied the man's demeanor, the way he held his gaze, the way he didn't blink. "Was anyone else hanging around her?"

Mosely's mouth flattened. "Yeah, that loser Theo. But she soon figured out his game. He didn't care enough to hurt her. And when I went back inside, I saw him reeling off with another woman to his cabin."

He thought back to the memories Elin had. "Let me see your hands."

Mosely stared at him, then extended his hands. "No scratches."

"Like that's what I'm looking for this far out from the attack. What about that ring, Mosely? You wear it all the time?" The ring had an *R* on it, and Marc dropped his hand a few inches closer to his gun. "My partner Will came to see you, didn't he? You knew you had to get rid of him, didn't you?"

Mosely took a step back, then the hand holding the hammer rose again, and he sprang toward Marc.

Marc sidestepped the blow and drew his gun, but Mosely's arm came down too fast. The hammer smacked into the side of Marc's head, and as he sank into darkness, he heard the man laugh before his footsteps faded into nothingness.

❧ Thirty-Nine ❧

The rest of the afternoon stretched luxuriously in front of Elin. She'd dropped the car off to be serviced, and it wouldn't be ready until three. She didn't feel like shopping, even though the thought of planning the wedding enticed her. What she really wanted was an ice-cream cone and to visit with friends. Her call to Sara dumped her into voice mail.

With no choice, she bought a cone and ate it by herself at the picnic table by the road. Her phone rang, and she dug it out of her purse. Marc's mother's name came up on her screen. "Hey, Christine."

"Elin, thank goodness I got you. I didn't want to worry you, but it's your mother."

"What's wrong?"

"She seems to have forgotten who I am and where she is. She's locked herself in her bedroom and is wailing like a banshee."

Elin's stomach plunged. "My car is in the shop." She noticed the bike-rental shop right next door. "But I can rent a bike and get to the ferry. I'll be there as quickly as I can."

"I'll let you know if things change."

Minutes later, Elin pedaled out of town toward the ferry dock. There wasn't much traffic today since it was the middle of the week with the next ferry not due in for two hours. The breeze lifted her hair and filled her nose with the scent of wildflowers. Her leg muscles burned with the unfamiliar task of riding a bike, but in a good way. She'd spent way too much time at a desk.

She eased up on the speed a bit when her heart began to thump in her chest. The doctor had given her the go-ahead for a normal life, but it wouldn't pay to rush into exercise too quickly. Several cars passed, slowing down as they came abreast of her. The road entered a stretch of no houses, only maritime forest on one side and seagrass mixed into sand dunes on the other. The roar of the waves and the sound of the birds lulled her as she rode along.

Her phone rang, and she stopped to answer it. Christine again. "Josie coaxed Ruby out. She seems fine now. I hope I didn't worry you too much."

"Oh, good. Would it help if I talked to her?"

"I think it's better if we don't rock the boat. I'll call you again if I need you."

Elin ended the call and exhaled. Thank goodness. She wheeled the bike around in the other direction and headed back toward town.

Something thumped, and she thought she'd run over a rock, but then the front of the bike wobbled, and she realized the tire was flat. Great. Several miles from town without a car in sight.

She dismounted and knelt by the tire. A nail gleamed in the side of the tire. She pulled out her phone and tried to decide who to call. Maybe the bike shop?

A truck slowed, and she glanced over to see a man smiling as he ran his window down. She smiled back, relieved she wouldn't have to walk this thing back to town. But a prickle of unease settled along her spine at the sight of his blond hair, which was stupid. Lots of guys had blond hair.

He parked the truck. "Got a flat?"

The sound of his voice made her take a step back, though she couldn't put her finger on why. "A bad one." She pointed out the nail.

He opened his door and got out. "I'll throw it in the back of the truck and take you to town. I was heading in for groceries anyway."

"Uh, no thanks. My friend is coming this way shortly. I'll just wait."

"You mean Marc?" An easy smile lifted his mouth. "I don't think you'll see him for a long time, and if he survives the fire, he'll have a pretty nasty headache from that hammer I hit him with. Though I don't think he'll survive the fire."

It took a moment for his words to soak in. She had to find Marc, save him. She whirled to run into the maritime forest, but his hand clamped down on her arm as she went for her cell phone. She tore at his strong fingers, but he propelled her toward the truck as if she weighed no more than a child.

"You're Ryan Mosely," she gasped.

"You're too smart for your own good." His fingers tightened on her arm. "You're even prettier up close."

Before she could react, his other hand came up, and she caught a whiff of chloroform on the cloth he moved toward her face. She went limp as if she'd fainted and shut her eyes, hoping he wouldn't dope her. His grip loosened, and she dropped to her knees and rolled under the truck.

He made a grab at her but missed, and she scooted into the center where he'd have to crawl to reach her. She could see his boots, then he dropped to his knees and peered at her.

His face contorted with rage. "I'm going to make you very sorry you gave me so much trouble."

He stood back up, and she watched his boots go around to the back. The tailgate scraped and banged as he opened it. Did he have a gun or something back there? She quickly sidled to the same side she came in under, hoping he'd think she would try another exit.

In a flash, she was on her feet and running for the forest. A shot whizzed over her head, and she hit the knee-high grass on her belly.

Then a shout came to her ears, a different male voice. She peeked up over the top of the weeds and saw Ben's truck parked behind the green one.

The rifle in his hands barked twice, and Mosely crumpled to the ground.

Elin jumped to her feet and swayed as the blood rushed from her head. Ben had saved her. She hurried toward him. "Mosely was going to kill me!"

"I know." He put the gun down to his side. "I saw him aim the rifle at you. I was going hunting and had my rifle with me." He raked his blond hair back with a hand that appeared a little shaky. "Are you all right? Did the bullet hit you?"

"No, no, I'm fine. Just scared." When he put his arm around her, she let him lead her to his truck and seat her in the passenger seat. "Sorry to be so shaky. I–I didn't think I'd be able to get away."

"Let me get you to town and have the doctor look at you. You're white and shaking." He went around to the driver's side and got in.

"What about Mosely?"

"He's dead. I'll have the sheriff come out and collect the scum."

She exhaled and leaned back against the headrest. "Thank you, Ben."

"You're welcome."

Several sandwich wrappers lay crumpled on the floor, and she banged her foot against a pipe wrench.

"Sorry it's such a mess." He ran up his window and cranked up the air-conditioning. He started the truck and accelerated away.

She grabbed her seat belt and reached down to lock it into place. A folder lay on the floor with pictures spilling out of it. Photos of her. Standing in the window at Seagrass Cottage, one even in her nightgown. Something squeezed in her chest, and she glanced up to see Ben staring back.

His gaze went from her to the pictures and back. Without expression, he reached to his door and clicked the lock on the doors, then flipped the child-protection switch before she could unlock her door.

"You killed Laura." She couldn't wrap her head around it. Not Ben, her own brother-in-law. "Why?"

"That was Mosely, not me." His voice betrayed no emotion. "But I'd finally had enough of your rejection. I thought all the stink you made about remembering Laura's death would be the perfect diversion. I could kill you and everyone would assume it was the same man who murdered Laura."

Elin could barely force the words out. The darkness in his eyes sapped all the heat from her body. "And Lacy? Was that Mosely too?" When he shook his head, her knees nearly gave out. "You?"

"It was her fault. I stopped by thinking you were there, and she slapped me when she found me in the kitchen."

"I don't believe you. You had a red wig with you and made her put it on. You planned it all along."

His eyes were fathomless, cold and emotion-less. "Shut up, Elin."

She tried to yank up the lock on her door, but it wouldn't budge. Even her window wouldn't roll down. "Let me out of here."

"I can't do that. You never should have broken up with me to go with my brother. That *ruined* everything, Elin. Everything."

He terrified her. "You don't want to hurt me, Ben. You're my brother. You and I only went out a few times. It was a long time ago." She wished she'd said nothing when he shot a look of such venom her way. She cringed back against the door.

"You've always been mine, and you always will be. My brother had no right to take you away. I made sure he paid though."

Elin couldn't breathe as she thought through what he'd said. Tim had suffered a heart attack and died within hours of Ben's visit. "Did you kill Tim?"

The truck bounced over ruts, and he gripped the wheel and wrenched it back into the middle of the path. "He didn't deserve to live with what he was putting you through."

She remembered how Tim had shouted at her the day Ben was there. She'd buried so much of Tim's treatment, thinking she deserved it, accepting the penance. "Oh, Ben, I don't know what to say. He was your brother."

"Half brother. Once he came along, Dad never bothered much with me. First Tim took my father, then he took you. He deserved what he got."

"H-How did you kill him?"

"An injection of adrenaline. He was sleeping and I shot it between his toes, then left. I bet you never even saw the puncture mark."

"I didn't." Her mouth felt like cotton. "Neither did the coroner, evidently. Where are you taking me?"

"Where we can be together forever." The corner of his mouth twisted into a sinister smile. "They'll find us sooner or later, you know. But it will be too late. We can be together in eternity."

"Y-You're going to kill me?"

He shot a glance her way, a softer one filled with pleading. "I'll make it painless, my darling. You'll fall asleep in my arms and we will go together. Just like Romeo and Juliet."

If she could just get to her phone. She glanced at her purse on the floor where her phone peeked from a side pocket. Maybe once he got out of the truck, she could grab it and dial 911.

He must have seen her glance, because he reached down and slipped her phone loose. Rolling down his window, he tossed it out into the weeds. "No one can be allowed into our final time together."

A scream built in her throat, but there would be no one around to hear. She didn't want him to see her terror. "I'll explain everything to them, Ben. Just let me go."

Shadows gathered in the truck as it entered a patch of trees. When he didn't answer, she yanked again on the door handle. Bushes scratched at the sides of the truck as it rolled deeper into the forest. Up ahead, the sunshine sparkled on grass.

A small seaplane sat in the clearing. An old metal hangar sat at the side of the road. He grabbed a garage-door opener and pressed the button. The door rose and he drove inside, where he parked the truck and grinned. "It's go time."

Something thick choked Marc's throat, and he coughed. His head pounded like someone had used it for a punching bag, but he managed to open his eyes. Thick smoke roiled at the ceiling, and flames shot up the drapes at the windows.

Fire.

He staggered to his feet, then fell back to his knees as the smoke stole his breath. He had to get out of here. It all flooded back to him—Mosely, the attack. He must have set the fire and left Marc to die.

He crab-crawled back toward the kitchen where he'd entered. The smoke lessened a bit once he got through the kitchen door. He got to the front door and threw it open. The fire roared louder behind him at the fresh influx of air, and he rushed outside. Drawing in a fresh lungful of oxygen, he stumbled twenty feet away, then turned to watch flames licking around the edges of the metal roof and bursting out the windows. There was a final roar as the flames ate up the logs.

Mosely would go after Elin. He knew it. Fumbling for his keys, he paused long enough to throw up in the bushes, then hurried toward his Tahoe. He had to get to her.

Sara felt as though she could float along the walk to Seagrass Pier without touching the ground. The ring on her hand already felt part of her. She wanted to share her joy with Elin. With her bare toes in the sand and the sun on her face, she walked along the sand toward the house. Gulls squawked overhead, and the salty spray swirled around her ankles with every incoming wave.

Life couldn't get much better than this.

She saw no activity at the house, and no one came to the door when she pressed the bell. Cupping her hands around her eyes, she peered into the window and saw only an empty living room. She probably should have called. She walked to the top of a dune and looked into the harbor where she'd docked her boat. The boat she'd thought was Elin's was one she didn't recognize. Someone was here then, but who? And why was the door locked and everything so quiet?

Unease stirred, and she fished her key out of her

purse, then went to the back door and unlocked it. Stepping inside the kitchen, she opened her mouth to call out, then stopped. Wait, maybe that wasn't a good idea. If there was an intruder, he would be alerted to her presence.

A sound upstairs caught her attention. A sliding, scraping noise as if someone had opened a drawer. She pulled out her phone, then dialed the sheriff's office. She told the dispatcher she'd discovered an intruder.

"Tom is out on a call right now, Sara, but I'll send him along as soon as I can. You're sure it's an intruder?" Mindy Stewart asked.

"I heard someone upstairs, and I don't recognize the boat. I think it should be checked out."

"Okay, I'll tell Tom. Let me know if it ends up being nothing." Her tone indicated she thought that was likely.

"I will." Sara hung up. Putting her phone on vibrate, she went back to the living room and tiptoed to the bottom of the stairs. Wisdom would tell her to leave, but what if Elin was in danger upstairs? Marc or his parents could have taken all the boats. Elin might still be here.

Sara looked around for a weapon, but before she found anything, she heard steps coming toward her. Spinning on her heel, she darted for the closet in the hall and left the door open just a crack.

Kalianne came into view. Sara held her breath and watched the woman pull out her cell phone and make a call. She strained to hear, but Kalianne's back was to her, and her voice was muffled. Opening the door a bit more, she leaned forward.

"I can't find it, Devi, and Elin is gone. I'd hoped to find her here with Marc and his parents gone, but there's not a soul here. I need to get out of here. Our faces are plastered all over town. Someone is bound to see me. What if the map doesn't exist any longer? There's no guarantee the old woman found it and hid it. I can't believe it wasn't in that stupid pouch!"

What map could she be talking about? Thank the Lord Elin wasn't here.

Kalianne listened a few moments. "Who is this Ben Summerall and why would he have taken Elin?"

Sara's eyes widened. *Ben* had Elin? She couldn't quite wrap her head around that.

"Where does he have her?" Kalianne stared at herself in a wall mirror and used her free hand to fiddle with her hair. "Okay, I'll meet you there. Where's the turnoff to the old airstrip?" She listened a few more moments. "It'll take me half an hour. If you can get there first, do it. I think the diary is in her purse. If we can just get that, maybe it will be enough. There might be details from the map."

The diary. Sara had been a little bored with the old history, so she hadn't paid much attention.

What would Devi want with it? Surely he didn't think the map led to anything real.

Kalianne clicked off her phone, then went down the hall to the powder room. Sara waited until the door closed, then eased out of the closet and exited the house as quietly as she'd entered. She called the sheriff's office again and told Mindy what she'd overheard.

"The sheriff will apprehend Devi on the road. Can you stop Kalianne there?" Mindy asked.

"I'll see what I can do." Sara ended the call and turned back toward the house.

It would do no good to call Josh since he was out on patrol. She eased through the back door and pulled a small pistol from her purse. The door to the powder room was still closed. When the sound of water running stopped, Sara raised the barrel of her gun and waited.

Kalianne's eyes widened when she opened the door and saw her. She attempted a smile. "Sara."

"Alive and well, no thanks to you. Put your hands up."

❧ Forty ❧

The ferry docked with Marc first in line to drive off. He pulled out his phone to call Elin for the fifteenth time. Why wasn't she answering? Had Mosely already gotten to her? His phone rang, and he glanced at the screen, praying it was Elin since she'd had so many missed calls, but the display showed Sara's name.

He thumbed it on. "Sara, have you seen Elin?"

"Where are you?" Her voice rose to a nearly hysterical decibel.

"Just leaving the ferry. What's wrong?"

"Ben's got Elin!"

Ben? Not Mosely? His breath hitched in his chest. "Tell me."

Sara launched into what she'd heard. "The sheriff should be there soon. He's looking for Devi too."

"I'm close to the old airfield, I think. Tell me where to turn off." He scanned the landscape as she told him to look for a nearly overgrown path. "I think this is it. There's an old gray fence post on the right side."

"That's it! Call me if you find her."

Marc dropped his phone into the passenger seat and gunned his Tahoe down the road. On the way to his destination, he saw several cars parked behind a familiar green pickup. Mosely's. A body lay sprawled in the ditch, a red patch spreading from his chest. Marc recognized the shirt on the victim even though he couldn't see his face. It was Mosely.

He accelerated past another two miles, then whipped his Tahoe into the narrow, overgrown cow path that headed toward the trees. It didn't appear like any kind of airfield, but maybe there was a big clearing on the other side. The weeds lay beaten down in wheel tracks ahead of him, so it looked like another vehicle had been through here recently.

Something white gleamed in the path ahead of him. An iPhone? He stopped the SUV and jumped out to retrieve it. When he turned on the screen, a picture of Josie popped up as the background. This had to be Elin's! He leaped back into the Tahoe and floored the accelerator. The vehicle's back tires spun in the sand, then gripped and shot the SUV forward.

As he entered the trees, he scanned the area hoping to see a house or cabin. Or even another vehicle, but only stands of live oak lined the path. The road was so narrow through here he had to let up on the accelerator. The shrubs brushed against his big vehicle as he rolled through.

Where was Elin?

❧ Forty-One ❧

The gloomy interior of the hangar made it hard to make out more than the looming shapes of workbenches and tools scattered around the perimeter of the large building. Elin sat on a carpet square in the corner with her hands tied behind her. She worked at loosening her bonds, but all she'd managed to do was bloody her wrists.

Ben worked at something in the corner, but she couldn't see what. He'd tied her up before he unlocked the truck, and she hadn't had a chance to try to escape or grab a metal tool as a weapon. She prayed for God to help her, but no great inspiration came to her. There seemed to be no way out.

Ben stepped away from the corner, then exited the cabin without a glance her way. Where was he going? When he disappeared from view, she staggered to her feet and raced to the workbench. There had to be a knife or something she could use to cut the rope. Was that a drywall knife under a piece of wood? She turned around and felt along the workbench until she felt the cool outline of the knife.

It took a few moments to expose the blade and several more to figure out how to press the blade against the rope without cutting her skin. Keeping an eye on the door, she sawed furiously at her bonds. It seemed an eternity before the rope fell away.

She looked for a place to hide near the door. Once he came in, maybe she could make a run for it. An old airplane wing sat perched on its end near the door. She slid behind it and waited.

When she heard his footsteps again, Elin shrank back into the shadows behind the plane wing.

She had to get out of here before Ben carried out his plan. His form blocked the tiny bit of light as he entered. She prayed the shadows would make him wait for his eyes to adjust before he realized she wasn't in the corner.

He moved her direction. She shoved the wing out of the way, and it toppled forward. As she darted toward the door, the wing crashed to the floor. Elin slammed the door behind her as she ran for the trees.

Behind her, Ben shouted, and she dared a glance back. The door was still shut so she prayed the airplane part blocked the passage for a few more seconds until she could melt into the shadows of the forest.

The glass in the door rattled, and she put on an extra burst of speed and plunged into the coolness of the shade. Ben yelled behind her, but she didn't waste any time looking back this time. Running faster than she thought possible, she darted around trees and leaped over shrubs in her way. Where could she hide? A low-hanging live-oak branch beckoned her, and she leaped atop it and shimmied up into the leaves.

She climbed as high as she could, until the branch began to thin enough she feared it might not hold her. Then she scooted against the main trunk and held her breath, praying all the while he hadn't seen her mad scramble into the tree.

She pressed her face into a covering of moss

and waited. Some scuffing came below, and she peered down to see Ben standing with his hands on his hips as he looked around.

"Elin? It won't do any good to hide. I'll find you sooner or later. You can't escape."

Don't look up. She barely dared to breathe. The thick leaves should obscure her from view, but she wore a bright orange top that might be seen.

"This is all your fault, you know. I couldn't let you marry Marc, now could I? His death is on your conscience, not mine."

She squeezed her eyes shut. Could Marc be dead? Wouldn't she know it, feel it somehow? *Please, God, let him be all right.* She opened her eyes and pulled in oxygen.

"I was surprised you didn't guess it was me. I gave you so many clues. Especially the song 'Music of the Night.' Remember when we went to see *The Phantom of the Opera*?"

Had they? She didn't really remember it.

Ben's gaze went to the base of the tree. Even from here, she could see the scuffed-up dirt where her foot had found purchase. His head went back, and he stared into her face.

"Come out, come out, wherever you are." Then he put his foot on the lowest branch and began to climb.

Marc's headache had abated some, and he fought with the wheel as his Tahoe hit the potholes.

Through the trees, Marc glimpsed an old airplane hangar and an airfield beyond it. Could Elin be inside? He stopped his vehicle and got out.

A woman's scream echoed from the woods, and he whipped around. It sounded like Elin.

He ran in the direction of the scream and entered the coolness of the shade from the big trees. Did he dare call out for Elin, or would it alert Summerall? Though Marc didn't want her in danger, he willed her to make some kind of sound. Scanning the underbrush, he looked for prints or a trail of some kind. Anything that would tell him which direction to move.

Cocking his head, he listened for thrashing or breathing. Nothing but birdsong and the wind in the leaves came to his ears. He saw some crushed weeds by a bramble bush and walked in that direction. There was matted grass on the other side of the bushes, so someone had come this way recently. Following his instincts, he hurried farther east.

"Stay away from me!" Elin's voice came from his left this time.

He got a better bead on the direction and set off toward her. She'd sounded high up, so he scanned the trees. Most were too small to climb, but a large live oak with low-spreading branches was about thirty feet ahead. His gaze touched on the big branch that almost reached the ground, then traveled up the tree. He caught a glimpse of orange, then saw Elin scrambling back from another figure that crawled toward her.

Summerall. He had a syringe in his hand and a smile on his face that could freeze someone's blood.

"Ben!" Marc leaped onto the first branch. "It's all over. Come down from there."

Summerall didn't even look in his direction. He continued to advance on Elin with the syringe. "It's not too late, Elin. Come to me. We can be in eternity together. I love you. I know you love me too."

He was going to reach Elin before Marc could stop him. He reached for his gun, only to realize he'd left it on the seat of the Tahoe. He glanced around for some kind of weapon and grabbed a stout branch.

"Ben!"

At Marc's shout, the man stopped and glanced at the ground. His cold gaze swept over him, and he smiled. "I really wanted to kill you myself. I'm glad I get the chance."

He released the branch he clung to and dropped to the ground like a cat. He set the syringe on a rock. His smile widened as he flexed his hands and leaped toward Marc.

Marc feinted back, but Summerall came right after him. A hard blow to his neck with the side of Ben's hand left him gasping for breath. Ben darted back, then swung around with a back kick that struck Marc in the stomach and drove him to his knees.

His vision dimmed, and he fought to draw in enough breath. Could he even beat this guy? Marc struggled to his feet. Summerall's smile never faded as he danced around Marc.

Elin dropped to the ground, and he shook his head when she started toward Ben. She paused and glanced around. Before either of them could find a weapon, Summerall made another move, and Marc found himself on the ground with the guy's knees on his chest and his forearm across his neck.

Marc strained to find the leverage to throw Summerall off. His lungs cried out for air, and his vision was already starting to cloud.

"No!" Elin grabbed a stick and walloped Summerall on the back with it.

The distraction rattled the guy enough that the pressure on Marc's throat eased. He flung out his hands and touched a rock. With the last of his strength, he gripped it and smashed it into the side of Summerall's head.

He fell off Marc and hit the ground with his eyes closed and his mouth slack. Marc got up as Elin rushed into his arms.

"I thought Mosely had killed you," she muttered into his chest.

He pulled her tight and pressed a kiss against her hair. "You can't get rid of me that easily."

❧ Forty-Two ❧

Twilight cast gold and yellow highlights over the darkening water. Gulls swooped over the water looking for a last-minute meal. The tranquility eased the tension from Elin's neck and shoulders as she sat with Marc on the edge of the pier looking out into a sea that seemed to go on forever. What a day it had been.

She leaned her head against Marc's shoulder. "I can't believe it's over."

He pressed a kiss against her temple. "You're safe."

"I keep seeing Ben's expression as he crawled toward me with that needle in his hand." She pressed her face against his chest for a moment, then looked up. "He killed Lacy too."

"I know." His arm tightened around her.

"What about Mosely? He strangled Laura." She shuddered, remembering her struggle with him.

"I think he'd done it before. The guy was a psychopath. No regret at all." He kissed her forehead. "He can't hurt you anymore."

"Ben said he was dead, but I wasn't sure."

"One shot through the heart and one through the head. Mosely's not going to hurt another woman."

"Let's get our daughter home with us."

The light in his eyes intensified. "I like the

sound of that. 'Our daughter.' And we'll be a family." When she didn't smile back, he frowned. "What's wrong, honey? I thought you'd be so relieved to have this over."

"Is it over, really? Or am I always going to have some of Laura's memories? Will I ever go back to hating coffee? Or watching my favorite movies?" She searched his gaze. "Am I even the person you think you love?"

His warm hand circled her cheek, and he rubbed his finger over her lips. "You're talking about unimportant things, Elin. Tastes come and go. The places we find our identities can vary depending on what part of our lives we're in. Look at my parents. For years, my dad's identity was in his job. Now he's content to be a grandpa, and the law isn't nearly as important. You've been a mom and a wife. You've been a single mom struggling to do it all on your own. You're your mother's caretaker. All those responsibilities change us and shape us, but you're still *you*. You have the same giggle. You still rescue stray animals and give whatever you have to help others. Your heart is as big as the ocean and just as clear."

His words caused warmth to spread from her heart down to the toes she dangled above the water. "You're not afraid to marry me? What if I change even more?"

"What if I do? We all change as we go through life. It's part of what makes living interesting. The trick with loving someone is to nurture those changes and encourage one another to be better people. I think the Elin-and-Marc team will be unstoppable."

His lips came down on hers, and she lost herself in the swirling sensation of want and need his kiss elicited. She wound her fingers into his hair and poured herself into showing him how much she loved him.

He broke the kiss with a sharp exhale. "Mercy, you'll be the death of me. Let's get this wedding planned and soon."

"How soon?" Her smile felt as though it would split her face.

"I'm not doing anything tomorrow. How about you?"

"I haven't even begun to look for a dress. Or a caterer or flowers."

"You want all that stuff?" He slapped his forehead. "How long will it take to plan?"

"I think Josie will be disappointed if she doesn't get to be a flower girl. And this will be fun for your parents. You're their only boy. They will want to make a big deal of it for Josie's sake."

"You have them pegged pretty well."

"And there's Sara. I don't want our wedding to overshadow hers."

"Don't tell me you're going to make me wait until they get married?"

She chuckled at the alarm in his voice. "No,

but I don't want ours to be so big that Sara feels left out."

"You want a double wedding?"

She shook her head. "I want Sara to bask in the glow of her *own* day."

His eyes darkened and he cupped her cheek. "See, that's exactly what I mean. You always think of others. Who you are hasn't changed, Elin."

When he kissed her again, she knew he was right. The way she felt inside was still uniquely *her*. The way God had made her. The good and the bad. If Marc could love her, warts and all, she would be content with that.

She wrapped her arms around his neck. "Let's call your parents and tell Josie."

"In just a minute. I'm not ready to let the world in just yet."

❧ A Note from the Author ❧

Dear Reader,

I think we women get too focused on trying to be everything to the people we love. We get tied up in how we look, what we wear, how we decorate, and our various roles in life. I know my roles have morphed through the years. But the cool thing I've come to realize is that they are supposed to. How boring it would be never to grow and evolve as a woman and as a Christian.

As I've gotten older, those things I mentioned have become less important (though I still don't like to be seen without my makeup!), but one thing I know—my real identity is in Christ who teaches us how to love others. When I go on to heaven, I want my legacy to be one of shining out love.

I've had a great example of that in my life. Diann Hunt recently lost her battle with ovarian cancer. But even as her body grew weaker, her spirit grew stronger. The lens shining out Jesus became so highly polished and brilliant that it was nearly blinding.

So I'm resolving to work on my real identity, a daughter of God. How about you?

E-mail me and let me know what you're working on. I love to hear from you!

Love,
Colleen
colleen@colleencoble.com

Reading Group Guide

1. Elin and Marc made a poor choice the night Josie was conceived. When Elin found out she was pregnant, do you think she did the right thing?

2. Do you know anyone who has had an organ transplant? Have you ever seen any evidence of cell memory?

3. Sara tried to forget about Josh by dating another man. What did you think of that?

4. Sara and Elin didn't believe Josh was guilty of the murder based on how they felt about him. Do you ever make judgments that way? If so, have you ever been wrong?

5. Having a loved one with dementia is hard. Have you ever experienced it? if so, what was the hardest part for you?

6. Scents can be very evocative of feeling. Is there any scent in your past that brings a specific time and feeling to mind?

7. Marc wanted to be part of Josie's life enough to marry to protect her. Why would that be a tough plan to follow?

8. Why do you think women can be attracted to bad boys like Ryan Mosely?

9. The book's theme is about identity. What do you think identity is?

⚛ Acknowledgments ⚛

I'm so blessed to be a part of the terrific Thomas Nelson dream team! Through their tireless hard work and commitment, *Rosemary Cottage* hit the *USA Today* bestseller list, which was a super exciting day. They really are my dream team!

I can't imagine writing without my editor, Ami McConnell. I crave her analytical eye and love her heart. Ames, you are truly like a daughter to me. Our fiction publisher, Daisy Hutton, is a gale-force wind of fresh air. She thinks outside the box, and I love the way she empowers me and my team. Marketing director Katie Bond is always willing to listen to my harebrained ideas and has been completely supportive for years. Fabulous cover guru Kristen Vasgaard works hard to create the perfect cover—and does. You rock, Kristen! And, of course, I can't forget my other friends who are all part of my amazing fiction family: Amanda Bostic, Becky Monds, Jodi Hughes, Kerri Potts, Heather McCulloch, Laura Dickerson, Elizabeth Hudson, and Karli Cajka. You are all such a big part of my life. I wish I could name all the great folks at Thomas Nelson who work on selling my books through different venues. I'm truly blessed!

Julee Schwarzburg is a dream editor to work with. She totally gets romantic suspense, and our partnership is a joy. She brought some terrific ideas to the table with this book—as always!

My agent, Karen Solem, has helped shape my career in many ways, and that includes kicking an idea to the curb when necessary. Thanks, Karen, you're the best!

I'm so grateful for my husband, Dave, who carts me around from city to city, washes towels, and chases down dinner without complaint. My kids —Dave and Kara (and now Donna and Mark)—and my grandsons, James and Jorden Packer, love and support me in every way possible, and my little Alexa makes every day a joy. She's talking like a grown-up now, and having her spend the night is more fun than I can tell you.

Most important, I give my thanks to God, who has opened such amazing doors for me and makes the journey a golden one.

About the Author

RITA finalist Colleen Coble is the author of several best-selling romantic suspense novels, including *Tidewater Inn*, and the Mercy Falls, Lonestar, and Rock Harbor series.

Center Point Large Print
600 Brooks Road / PO Box 1
Thorndike ME 04986-0001 USA

(207) 568-3717

US & Canada:
1 800 929-9108
www.centerpointlargeprint.com